Readers love
the Brandt and Donnelly Capers
series by XAVIER MAYNE

Wrestling Demons

I0669263

"Xavier Mayne has an unquestionable talent for making me fall in love with all of the characters in a book."

—The Novel Approach

"*Wrestling Demons* is a realistic, compelling tale about two boys who learn some harsh truths about the world and their own community, but also learn some beautiful things about the nature of love."

—Top2Bottom Reviews

"It reached out and drew me close—made me feel comfortable with some old and new friends. Loved it!"

—Hearts on Fire Reviews

Frat House Troopers

"This is one book that will make you laugh your ass off."

—MM Good Book Reviews

"It's sassy, sweet, and joyful."

—Rainbow Book Reviews

By XAVIER MAYNE

The Accidental Cupid (*Dreamspinner Anthology*)
Husband Material

BRANDT AND DONNELLY CAPERS
Case File One: Frat House Troopers
Case File Two: Wrestling Demons
Case File Three: A Wedding to Die For

Published by DREAMSPINNER PRESS
http://www.dreamspinnerpress.com

A WEDDING TO DIE FOR

XAVIER MAYNE

Dreamspinner Press

Published by
DREAMSPINNER PRESS

5032 Capital Circle SW, Suite 2, PMB# 279, Tallahassee, FL 32305-7886 USA
http://www.dreamspinnerpress.com/

This is a work of fiction. Names, characters, places, and incidents either are the product of author imagination or are used fictitiously, and any resemblance to actual persons, living or dead, business establishments, events, or locales is entirely coincidental.

A Wedding to Die For
© 2014 Xavier Mayne.

Cover Art
© 2014 L.C. Chase.
www.lcchase.com
Cover content is for illustrative purposes only and any person depicted on the cover is a model.

ISBN: 978-1-63216-469-8
Digital ISBN: 978-1-63216-470-4
Library of Congress Control Number: 2014947593
First Edition December 2014

Printed in the United States of America
(∞)
This paper meets the requirements of
ANSI/NISO Z39.48-1992 (Permanence of Paper).

For J, as with everything in this life.

ACKNOWLEDGMENTS

I'd like to thank the most diligent and generous first reader ever, George Schober, whose contributions go far beyond the grammatical infelicities that he spies, hawklike, among the reeds and rushes of my prose.

CHAPTER ONE
THE BELL TOLLS

"NO. I can't do it." The man crossed his arms across his chest and shook his head gravely. His words had really left no doubt, but in case they had, his body language would have extinguished it with brutal alacrity.

It was hardly the demeanor one expected from a baker.

"I don't understand," said one of the two men sitting at the dainty pink-and-white cafe table. "Are you overbooked for that week, or…?"

"No, I just can't do it." The baker's tone was even and businesslike, but his refusal was adamantine.

"But," offered the other man sitting at the ridiculously precious table, its lace tablecloth woven with shiny strands of pink ribbon, "the piece in *City* magazine was so amazing—we just loved your designs. We were really hoping to have one of your cakes."

"You'll have to find someone else," the baker replied, darting a glance through the front window of the shop as if concerned that someone might see him talking to the two well-heeled gentlemen.

"But why?" rejoined the first man, his tone mystified.

The baker sighed and shook his head wearily. "I don't do weddings like… yours," he said, almost under his breath.

The change in expression on the faces of the two men could not have been more sudden, or more drastic, had they been splashed with cold water. They sat back, shocked and offended, and then looked at each other in dismay.

"Excuse me?" said the second man, the excitement in his voice replaced with an icy crispness. His hands balled into fists atop the doily tablecloth.

"We're just wasting each other's time here," the baker said, rising to his full five-and-a-half-foot height of imposing pudgy grandeur.

"I don't think you know whom you're dealing with," the groom said, rising as well. As he was well over six feet of refined athleticism, he towered over the baker.

As stubborn as the baker had seemed while sitting, he became positively inflamed when having to look up at his foe. "I know perfectly well who I'm dealing with. I watch Channel 3 news—or at least I did until today. Now you should know who *you're* dealing with. My family has run this bakery for three generations, and we are God-fearing, upstanding citizens. I will make a cake for any man and woman in this town who wants to get married, but the day two tuxedos go on the top of one of my cakes is the day I close this place down."

"That, my good man, can be arranged." The second groom, his voice even and calm, rose from his seat to face the baker. "You may have seen my fiancé on the nightly news, but unless you've found yourself on the losing end of a lawsuit, you've never seen me. Shortly you shall."

The baker sneered. "You're going to sue me into making you a cake?"

"No. But I am going to sue you for violation of Section 28 of the state constitution. In case you aren't aware, that section has recently been found by the state supreme court to guarantee access to public accommodation to all citizens, including those who are gay, lesbian, bisexual, and transgender."

"I'm not going to make wedding cakes for that parade of freaks— on my mother's grave I'm not."

"Then we will see you in court." The attorney turned to his fiancé. "Now, my love, we have a florist to see, don't we?" The men turned to leave.

"Good luck with that," the baker growled to their backs as they walked to the door. "Most people in this business agree with me."

The second groom turned back as they stepped out of the bakery. "Then we will be busy in court, won't we?"

The baker shook his head and stomped back to his kitchen as the grooms walked past the shop's front window.

"CAN YOU believe that guy?" The news anchor's voice was livid, but his face gave no sign that he was in any way upset—he often referred to this as his Botox face, devoid of emotion in case the camera was still on him during a commercial break. "Apparently not everyone has gotten the memo that the Dark Ages are over."

"Calm down, love," soothed the attorney as the two men walked down the block and around the corner. "We'll get him sorted out quickly with a saber-rattling letter. I'll spell out just how much trouble he's heading for, and he'll come around."

"But the court ruling on Section 28 was supposed to guarantee we would be treated like anyone else. Now we have to sue someone for the privilege of having him make a cake for us?"

"But just a few years ago, we never imagined that we'd be able to get married at all. Things move slowly until they don't; that's how the law works sometimes."

"I know, I know—you're right, as always. I just wish I were as calm as you are about it. I so wanted to reach across that lace-drenched table and strangle the homophobia right out of his fat head."

"This is why people get married, love—to complement each other. I keep you from strangling bigoted bakers, and you remind me that not everything can be solved with a subpoena."

"But I love your subpoenas! Mainly because it sounds like penis."

"My God you are a big child. But I love you."

They kissed and then looked up to realize they had arrived at the florist who, they hoped, would provide the flowers for their wedding. They opened the door with a tinkle of the ancient brass bell mounted on the jamb and approached the counter.

"We have an appointment with Monty. For a wedding?"

The diminutive woman behind the counter smiled up at the men. "And who's the bride who would trust her flowers to the groom and his best man?"

The anchorman took a deep breath. "It's our wedding," he said with the winning smile he used to introduce cloying human-interest stories on the newscast—something involving a baby squirrel water-skiing or a kindergarten chess champion raising money for the blind.

The woman's smile vanished. She turned without a word and walked into the back of the shop.

"Oh, shit," exhaled the news anchor. "That didn't look so good for us, did it?"

"Let's not leap to conclusions," the attorney replied. "Give folks the benefit of the doubt, right?"

The first man took a deep breath and nodded.

"Gentlemen, I'm Monty." A whippet-thin man with salt-and-pepper hair cropped close to his head bustled out from the rear of the shop. Stray bits of greenery clung to his clothing, as if he had been standing too close to some kind of floral explosion. "How can I help you today?"

The news anchor dialed the human-interest smile back up to full wattage. "Pleased to meet you, Monty. We're here to talk about flowers for our wedding."

"Okay, so, that's the part I don't think I understand. When you say 'our wedding,' you mean...."

"The two of us," the attorney announced in a tone that had no doubt struck fear into many a defendant. "We are getting married in June and would like to retain your services for the floral arrangements. We are planning to spend at least forty thousand dollars on centerpieces and decorative elements. Are you available?" This last was less a question than a challenge.

Monty turned and looked into the workroom, visible through the swinging doors behind the counter. The small woman who had been at the counter stared back at him through narrowed eyes.

"I'm so sorry, gentlemen," Monty said to the men. "We're simply not available to provide flowers for your... wedding."

"Booked up for the entire month, are you?" the attorney replied. "Do you get many forty-thousand-dollar wedding orders? That's not worth a little overtime?"

"It's not that," Monty said in a low voice. He glanced toward the back of the shop again, just for a second. "We don't... uh... support that kind of... um...."

The news anchor took a breath as if to finish the florist's sentence for him, but the attorney put a hand on his arm and gave one slight shake of his head.

The florist took another breath and forged ahead. "We don't provide services for nontraditional weddings," he said finally.

"Two people, friends and family, vows," the attorney replied. "I don't see that we're after anything at all nontraditional, Monty."

Monty closed his eyes and took a deep breath that seemed to help his agitation not a bit. "I'm afraid I can't help you," he said, a note of genuine apology in his voice.

"Are you aware of Section 28 of the state constitution?" began the attorney in what had suddenly become a rote lecture.

"WELL, AS wedding planning goes, this day was about the worst imaginable," the news anchor lamented before tipping back his wine glass. "I worried about you turning me down, but I never dreamed that we would be rejected by both a baker and a florist on the same day."

The men had sought refuge in a more Adam-and-Steve-friendly locale: their favorite wine bar on Alta Avenue. They had done some serious damage to an astringent chardonnay and were contemplating an assault on a cheeky gewürztraminer.

"Worry not, my love," the attorney soothed. "We'll get them sorted. I just have two letters to fire off first thing in the morning, and you'll see how quickly they cave. This time next week they'll be begging us to come in for a consultation."

"Not sure I want them to do it now. Maybe we should just find someone on the Avenue to do it instead?"

"They're who you wanted, and all you've talked about for weeks is how anyone who's anyone has flowers by Monty and a cake by Capella's. I want you to have everything you want, love, because you're only getting married once."

His fiancé smiled.

"Because if you try to divorce me I will take you apart in court, piece by gorgeous piece," the attorney added with a wink.

"It's amazing no one's marched you down the aisle already, what with your gift for sweet talk."

"NOW, DARLINGS, I love a good mystery as much as anyone—oh, the hours I've spent trying to figure out which member of One Direction is the straight one—but this is too, too much! I'm simply going to *expire* if you don't tell me your big news right this very second, which as I'm sure you would agree would make quite a scene in this lovely and expensive boîte that my beloved Nestor and I could never afford to enter were we not invited."

Brandt smiled at Donnelly, and they shared a laugh. Bryce's performance was, as expected, a typhoon of aggrieved delight. "Bryce, it's been all of an hour since I asked you to meet us here."

"An hour that I spent feverishly imagining every possible eventuality. Why, my mind was so occupied I don't think I was able to do a second of actual work after reading your text. Thank goodness it was slow in the shop."

"Not many people wiling away a late Monday afternoon browsing the racks at Grindstone?" Donnelly asked.

"The only people in the store were a few college boys doing some kind of scavenger hunt thing. They weren't interested in the clothes at all. They just piled into a dressing room together and mooned the mirror while one of them reached around with a camera."

"They mooned the two-way mirror that you use for... loss prevention?" Brandt queried with a smirk.

"One cannot be too careful these days—we must be vigilant," Bryce stated with an almost manly vigor. "Thanks to our professional observational techniques, in case we are ever called upon to identify them in a lineup, we are ready to serve."

"Committed their buttocks to memory, did you?" teased Donnelly.

"And to the Instagram," offered Nestor, brandishing his phone.

Brandt laughed and left aside the potential privacy issues brought up by Bryce and Nestor's itchy shutter fingers. The men had proven themselves invaluable in several investigations over the past year, and despite their flamboyance, their discretion could be relied upon in a pinch.

"Now, at the risk of being tiresome, I must ask again," Bryce resumed. "For what momentous disclosure have you summoned us? Keep a lady waiting long enough and your chivalry may be subject to question in the streets."

"First, let's get something to drink." Brandt waved, and a waiter sped across the room to appear, somewhat breathlessly, at his side. His ability to instantly command attention from any man on Alta Avenue had been somewhat disconcerting when Brandt first noticed it last year, but as he had become more comfortable in the gay world of the Avenue, he came to see this as a benign superpower that he was careful not to abuse. He turned and smiled sunnily at the waiter.

"What can I get for you gentlemen today?" the waiter asked, generously including all four seated at the table though never taking his eyes from Brandt.

"We'd like a bottle of champagne, please," Brandt replied with a playful hint of ceremony in his voice.

"Celebrating a special occasion?" the waiter queried, an eyebrow raised in playful interest.

"Yes, we are," Donnelly replied. His intonation told that he was perfectly reconciled to Brandt getting the raised-eyebrow treatment from Messrs. All & Sundry.

"Excellent," the waiter said with a knowing nod. "What's our budget, then? School teachers on holiday, or rappers celebrating a tax refund?"

Brandt burst out laughing. "Something along the school-teacher line, I think."

"Very good. I'll be back in a jiff."

"Champagne?" hooted Bryce. "The plot thickens. Though I am relieved to discover that the news must be good indeed, I'm still burning with curiosity. You are so cruel to drag this out, plying us with bottle after bottle of bubbly."

"I ordered one bottle!" Brandt replied.

"The night is young," Bryce pronounced, his head swiveling around the room, perhaps looking for anyone he knew who might witness him drinking champagne with the two strapping officers.

Brandt was relieved when the waiter returned to the table with the champagne almost immediately. He laid a flute in front of each man and then presented the bottle to Brandt for approval. It was a label rather nicer than he was expecting, but as this was a special occasion, he decided to indulge. He nodded, and the waiter popped the cork and poured all around the table.

Bryce was practically vibrating with excitement, quivering in his chair. Brandt wasted no time in putting him out of his misery.

"You two have become part of our lives over the last year, and we wanted you to be among the first to know that"—he turned and looked at Donnelly with what he knew was a sappy smile—"the love of my life has asked me to marry him, and I've said yes."

It surely violated a law of physics that Bryce could both suck in a huge, dramatic breath and emit a high-pitched squeal of excitement at the same time. But Bryce had probably passed physics by dint of various extra-credit projects he'd performed for his teacher after school hours. Brandt simply waited for him to breathe again.

It was a long moment.

Meanwhile, Nestor turned his beaming face to the fiancés. "Long have I been dreaming," he began solemnly, "of this very moment. I shall be honored to witness your souls unite as I have long imagined your bodies to do." His eyes grew unfocused, as if he were imagining it as he spoke.

Finally, Bryce seemed to have found the composure to speak, if only a single word. "*Among?*"

"Pardon me?" Brandt said, leaning toward Bryce.

"We are *among* the first to know?" Bryce's eyes glinted fiercely.

Brandt shook his head and smiled. He knew that Bryce's dudgeon would only hold out so long before being overwhelmed by his excitement. "We told our families, of course, but you are the first friends we've given the news to."

Bryce's expression instantly changed from Dour Countess to Tipsy Cheerleader. "Oh! Oh! Oh! This is so exciting!" He laid a hand at his throat and made a great show of catching his breath. Then, with the practiced elegant motion of a hand accustomed to wearing opera gloves trimmed with marabou, he raised his flute. "It has been my great honor and pleasure to encourage the two of you as you made your way from the dark recesses of heterosexuality into the glorious daylight of your love for one another. I cannot think of two people I would be happier to watch walk down the aisle. Blessings and congratulations, my dears. May every happiness be yours." Bryce raised his glass high, and then all four took a sip of the champagne, Brandt and Donnelly blushing at Bryce's effusion.

Then Nestor raised his glass. "The first day I see you, I know. You fight against it, but I know. Now you stand up together and the whole world know."

Brandt felt Donnelly's hand grip his, and when Brandt turned to him, he saw tears welling in his fiancé's eyes.

"You two are just the best," Donnelly said, his voice a little thick. "I'm so touched."

"You gonna get a lot more touched on the wedding night," replied Nestor in a light, singsongy voice.

"Now, to the important business at hand," Bryce interrupted the giggles occasioned by Nestor's ribaldry. "First we need to know the date so that we can back schedule and sort everything by priority. We'll need to convene a group of the city's finest purveyors of matrimonial necessities, plus that really hot DJ—you know the one I mean, Nestor?"

Nestor nodded. "But, my love, they have not asked for our help."

Bryce froze, his face pale with shock. His lips moved, but no sound emerged.

"Of course we would be so grateful for your help in planning the wedding," Brandt blurted, eager to head off a meltdown.

Bryce closed his eyes and took a deep breath. "A very sensible decision," he said once he had exhaled and opened his eyes again. "And we would be delighted to provide any assistance we can, of course. You are the very first of our select social circle to tie the knot."

"Not surprising, given how recently it became legal," said Donnelly, an edge to his voice. "It's so nice that our state has finally seen fit to extend human rights to everyone."

"I prefer to think that they simply weren't prepared for weddings as fabulous as yours will be, darlings," replied Bryce briskly, shaking off the political bitterness of Donnelly's remark. "And fabulous it shall be. Now, what's our date?"

"We haven't really picked one," Brandt said, looking at Donnelly with eyebrows raised. Donnelly shrugged in response.

"Well, since it's April, and given the logistics we're facing, I'd say the absolute soonest would be November. Next year."

Brandt and Donnelly both startled back in their chairs.

"A year and a half?" Brandt asked.

"Bryce, you know we love you, but we aren't looking for a Disney-princess-level event here," Donnelly said gently. "We'd be happy with something small and simple."

Bryce's visage clouded.

"With your trademark elegance and style, of course," added Brandt.

"Well, perhaps if we get started immediately and call in a few favors, we might be able to do next June," groused Bryce with an unconvincing pout.

"We really need more than a year?" Brandt asked.

"All of the best people are booked a year in advance at the very latest. We'll be scrambling just to find anyone at all who will meet my—sorry, your—standards. And we will be hard-pressed indeed to find the right wedding planner, which we must absolutely get started on right now."

"Wait, I thought you were going to plan—"

"Oh honey, no! Think of us as your personal assistants, guiding you to the most fashionable and fabulous choices. Nestor and I are well acquainted with which caterers have the most muscular waiters, but for the heavy lifting, you need to engage a professional. I will start arranging audiences with the finest consultants *tout de suite*."

Bryce and Nestor beamed at the engaged couple, fidgeting with excitement.

"We're really doing this, aren't we?" Brandt asked Donnelly.

"We are. God help us, we are."

"YOU KNOW anything about this task force?" Donnelly asked Brandt as they drove to work the next morning.

"Just what the chief said in that e-mail yesterday. Not a lot to go on."

"I kind of like what we've been doing lately, helping local law enforcement with sensitive investigations. I hope they're not going to take us off that and put us on highway patrol or something."

"If I know the chief, what he has in mind is going to be more challenging than aiming a radar gun at traffic on the interstate."

"I hope so," Donnelly replied. "But the last time he had a special project for us, you ended up doing naked videos. Not sure I'd be up for that again."

"You saying you wouldn't want me to make a sexy video? Are you getting tired of seeing me naked, Officer Donnelly?"

"If you were naked, I would gladly spend any number of shifts sitting by the side of the road doing speed enforcement."

"I haven't reviewed the uniform standards for a while, but I'm going to go out on a limb and guess that that would be a violation."

"That would be the least of the violations, I promise you," Donnelly replied with a growl. He slid his hand up his partner's thigh and gave him a squeeze.

"I like the way this is going. But, seeing that we're in the parking lot of headquarters, I think we should probably just stay fully clothed and get to our desks. Sound good?"

"As long as you'll be naked before this day is over, I'm good to go."

"Promise." Brandt leaned over and kissed his partner. "Now, let's see what the chief has in store for us."

Fifteen minutes later Brandt and Donnelly were sitting across the desk from the chief of the state police, waiting for him to return from a meeting down the hall.

"Every time I sit here, I remember when he gave me that undercover assignment," Brandt whispered to Donnelly. "My entire life changed when he told me I'd be infiltrating a porn operation."

"Yeah, that changed a lot for both of us," Donnelly whispered back. "But I wouldn't have it any other way."

Brandt winked and grinned but said no more as the chief strode in and took his seat behind the desk.

"Brandt, Donnelly, good to see you. And great work, by the way, on sorting out that mess in Woodley. Read your report, and I'm very impressed."

"Thank you, sir," replied Donnelly for both of them.

"What you did to help out the Woodley PD got me thinking about how we might take a more proactive stance on those issues, and I had a meeting last week with the new attorney general. I proposed a new task force, and she's on board. I'd like the two of you to head it up."

Brandt expected more information, but the chief seemed to be waiting for a response. "We're honored, sir, and we're ready to serve. But what, exactly, would we be doing?"

"I'm sure you're aware that people across the state are starting to file lawsuits to compel businesses and organizations to comply with Section 28."

"Yes, we've been following the news," said Brandt.

"Good. Now, this is the first time in a long while that a provision of the state constitution is running contrary to the law in many municipalities. We haven't seen state preemption like this since the Civil Rights era. And it's causing friction in more traditional communities."

"You don't have to tell us," Donnelly replied with a wry chuckle. "We spent enough time in Woodley to know what that 'friction' looks like."

"What we need, and what the attorney general needs, is a state-level resource to go to these communities and be very clear with them on what the constitution requires in terms of equal treatment. And that's what we'd like the two of you to do."

"So, we'd be responsible for Section 28 enforcement?" asked Brandt.

"Yes, but more than that, you would serve as a resource to local law enforcement on their obligations with regard to equal treatment, helping them update policies and training. You would advise local businesses about the need to bring their workplace practices into line. You'd also meet with politicians and local governments to support them as they work to bring the legal code and regulations into compliance with the court ruling. What we want to avoid is a long and costly string of lawsuits clogging our court system, which a simple and forceful explanation of the law would serve to prevent."

"It sounds like something that lawyers would be more suited to," replied Donnelly. "Why send state troopers to do it?"

"Because the two of you have been on the front lines. You've already shown what you can accomplish in Woodley, and I think you're the right men for this. And the attorney general agrees. Now, you will have access to the district attorneys across the state if you need help from a lawyer. But we're operating under the assumption that it's better to consult constructively than it is to go in with lawyers blazing and read them the riot act." The chief sat back in his chair and smiled at the men. "Well, what do you think?"

Brandt and Donnelly exchanged a look.

"We're definitely on board, Chief," Brandt answered on behalf of both. "Looks like a great opportunity to do some important work."

"Excellent. Now, let me show you the first situation that needs your attention." The chief turned to his computer and brought up a browser window. "This press conference was held yesterday afternoon." He clicked the video frame, and the picture came to life.

CHAPTER TWO
TOLERATING INTOLERANCE

ON THE wide marble steps of the city's grandest courthouse, a young but distinguished-looking man in an expensive suit stepped to a clutch of microphones. He was joined by a tall, strikingly handsome man in an even more sharply tailored suit. They stood for a moment and waited for quiet.

"Thank you for coming today," the first man said. "My name is Peter Laurence, an attorney with the firm of Filbert Laurence & Stone. As you are no doubt aware, Section 28 of the state constitution was the subject of a landmark ruling two years ago by the state supreme court. In that decision, the court declared unequivocally that the constitution requires equal treatment of all citizens, regardless of sexual and gender identity. Then, less than a year ago, a subsequent ruling clarified—unnecessarily, in the minds of most people, as this conclusion should have been obvious—that equal treatment requires equal access to marriage."

There was some shuffling and muttering among the assembled audience, but they settled back down quickly. The man continued.

"While the court's rulings have allowed my fiancé and myself to obtain a marriage license for our upcoming wedding," he said, nodding to the man next to him, who flashed a winning but serious smile, "we have been frustrated in our efforts to secure the services of several well-known businesses. When we met with them, they informed us in no uncertain terms that they would not provide services for our upcoming wedding because we are a gay couple. We informed these businesses by registered letter of their constitutional obligation to provide equal access to public accommodation, but we have to date received no response. We regret that we must now pursue legal recourse to compel them to comply with the law. Accordingly, we have this afternoon filed a civil claim. Yes?" Laurence looked to a reporter in the crowd with his hand raised.

"Are you seeking damages? Do you intend to run these companies out of business?"

"No, not at all. We seek only to have the same opportunities that straight couples have in planning their wedding."

"But what about businesses who object to working on gay weddings due to what some of them describe as their 'sincerely held religious beliefs'?"

The lawyer nodded, as if he'd been expecting this question. "We do not seek to change the conscience of the men and women who run these businesses. They are free to disapprove morally of our marriage if that is their preference. But what they cannot do, and what the constitution does not allow them to do, is to discriminate on the basis of sexual or gender identity. If these businesses refused every African-American or Latino couple who wanted to use their services, we as a society would condemn them as racist, and they would be driven out of business in short order. We are simply asking to be treated as any other couple would be."

Another reporter waved a hand. "Mr. Sampson, do you think your position as a public figure will influence how the court, or the public, views your case?"

The other man stepped to the microphones. "I stand before you as a citizen, not as a news anchor. My claim to the full range of rights that come with citizenship docs not depend on my being on television. If our fight has a higher profile because of my job, then we may be able to have a larger impact across this great state of ours, and I am glad of that. My grandparents suffered under unjust Jim Crow laws. And I am proud to say that one of my grandfathers was a Freedom Rider, arrested multiple times as he and several hundred other brave men and women challenged the shameful 'separate but equal' doctrine. Today, we are simply carrying on their work, forcing a change when injustice won't be otherwise rectified." By the end of this speech, he was in full-throated declamation, using the pitch and timbre of his voice to bring the press event to a dramatic climax. He had also managed to deliver a perfect fifteen-second sound bite that would find its way onto all of the evening news broadcasts, including that of his own station.

"We expect the court will move quickly to rule in our favor and cement equal rights protections for all citizens," the lawyer summed up. "Thank you for your time."

THE CHIEF closed the browser window and looked up at Brandt and Donnelly. "I assume you saw the coverage on this last Friday?"

The men nodded.

"They make quite a team," Brandt said. "Laurence has a fearsome reputation in the courtroom, and Sampson has a huge fan base across the entire region."

"They will win this suit," the chief said simply. "It's clear that the court has been trending this way for the past couple of years, and the governor and the attorney general certainly want that to continue."

"Then," Donnelly said, somewhat uncertainly, "if the outcome is pretty much determined, I'm not sure how we can help."

"While there's no doubt how this will end, the wheels are going to move slowly—and expensively. If you can get the businesses named in the suit to see that there's no way they can win it, there will be two benefits: first, the court won't have to spend the time and money on a civil action that is basically pointless and can instead take real cases that actually will help settle valid questions of law; second, the state can avoid another protracted media circus that makes everyone else in the country think we're some kind of redneck backwater. It just looks bad for us that these equal rights issues keep getting dragged into court, and the governor wants them to stop."

Brandt nodded. "I think we all agree with the governor on that one." He turned to his partner. "Ready to go forth and exercise our moral suasion?"

"Ready," Donnelly replied with a grin. "And thank you, Chief, for this opportunity. I'm sure we don't have to tell you how important this issue is to us. You've made sure this is a supportive environment for us, but not everyone is so lucky—yet."

The chief acknowledged Donnelly's appreciation with a solemn nod.

"We'll do our best to defuse the situation," Brandt said, rising. "Thank you for your confidence in us, sir."

They shook hands with the chief and headed to their desks.

Once there, Brandt flipped open his computer and punched up the judicial database. In a moment, the complaint that Peter Laurence had described to the press was on his screen. The first page of the pleading gave him what he needed to know.

"Defendants are Montgomery Floral and Cakes by Capella," he read off to Donnelly, who typed the names quickly into his own laptop and scanned the results.

"All right, I've got addresses. They're both in the same neighborhood. Hmm," he mused, reading further through the search results.

"Whatcha got?" Brandt asked, walking around to Donnelly's side of the desk.

"Both have been going for decades," Donnelly replied. "Looks like third generation for Montgomery, and Capella's has been around almost as long. But for such old-school businesses, they're certainly popular; there's a ton of pictures of their work here, tweeted out by a who's who of the hip and wealthy." He paused, and frowned at the screen.

"Find something?" Brandt asked, leaning over his partner's shoulder.

"There are petitions going against both of them. Several thousand sigs on each, but that's not as big a problem as this," Donnelly said, pointing to his screen.

"Boycott the Bigot Baker," Brandt read aloud, then scanned down the page. "Is that a list of people who have cancelled their cakes?"

Donnelly nodded. "Dozens, and this site started up only a week ago." He clicked into another browser tab. "There's one for the florist too."

Brandt shook his head. "This is gonna hurt them a lot more than the lawsuit will."

"Hard to believe that people who can create such amazing cakes and bouquets can have such ugliness in their hearts." He nodded toward a browser window full of pictures of lavish floral arrangements and fantastically decorated cakes.

"Wow," Brandt whispered, genuinely impressed.

Donnelly turned to look up at his partner. "Give you any ideas?" he asked, mischief in his voice.

"What, you want to start our wedding planning by getting a court order for a cake and flowers? How romantic."

"I'm just saying that this cake with the royal blue fondant is pretty awesome," Donnelly said, nodding toward the screen.

"How about we do our day jobs, and then we can think about our wedding after work, okay?" Brandt asked with a nudge to Donnelly's ticklish ribcage.

Donnelly laughed and dodged away playfully. "All right, slave driver. Lead on."

"CAN'T SAY I even knew we had a wholesale flower district," Brandt mused as they stepped out of the car. He had parked across the street from a Victorian-looking iron-and-glass building that stretched down the entire block. Over the wide entrance, the words "Flower Mart" sizzled in purple neon letters three feet high.

"Yeah, I could kind of tell that by how many times you haven't brought me flowers," Donnelly replied with a smirk.

"I'll remember that next time I'm tempted to bring home play-off tickets. Apparently you would prefer camellias to courtside seats."

"On second thought, scratch the flowers. A smooch on the kiss cam is romantic enough for me."

They walked along the sidewalk for about half a block and then turned a corner and found their destination: Montgomery Floral, a broad and imposing storefront with beveled-glass windows glinting in the midmorning light. Aside from its deep green color, it gave no sign that it was a florist's shop.

"Hmm."

Donnelly turned to Brandt. "What is it?"

"It doesn't really look like a florist, does it? I guess I was kind of expecting racks of flowers and people bustling around making bouquets."

"This isn't really the kind of place where people just stop by on their way to the train to pick up some flowers. These guys do the big showy stuff and leave the nosegays to others."

Brandt looked at his partner. "Nosegays? You been reading Jane Austen again?"

"Can't a guy break out some vocabulary without being harassed? My goodness." With a chuckle Donnelly stepped toward the door of the shop.

Brandt followed, shaking his head. He pulled the door open, and they stepped into an elegantly appointed but mostly empty room. A long marble counter stood to one side, and large, extravagantly framed photos of floral arrangements lined the wall opposite. "Still no flowers," he muttered to Donnelly as they looked at the pictures.

"But you can sure smell them, can't you?" Donnelly took a deep breath and closed his eyes. "Roses, lilies, and evergreens," he said during a long, wistful exhale.

"I really do have to bring you flowers sometime. Just to watch you get a floral boner."

Donnelly whacked him in the stomach with a lightning-fast twitch of his arm. "Good God, how did I fall in love with such a... *man*."

"Can I help you?" asked a voice behind them.

They turned to find a man smiling at them from behind the counter. He seemed to be in his early twenties, and he was wearing an impossibly white button-down shirt with the sleeves rolled halfway up his forearms. He looked to Brandt as though he had never touched anything that grew in dirt, much less worked in a florist's shop.

The officers stepped toward the counter.

"Good morning. I'm Ethan Brandt and this is Gabriel Donnelly. We're with the state police."

The young man's smile vanished for an instant but then flashed back into view. "I'm Roman Montgomery. What can I do for you?" he asked with careful cheer.

Brandt noticed the flicker in the young man's eye contact, as if he were trying very hard not to look toward the back of the shop—or not to be seen to be looking in that direction. "We're here about the lawsuit filed last week. We'd like to talk to the owner, see if we can't keep this from becoming a long legal ordeal."

The man exhaled with such relief that he seemed to shrink a full inch in height. But when he took another breath, his manner hardened. "We've been told not to talk about that," he said in a low, even voice.

"Told that by your attorney, I assume?"

"Yeah," the young man replied vaguely.

"I see," Brandt said, nodding in a manner he intended to look thoughtfully surprised by the young man's answer, though he'd fully expected that this would be the response he would get. "I'm sure that's sound legal advice, but there are some things that you should know before you spend any more money on lawyers."

"Wait here for a moment?" Roman said. He turned and walked through the swinging doors into the back of the shop.

"What's your take?" Brandt asked his partner.

"He didn't seem happy to see us, for a start," Donnelly replied.

They waited in silence for a full minute.

From the back of the shop strode a lean, sprightly man in his fifties. Though his gait was purposeful, his face wore at least a veneer of cheer. "I'm the owner," he said, walking around the counter to stand before the officers. He extended a hand and firmly gripped those of Brandt and Donnelly in turn.

"Mr. Montgomery, then?" Brandt ventured.

"Please, call me Monty," the man answered. "Now, Roman says you've come to talk about the lawsuit?"

"Yes, sir, we have," Donnelly said. "I'm Gabriel Donnelly, and this is Ethan Brandt. We've been asked by—"

"I'm sure Roman told you," Monty interrupted, "that we've been advised not to talk with anyone about the case."

"Yes, he did say that," Brandt replied. "But the state attorney general has sent us to talk with you about finding a way to avoid going to court."

Monty's eyebrows peaked in surprise. "Why would the attorney general do that?"

"Because there's no chance you will prevail in this case," Donnelly said, in a tone that, while gentle, nonetheless left no doubt as to his seriousness.

"That's not what our attorney says," Monty objected.

Brandt studied his face for a moment. He had expected the defendants in this case to be combative, even openly bigoted; he had not expected this naiveté. Monty seemed genuinely mystified that anyone would suggest he might not win this case. "Monty, what your attorney told you is privileged, and I don't mean to suggest that you've been given bad advice. But I'm here to tell you that from the state's perspective, the law is clearly on the side of Laurence and Sampson."

"I don't see how that can be," Monty said, his voice still full of confusion. "Last time I checked, businesses are free to decline business if they wish. It's a free country."

"Yes, of course," Donnelly replied. "You can turn away potential customers for pretty much any reason. But what the law doesn't allow you to do is turn away every potential customer who belongs to a particular group."

"Even if that particular group violates my beliefs?" Monty asked.

Brandt was losing his patience. The florist was simply parroting talking points he'd probably heard on conservative radio shows without even thinking about what they meant. "How can a group of people violate your beliefs simply by existing?" Brandt demanded in a tone he'd tried to keep more civil than it came out sounding.

"Officer, we are a family-run business. And that family has been Catholic for longer than this country has existed. We don't believe that two men or two women should be allowed to marry each other, and we won't participate in it even if everyone else says it's suddenly okay."

Brandt took a breath, ready with an angry rejoinder, but Donnelly put his hand on his arm. "Monty, no one's telling you what to believe. Surely you've done wedding flowers for people you thought shouldn't be getting married? Divorcées, couples who might already have been living together without benefit of clergy, perhaps even a bride or two with a belly that seemed slightly enlarged?"

Monty, despite the grim look on his face, allowed a small chuckle to escape. "Yes, but they were heterosexual couples."

"But they were getting married under circumstances that your church would not approve of."

Monty shrugged. "They weren't getting married in my church."

"And neither is the couple who has filed the lawsuit," Brandt said, having gotten the edge out of his voice at last. "They are having a civil ceremony. They're not asking your—or any—religion to sanction their marriage."

Monty seemed for a moment to have run out of steam. But he recovered quickly. "I understand that it's their right to get married—

though how that happened I still don't get—but it should also be my right to turn down the business."

"If they wanted to get married on a weekend when you're fully booked, that's fine," Brandt replied. "Send them to another florist. If they want a kind of flower that you don't stock, they can look elsewhere. But what you can't do is—well, exactly what you did. You can't send them away just because they are a gay couple."

"Monty, we're not here to argue with you," Donnelly said. "We're here to see if there's any way we can calm things down and settle this before it gets to court."

Monty closed his eyes and rubbed the bridge of his nose. "This is a nightmare," he said under his breath. When he opened his eyes, they looked tired and were starting to redden. "We had a dozen cancellations last week and three more already this morning." He turned and walked to the wall of photos behind the officers, as if he didn't want them to see his haggard expression. He pointed to the far left side of the wall where black-and-white photos showed the shop's early days. "My grandfather started this business just before the Great Depression. Great timing, right? But he made it through by sticking with his values and trying to do the right thing. My father grew up in this shop, just like I did. And we've tried to keep to my grandfather's founding principles. My dad did the flowers for the first interracial wedding this city ever saw, and he did it for free because it was the right thing to do. People thought he was trying to stir up trouble, but he told them the Bible didn't say brides and grooms had to be the same color."

Brandt and Donnelly stood silent while Monty reminisced.

"I guess you know you're old when the world starts changing whether you want it to or not," he mused, turning back to the officers. "I just don't know how to get right with this. If I take this job, I'm violating my principles. If I don't… well, no business can take the kinds of cancellations we're seeing for very long." He shook his head and looked out the window for a long time. "I honestly don't care what these two guys do in the privacy of their own home, I really don't. Back when the marches and the—I guess they call them 'pride' parades—started, live and let live was enough. But that's not enough anymore, is it? Now I either have to say congratulations to the happy couple or lose the business that my family has put our blood, sweat, and tears into for the last almost hundred years." He fell silent again for a moment. "And that stinks, gentlemen—that really stinks."

Monty stared out the window, not seeming to focus on anything in particular, for a long moment. Then he took a long breath and seemed to return to himself. "The lawsuit is the least of my problems right now. If I don't get in front of this boycott thing, I'm going to be closing the family business within a month." He shook his head, but the anger seemed to be draining out of him. "I'll do the damn wedding. Tell them to call off the dogs. I'll do it."

"You're making the right choice, Monty," Donnelly said, his voice full of compassion.

Monty fixed him with a hard stare. "I don't believe that, not for a second. I'm making a choice to survive, even though it goes against everything I believe."

Brandt wanted to bring this meeting to a close before Monty could prove himself an even more intractable bigot. "We'll get word to Laurence that you're ready to meet with them about the wedding arrangements."

"Great. And I'll spend the day learning how to 'tweet,' or whatever the hell you call it, trying to convince anyone who hasn't already cancelled that I'm not some kind of satanic bogeyman bent on destroying all that's good in the world. Sounds like a great time." He turned to the portrait of his founding grandfather. "Sorry, Granddad. Looks like to stay in business, we gotta sell out."

"Thank you for your time, Monty. Please let us know if there's anything we can help with." Brandt handed his card to Monty as he said this.

Monty grunted, looking at the card. "I think you've done quite enough already."

A FEW blocks from the flower district, Brandt and Donnelly found the building that housed Cakes by Capella, a large brick bakery fronted by a delicate shop complete with lace curtains and elaborate glass display cases bearing samples. Their entrance was heralded by the tinkling of a bell above the door, and they stepped into the small, precisely decorated room.

"What does your watch say?" Brandt asked. "Because according to this place, it's 1880."

"A bit precious, isn't it? And yet from the look of the cakes they've made lately, they're on the cutting edge." Donnelly stepped up to the display case and tapped the silver bell that sat atop it.

Soon they were joined by a young woman in a crisp white uniform—she would not have been out of place in a Victorian hospital ward. "Welcome to Capella's," she said brightly. "How can I help you?"

"Good morning. I'm Gabriel Donnelly, and this is Ethan Brandt. We're officers with the state police, and we'd like to talk to the owner, please."

The young woman's eyes widened, and while she may have intended to say something like "I'll be right back," she only made the slightest squeaking noise before bolting for the back of the shop.

"Our arrival always brings such good cheer, don't you find?" Brandt asked with a wry smile.

"I think we can forgive them for thinking we've shown up to rub salt in their wounds," Donnelly replied. "Let's just hope we can move things along as easily as we did with Montgomery."

"Somehow I think the forces of tradition might be a little stronger here," Brandt mused, looking about the grandmotherly parlor. He was interrupted in his contemplation of the varieties of lace doily on display by the rapid-fire clicking of approaching heels on the hard tile floor.

The young woman in white reappeared in the doorway, but then stood aside while a large older man in an apron bearing a rainbow array of splatters marched purposefully through. He was followed by a young man in crisp, clean whites scurrying to keep up. The larger man rounded the counter at a brisk stomp and strode over to the officers, looking very much like a rhino advancing on a trespassing Land Rover. The younger man stayed safely behind him.

"What?" the man spat, challenge in his eyes.

"Mr. Capella?" Brandt asked, holding out his hand. The man did not move to take it but grunted and gave a single jerky nod. Brandt continued. "I'm Ethan Brandt, and this is Gabriel Donnelly. We're from the state police."

"So?"

"We're here to talk with you about the lawsuit filed last week. By the—"

"By the two faggots," Capella grunted, finishing Brandt's sentence.

"There's no need for—" Donnelly started, advancing on Capella with his hands clenched tight, but Brandt put a hand on his arm and he stood down.

"Mr. Capella, we've been asked by the attorney general to talk with you today, to see if there's some way we can avoid a drawn-out court battle that will only cost you and the state a lot of time and money. The verdict," he continued, his voice stiffening, "is not in doubt."

"The hell it isn't," Capella snarled. "I've gotten a hundred e-mails in the last week from conservative groups all over the country backing me up. Cases like this are won every day, and I'm going to win this one."

"No, you aren't," said Donnelly evenly. "The law is clear. The court precedent is clear. The will of the people of this state is clear. You won't win this case."

"We'll just see about that. I think you'll be surprised what one man can accomplish when he stands up for what is right." Capella waved his hand dismissively and stepped away from the officers.

"How long are you willing to stand by while your customers go elsewhere?" Brandt asked in as conversational a tone as he could muster.

Capella stopped in his tracks. He turned slowly back to face Brandt.

"Are you threatening me? My business?" Capella's voice was deeper now and deadly serious.

"Not at all," Brandt said lightly. "But I assume that the cancellations are going to start to pinch, if they haven't already."

"I haven't had any cancellations," Capella replied with a sniff. "In fact, I've gained a couple of customers who appreciate my standing up for traditional values."

The young man who had followed Capella into the room shook his head so slightly that Brandt wasn't sure at first that he had seen it. He nodded encouragingly, hoping to draw the man out.

Capella noticed the motion and turned toward the other man in baker's whites. "Justin?" he demanded, squinting angrily.

The younger man paled visibly and seemed to shrink under the withering gaze of the larger man. But he stood his ground.

"Dad," he said nearly inaudibly. "We've lost six weddings so far."

"No we haven't!" Capella snapped.

But Justin nodded slowly while studying the floor, as if expecting to be struck at any second.

Capella's mouth dropped open, and he emitted a sound like he'd been punched in the gut. "Why didn't you tell me?"

"I tried." The young man cleared his throat and took a deep, steadying breath. "Every time I'd bring it up you'd just yell at me about how angry you were and how everyone else was wrong, and I couldn't get you to listen to me."

Capella closed his eyes and sighed. But this defeated reaction didn't dissuade his son; rather, it seemed to spur him on.

"We're getting killed on Twitter, Dad. There's so much anger out there. Even the people who haven't already cancelled are talking about how they're going to. We'll be lucky to keep half of the weddings we have on the books if we don't stop fighting this."

Capella held up a hand to silence his son, but this motion was not nearly as forceful as the one he had made previously. "Stop. We don't do anything until I talk to the lawyer."

"Dad, we have to do what the officers say. And we have to do it right now."

His father's eyes sprang open. "Like hell we will!" he roared, and pushed past his son—or rather walked right through him, shoving him off to the side on his way out of the room.

Justin watched his father storm out, then turned back to the officers, his eyebrows peaked in apology. "I'm sorry about my dad. This has got him really worked up."

Donnelly nodded empathetically. "I know it probably feels like he's being attacked on all sides right now, but you're doing the right thing by pushing him. It'll be for the best in the long run."

Justin gave a half-hearted chuckle. "You don't have to convince me. His generation completely freaks out about sex, even the normal kind. People my age—" He stopped and looked at Brandt and Donnelly "—our age, I mean… well, it's just not that big a deal." He straightened his apron, which had been knocked askew by the impact of his fleeing father and then smiled at the officers. "I'm so glad you came to talk with him about this. I was getting nowhere."

"Is there anything else we can do?" Brandt asked.

"He'll come around. He just needs a little time."

"Here's how to reach us if you need anything." Brandt handed him a business card.

Justin looked at the card for a moment. "This is really your job? Going around and telling people not to be bigots?"

"Oh, it's much more complicated than that," Donnelly replied. "There's also, you know, a form we have to fill out. Police work."

Justin laughed. "Sounds very important. But seriously, I think what you're doing is awesome."

"I take it you don't share your father's view on 'traditional values'?"

"That's one way of putting it," Justin replied. "We don't see eye-to-eye on many things these days."

"Well, I hope he comes around to your way of thinking," Donnelly said. "Can you keep us posted?"

Justin tapped the business card in his hand. "I will—just as soon as I drag my dad into the twenty-first century."

"Thanks, Justin. It was great to meet you," Brandt said, extending his hand.

"You too." Justin shook both officers' hands and, with a deep sigh, turned to head into the back of the shop.

Brandt and Donnelly left the shop and walked back toward the floral district, where they had left their car. "Well, one win and one maybe," Donnelly said as they turned the corner. "Not bad for a morning's work."

"What did you think of the Capella family?" Brandt asked.

"The dad seems really angry, but the son…."

"Hmmm?" Brandt prompted, eyebrows raised.

"Our Justin seemed like a pretty strong supporter," Donnelly replied, somewhat carefully.

"My thought exactly. I wonder if there isn't something more that separates the two Capellas than a simple generational divide."

"Can you imagine growing up gay in a family like that?" Donnelly said with a shiver.

"Huh—I don't think I've ever really thought about what it would be like to grow up gay at all," Brandt replied. "I know you and I are kind of weird, since we grew up straight—or at least thinking we were straight. I probably would have been fine, since my family pretty much adopted you at first sight, but what would it have been like for you?"

"I think my parents and I would have made the Capellas look pretty calm by comparison. My brother Michael had exactly one conversation with my mom when he came out. It started with yelling and ended up with half of the good china shattered. They never saw each other again."

Brandt stopped walking. "Oh God—that's horrible."

Donnelly turned to his partner, a sad kind of smile on his face. "Yeah, it was horrible. And it made quite an impression on me, all of eleven years old. It's probably what kept me from seeing that you had fallen in love with me until it was obvious to everyone." He grinned and then kissed Brandt playfully on the nose. "Everyone's got drama in their past. But that's the best part about this new assignment: we get to make things better for those who come after us."

Brandt shook his head, beaming at his fiancé. "I am the luckiest man in the world."

"Damn right," Donnelly agreed and kissed Brandt again, this time on the lips.

They were interrupted by buzzing in Brandt's pocket, followed almost immediately by a similar sound coming from Donnelly's. They both reached for their phones and read the incoming message.

"Bryce?" Brandt asked.

"Yep." Donnelly looked up from his phone. "Ready to meet the first wedding planner?"

Brandt tried to make a convincing smile but burst out laughing when he saw Donnelly attempting the same maneuver. "We might as well get it out of the way. How bad could it be, right?"

Donnelly rolled his eyes as if he knew exactly how bad it could be but preferred not to say it out loud. They had until two o'clock to ponder.

CHAPTER THREE
BURYING THE HATCHET

"DAD, WE have to talk about this." Justin followed his father around the kitchen despite the older Capella's evident desire to avoid both his son and the subject of the gay wedding lawsuit.

"Look, we have a lot of work to do today. I can't take the time to call the lawyer right now."

"What's so urgent?" Justin asked, looking at the large calendar on the wall where the month's cake orders were posted.

"I gotta start on that wedding at the aquarium—they want the dolphins to be leaping over the main cake, and that means a lot of structure needs to be built." He knelt down and grabbed his toolbox from the shelf under the stainless steel counter.

"Dad, they canceled," Justin said softly.

Capella froze for a long moment, then set his toolbox slowly on the counter. Still facing away from his son, he took a deep breath and let it out slowly. "What?" he said, not really asking a question.

"They canceled Friday."

Capella picked up his toolbox and put it back under the counter. He turned to face his son. "Okay," he said, nodding to the calendar, "show me the damage."

Justin walked over to the calendar and plucked off the sticky note representing the aquarium wedding, three weeks away. He pulled five more notes off the calendar, ranging from a small wedding next Saturday to a huge winter affair just into next year.

"Those are the ones who have officially canceled. But judging from what I've been seeing online, we're going to lose this one, this one, and both of these"—he pulled off a series of sticky notes in turn—"and that's just through summer. I'd be surprised if we have more than a handful left by the end of the week."

Capella stood before the calendar and shook his head. "How did it come to this?" he asked quietly.

"It's a free country, Dad. People can do what they want."

"But how did this happen? When did this country decide that if you don't approve of sodomy, you don't get to run a business?"

"That's not what this is about."

"The hell it's not. I remember when this country stood for something, and faggots snuck around in the dark and didn't bother normal people. They knew better than to flaunt their perversion in public. Now, though, say one bad thing about the guy who wants to marry his pet goat and you're the enemy."

"We've never done a cake for a goat wedding, have we?" Justin asked, turning to his father in mock surprise.

"Shut up. That's not the point and you know, it."

"What is the point, then, Dad? We do wedding cakes. These people want to have a wedding. We don't have to approve of it, we just have to do it. And if we don't, then we won't have any of these to worry about either." He held out the handful of sticky notes representing lost business.

Capella turned to his son. "This is okay with you? Two men kissing and pretending like they're a bride and groom?" He looked about ready to expectorate in disgust as he spoke.

"It doesn't matter whether it's okay with me, Dad, that's what I'm trying to say. Whether or not it's okay with me, I can still make the cake and roll the fondant. The supply catalogs have carried two-groom toppers for years now. We can do this, just like any job we've ever done."

"I didn't ask you if you thought we could do it. I asked you if it was okay with you." Capella looked hard at his son. "Is it?"

Justin returned his father's piercing gaze. He squinted a bit and took a halting breath. "Dad—"

"I raised you with the right values," Capella interrupted. "You've been brought up the right way. Before you left for college I was sure of you—sure of what I had brought you up to believe. Then...." He paused for a moment and shook his head ruefully. "And then you went to college. Every time you came home I could feel that you had slipped further away from your roots, from the values that we raised you in."

"Dad, I'm still—"

"No, you aren't!" Capella barked. He took a step back as if surprised by his outburst but then stepped forward again to look into his son's eyes. "You aren't still the same boy I raised. I see the change."

"Times have changed, Dad. The people I went to school with, they don't care whether two men want to get married. They just don't care."

"But," his father said as he slowly brought a finger to Justin's chest, "do *you*?"

Justin closed his eyes and took a deep breath. "No," he said simply.

Capella pulled his finger back from his son's chest and let it drop limply to his side. He shook his head mournfully.

"Dad, I—"

"No." He shook his head more definitely now. "No. Don't talk." The baker turned and walked away from his son. He got about halfway through the kitchen before he stopped. "You do it," he said, facing away from his son. "I won't. If it has to be done, you do it." He resumed his shuffling progress through the kitchen and out the back door. It slammed shut behind him.

Justin stood silent, the sound of the heavy metal door echoing around him.

"Brandt."

The ringing of the phone had disturbed the officers as they sat at their desks writing up the morning's report. Brandt was actually glad to have the distraction—report writing was not really his thing.

"Officer Brandt, it's Justin Capella."

"Oh, Justin. Good to hear from you. What can I do for you?"

Donnelly looked up from his work with eyebrows raised. Brandt had never known him to be distracted from exercising his report-writing skills.

"I talked to my dad, and we're going to do the wedding. Can you get in touch with them? I haven't called the lawyer because… well, frankly the guy scares me. But I wanted to get the ball rolling because the wedding date is coming up and we need to get started."

"That's great to hear," Brandt replied, smiling and nodding to Donnelly. "I'll call the guys right now and let them know. And then you can put all the controversy behind you."

"That'll be a relief," Justin said with a sigh. "I just hope I can call off the social media attack dogs in time."

"Once you get the story out there, I imagine things will cool down pretty quickly."

"I hope so."

"If there's anything else we can do to help, please call us, okay?" Brandt said into the phone. He nodded and then hung up.

"Good news, then?" Donnelly asked.

"Very good news. Looks like both our florist and our baker have come around. This will make the chief happy."

"Well, once he reads this masterpiece of a report, he sure will be," Donnelly replied with a wide smile and turned back to his keyboard.

Brandt watched him type with a gusto that he simply couldn't understand. He smiled at the goofy love of his life and dialed the phone. When his call was answered, he snapped back to professional attention.

"This is Officer Ethan Brandt calling for Peter Laurence. … Yes, I'll hold."

"I'D FEEL better if Bryce and Nestor were here with us," Brandt said as he opened the door of the office complex corresponding to the address Bryce had sent them.

"Has wedding planning struck fear into the heart of the fearless Officer Brandt?" joked Donnelly.

"Can I be completely politically incorrect for a moment?" Brandt asked in a low voice as they walked in the direction indicated by the directory in the lobby of the building.

Donnelly nodded expectantly.

"I never imagined myself doing this," Brandt said.

"Getting married?"

"No, this—planning a wedding. I guess I always assumed that… well, that my fiancée would be doing all of this. You know, the kind of thing that… women like to do."

Donnelly sucked his cheeks in and nodded thoughtfully. "I see," he said through pursed lips.

"Not that I don't want to be here, doing this, you know. It's just that I didn't used to lie awake at night imagining the perfect wedding. I have no idea how we're supposed to do this. Like Laurence and Sampson, who have such strong ideas about cakes and flowers that they were ready to drag people into court to pursue their vision, or whatever."

Donnelly nodded again, a hint of a smile playing on his lips. "You know what I imagine about our wedding?"

"What?"

Donnelly stepped closer to his partner and put his lips to Brandt's ear. "You," he whispered. Then he stepped back. "That's it. If you're wearing a tux, that's great. If you're wearing jeans and a T-shirt, also great. If you're not wearing anything at all, well, that might be awkward for our guests, but I'd totally be on board. If there are flowers, that's awesome. I'm going to pretty much insist on cake, because for one thing, I love cake, and for another thing, I am going to completely smush a piece of that into your face at the reception—which can take place in a palace or at a gas station for all I care because by that time we'll be fucking married and no one will put us asunder. And that's it. Everything else is just frippery. But it's important frippery, because it will show the world—and God, and my mother—that we are married for real, just like all the 'normal' people who get married every day."

Brandt just goggled at this outburst.

"If it were just us, I'd be fine to run to the courthouse," Donnelly continued. "But we're not just doing this for us. We're doing it because it's an important right that the state has finally seen fit to grant us, and because by doing it publicly, we can set an example and make it easier for those who come after us. And because I want to prove to every man who's ever winked at you that you are mine." He leaned in again and pushed his finger into Brandt's chest, right at his heart. "Mine."

Brandt grabbed Donnelly by both shoulders, suddenly, roughly, pressing his fingers against the unyielding muscles. He lunged forward and kissed Donnelly with a ferocious desire, a surge of love and certainty that took his breath away—and Donnelly's as well, judging by his sudden intake of breath. They kissed for a full minute, not breaking their embrace even when two women walked past them in the corridor, deep in a discussion about life insurance.

Finally, when Brandt released him, Donnelly took a steadying breath. "Okay," he panted, "so I guess we're on the same page, then? About the wedding?"

"I would do anything, anything to be your husband," Brandt said, his voice reflecting the loopiness he felt in his head.

Donnelly beamed. "Then let the wedding planning commence, my love." He led the way down the hall.

They shortly arrived at the office of the wedding planner; standing before the door, they took a deep breath and nodded to each other, then entered. The office suite was decorated in a funky array of lush purples and reds, with leather furnishings that were perhaps more artistic than elegant. A receptionist smiled at them from behind an imposing desk.

"We're—" Brandt began.

"Mr. Brandt and Mr. Donnelly," said the receptionist in a British purr. "Or, shall I more properly say, Officers Brandt and Donnelly." She stood and walked around the desk on legs that would once have made Brandt a little light-headed; he was somewhat ashamed to admit that they had some of that effect on him still. But he shook it off and extended his hand, which she took delicately; she repeated this gesture with Donnelly, then pointed them to two extravagantly curvy leather chairs. "He will be with you shortly."

As the receptionist retreated to her desk, Brandt whispered into Donnelly's ear, "Do we even know who we're seeing?"

Donnelly shook his head. "Bryce didn't give a name."

"Typical. He's all about the mystery and intrigue."

Donnelly laughed and nodded. "All I know is that he was set up in business by someone Bryce called a 'wealthy benefactor,' which I can only interpret to mean 'sugar daddy.'"

"Does that inspire a lot of confidence?"

Donnelly shrugged. "What do we know? We just have to let Bryce be Bryce."

Brandt cast a quick glance around the room. "Clearly we are, or we wouldn't be in this purple den of matrimonial excess."

"Again," Donnelly replied, "if this is what it takes, I'm all in."

"Me too, me too."

"Gentlemen," called a male voice in greeting, and they turned to see their wedding planner approach. He was a slight but fit man wearing a precision-tailored suit and a well-practiced smile. "So pleased to meet you. I'm Lars."

The officers stood and offered their hands. Lars's grip was not quite as forceful as that of his receptionist.

"Oh my," he said wonderingly. "Bryce didn't do you justice."

"Excuse me?" Brandt asked.

"Oh, nothing. It's just that Bryce is normally quite adept at physical description, but this time the best he could give me was 'Captain America in street clothes, times two.' Which, as I said, doesn't even come close."

The men blushed and muttered in response to this not very subtle appreciation.

"Now, please, come into my office. Let me show you the wonders that await you on your wedding day."

They followed him down the hall and into the large room at the end. It looked more like a small theatre than an office, with rich red drapes covering the walls and a silvery screen at the far end. Lars closed the door behind them, and the only illumination was from small twinkling lights set into the ceiling.

"Please, sit, and let me show you my vision for your ceremony."

They took seats in the center of the room, and the screen lit up with the Lars's glittering logo; it sparkled brightly as he walked to the front of the room.

"Now, your wedding is the most special day in your entire life, and a wedding planned by my team of professionals will guarantee that everyone who attends will be talking about nothing else for weeks to come. First," he said, clicking the presentation remote in his hand, "the venue." The logo slide split in two and revealed a photo of the building that would house their nuptials.

"Wait, is that…?" Brandt wondered, shaking his head as he looked at the screen.

"Yes, it is!" Lars replied excitedly.

"So you're proposing that we get married… at the stadium?" Donnelly asked incredulously.

"It's the only place in the city that is large enough to contain my vision. Just wait until you see what I have planned!" He clicked the remote again, and the stadium faded away to be replaced by a picture of the football field it contained. Onto this canvas he had superimposed his concept. "Now, the march down the aisle has just been done to death, so I thought we'd go a different way."

Brandt squinted at the screen. "So, is that me on the horse?"

"Fabulous, isn't it? Of course it means the aisle will have to be wider than usual, and we'll have to be sure that there's nothing in the floral arrangements that might tempt him to stop and graze, but these are minor considerations."

"Yes, if I'm to be married on a horse, the rest of it is minor indeed." Brandt's voice was calm and even despite his rising horror.

"Oh, you aren't going to be married on the horse," Lars chuckled, as if the very idea were ridiculous. "You'll dismount once you reach the dais, and the hot air balloon has swooped down and deposited your beloved next to you."

Donnelly nodded, his face studiously serious. "Hot air balloon. Okay. But—now, I'm just thinking aloud here—wouldn't it be easier if I wore a jet pack and launched myself out there under my own power?"

"You'd think so, wouldn't you?" replied Lars with a knowing chuckle. "But take my word for it, jet engines and a tux with tails are a combination I'd recommend avoiding. The burn unit is no place for a honeymoon!"

Donnelly nodded as if trying to believe that any of this made sense. But Lars was still gathering steam.

"Now that our grooms are in place, we'll have the ceremony." He clicked the remote and a figure in black robes appeared at the head of the aisle, next to the grooms—and the horse.

Brandt leaned forward in his chair. "Is that David Beckham?"

Lars giggled with delight. "Just an artist's concept, dear—I don't think we'd be able to get him to officiate. But he makes for such a tall and strapping group, don't you agree?" He beamed at them with such intensity that they simply nodded, struck dumb by the "vision" Lars had put together.

"So then, love-honor-cherish, I do I do, and done. Now comes the fun part!" Lars clicked again and then took a step back, eyes intently focused on the fiancés.

Brandt felt his mouth drop open as if he were a cartoon character. He glanced to the side at Donnelly, whose hand was clapped tightly to his lips as if afraid his jaw was about to detach itself as well. Brandt swiveled his head back to the screen, and tried to make sense of the spectacle.

"So, we're sure about the fireworks, then?" Donnelly asked in a small voice.

"Oh yes! I have a connection on the city council—if you know what I mean," Lars answered with a wink, "so getting a permit for the pyrotechnics will be no problem at all."

"Will we be able to hear the choir over the explosions?"

"Certainly. Now, if there were just a few voices, they might be drowned out, but when you have this many it's not an issue. Plus, the stadium has a great sound system—when Celine Dion gave a concert there last year, no fewer than a dozen people ended up with burst eardrums."

Donnelly sat back, looking helpless.

"And… that's… another horse?" Brandt asked.

"Yes, of course! The two of you will ride back up the aisle on your majestic stallions, side by side."

Brandt winced. "You're certain the fireworks wouldn't spook them?"

Lars took a breath and looked at the screen with pursed lips. "Ah. Well. Yes, I'm sure we can get that figured out."

"Well, if the fireworks don't do it, I'm pretty sure the helicopter will," Donnelly murmured.

"Oh but the helicopter is *crucial*! It's how you make your big exit, and how we release the doves!"

Donnelly's eyes bugged out. "You're going to throw doves from a helicopter?"

"Not throw them, no! We're going to *release* them, so that they flutter away majestically into the sunset." Lars smiled broadly as if he had addressed every concern.

Brandt could no longer keep the laughter in his chest. It started as a chuckle, then erupted into a full-throated guffaw. Donnelly turned to him in alarm but quickly gave in to the same impulse and began laughing himself. Soon tears were running down the men's cheeks.

"What? What is it?" Lars demanded. "Did I miss something?"

Brandt wiped his eyes and tried to summon the breath to answer. "What you missed," he said, panting from the effort of stopping his (fully justified) laughter, "is that releasing doves into rotor wash is going to result in the guests being pummeled by birds crashing to earth. It will be like an explosion at a magic factory. Luckily, most of the guests will have already been blown out of the way by the helicopter taking off." He gave up trying to speak and began laughing again.

"These are valuable notes," Lars said with a sniff. "I'm sure we can tone down a few things."

Brandt and Donnelly, with great effort, recovered from their manic laughter and nodded as if they really believed Lars capable of toning down.

"Now, let's vision the reception!" he sang out, and clicked his remote.

"THANK YOU for coming to meet with us today," Peter Laurence said as he welcomed the man into his spacious corner office. "Please, have a seat."

Gregory Sampson was already sitting at the glass conference table. He rose and extended a well-manicured hand. "I'm Greg," he said in his resonant TV voice. "Pleased to meet you."

"I'm Justin Capella. Pleased to meet you, sir." Justin sat in a chair opposite the news anchor.

Laurence took a seat at the head of the table. All three men were silent for a moment. "I'm sorry that we had to go to such extreme measures to resolve our… issues," he said finally.

"No, I should be apologizing to you guys," Justin replied. "It was really stupid, what my dad did. If I had been home when you first met with him, I might have been able to head this whole thing off. But I was finishing my last semester, and I didn't get back home until two weeks ago."

"Congratulations on your degree. What did you major in? I'm sure it was something more useful than journalism," Sampson said with a chuckle and a roll of his pale blue eyes.

"Doubled in business and culinary arts," Justin replied. "Most people go to college to figure out what they want to do in life. I went because I knew exactly what I'd be doing for the rest of my life."

"You'll be the fourth generation to run the bakery, correct?" Laurence asked.

Justin nodded. "That's assuming I can rescue it from the nosedive Dad pushed it into. I've been working all day in the kitchen and all night on Twitter and Facebook, and all I can do is cross my fingers that I've done enough."

"Looks to me like you've been getting some good coverage on it," Sampson said encouragingly.

"Yeah, that piece in *AltaView* really helped us," Justin said.

"You read the gay weekly?" Laurence asked, eyebrows raised in surprise.

Justin nodded. "I figured it was the best way to tell whether our reputation was on the mend." He paused for a moment. "I wasn't expecting such a positive piece, though. It's almost like someone there was pulling for us."

"Well, sometimes things just work out like that," Sampson said with a wink at Laurence.

Silence fell on the group once again.

"So, I guess we're here to talk about the cake design?" Justin asked when the weight of the silence got to be too much. He ran his fingers along the edge of the black leather portfolio he'd brought with him.

"Yes, but we've also asked our florist to come to the meeting," Laurence replied. "We want to coordinate closely on the colors and designs, and we'd like the cake to incorporate some floral elements as well."

"Ah," Justin said with a nod. "Who's doing the flowers?"

Laurence's answer was cut short by the opening of the office door. His secretary showed in the person they were waiting for.

"Thank you for coming," Laurence said, standing and extending his hand. "I'm Peter Laurence, and this is my fiancé, Greg Sampson." The men shook hands. "And this is the man who will be making the wedding cake of our dreams—"

"Justin Capella," the new arrival said, causing Justin to turn around in his chair and look.

Justin's mouth dropped open, and he stood slowly. "Roman," he whispered. He put out his hand, but tentatively, as if he suspected he were about to reach straight through a ghost.

"Good to see you, man," Roman replied, grinning. "It's been too long." He pulled Justin into a hearty, back-thumping hug.

Justin, with a bewildered expression, hesitantly returned the other man's embrace. They disentangled and sat down at the table.

"So you two know each other?" Sampson asked. "I mean, obviously, but...."

"We haven't seen each other for a long time," Roman said, looking at Justin's still-surprised face. "But when you grow up in the wedding business, you know everybody."

Justin nodded and then looked away for a moment.

"Well, then, gentlemen," Laurence announced, "with that happy reunion accomplished, let's get to work."

"WELL, THAT was sure something," Donnelly said blandly on their drive back to the office.

"Yes, yes it was," Brandt replied, his eyes carefully on the road as he drove.

"I got kind of confused there at the end—I'm still not sure which parts of the reception are supposed to take place on the yacht. And where were all of those kids dressed in white holding candles supposed to stand?"

Brandt shrugged and looked helplessly at his partner. "Honestly, by that point I wasn't really taking in the details anymore. After the flash-mob dance number, I kind of lost it. There's no way the city would close an entire block of downtown so that our wedding guests could lip-synch Bruno Mars. And how did he think we were going to come up with the money for all that? It would cost a fortune."

Donnelly laughed. "I wasn't really thinking about how much it would cost, because you couldn't pay me enough to participate in that bizarre circus."

"So we're agreed that we need something a bit more tame?"

"Oh hell yes," Donnelly agreed and pulled out his phone. "I'll let Bryce know—oh, wait. Here's a text from him. He must have sent it just as we were getting in the car." He paused to read the message, then set the phone in his lap and looked at Brandt. "Apparently Lars called Bryce in tears because we didn't seem to appreciate his vision."

"I'll say this for Lars: he picks up on subtle signs," Brandt replied.

"Yeah, subtle like when you asked if he'd ever planned an actual wedding before," Donnelly said with a punch to Brandt's shoulder.

"Notice that he didn't answer that question?"

"You have a point there," Donnelly said with a tip of his head. He picked up his phone and typed away. "I'll let Bryce know that we're looking for something more normal...."

"Oh, don't use that word—you know how Bryce is."

"No worries. I have my autocorrect set to change the word 'normal' to a snoring emoticon. It offends him less." Donnelly finished typing, and a response arrived almost immediately.

"Oh dear," Donnelly muttered.

"What is it?"

"He says he has just the most perfect wedding planner in mind."

The men exchanged a wary glance.

"Couldn't be worse than Lars Vegas, could it?" Brandt asked, no trace of hope in his voice.

Donnelly nodded grimly. "I think that's pretty certain." He turned to Brandt, and his mouth turned up into a grin. "I'll bet the next one really will be perfect."

Brandt had no such confidence. "Of course it will," he said, putting his hand on Donnelly's leg and giving it a squeeze. "Of course."

CHAPTER FOUR
REUNITED

TWO DAYS later, Justin was alone in the bakery kitchen. The day's work was over, and the rest of the staff—including his father—had gone. Justin had developed the habit of staying later than everyone else so that he could spend time poring over the company's accounts, or making up supply orders, or—lately—monitoring social media channels for improvements in the reputation of Cakes by Capella. Over the last several days, the use of the #WeddingBigotBoycott hashtag had waned a bit, and several of the intended cancellations hadn't materialized. There were more sticky notes on the big calendar than there had been at any time since he returned from school.

He was startled by a knock on the back door. During the workday, this door was the main portal for suppliers, who wedged their delivery vehicles into the narrow alley behind the shop. But after about ten in the morning, a knock on that door was a rare event indeed. Justin got to his feet and walked through the corridor of wire shelving that held cake pans of every size and shape.

He peered through the peephole and then slid open the locks.

"Hey, Justin, you got a minute?"

"Uh, sure, come on in, Roman." Justin swung the door out into the alley.

Roman stepped into the kitchen and took a deep breath. "Ah, there it is. You were the only kid who came to school smelling like vanilla."

Justin pulled the door shut and locked it. "I can't believe you remember that, all the way back to third grade."

Roman stepped toward Justin and said quietly, "You're not the kind of person someone forgets." He turned and walked into the main part of the kitchen, leaving Justin standing with his hand on the door handle, stunned.

"I thought we should talk about the big gay wedding," Roman said as he pulled up a stool at the vast butcher-block table that formed the heart of the bakery. "Seems like a pretty high-profile deal, and I'm sure you want it to go as well as I do."

"I'm just kind of surprised that you're that concerned about it. You didn't seem all that thrilled with having to do it once they started talking about what they wanted."

Roman grunted and looked at the ceiling. "I'm not, to tell you the truth. My dad seems to have made his peace with the idea, but I just don't see the point in it."

"In what? People getting married?"

"No, in those guys getting married. Any guys getting married. I just don't see why they want to do it."

"They want to get married for the same reason anyone gets married." Justin looked hard at Roman, trying to remember whether he'd been such a jerk in third grade. "Look, you may have a problem with guys being together, but they have as much right as anyone—"

"I don't have a problem with guys being together," Roman interrupted. "Are you kidding me? Especially those two guys. I mean, did you get a look at them? Can you imagine what they look like when they're going at it? Damn."

Justin slumped back against the table, gripping it for support. His mouth went slack, and he squinted at Roman. No sound came from his lips.

Roman plowed ahead. "That lawyer's in pretty good shape for being, you know, a lawyer, but the TV guy? Holy shit. Don't tell me you didn't notice the way his shirt clung to him. Fuck, I was hard the entire time they were droning on about the exact shade of blue they wanted. The bluest things in that room were my poor fuckin' balls!"

Justin felt behind him for a stool and then thudded down onto it. He goggled speechlessly at Roman for another long moment. "You're kind of freaking me out right now" he was finally able to say.

"Yeah, I can see that. Sorry. I just didn't think I needed to sugarcoat it with you. Because you… like, get what I'm saying… right?" Roman nodded at Justin with eyebrows raised.

Justin blushed hotly and looked away. But he took a deep breath and made the slightest of nods.

"Good man. I knew it." Roman reached for a leftover bit of bright pink fondant and started to play with it like clay, molding and rolling it between his hands.

"So if you're—if we're both...." Justin cleared his throat and began again. "Why do you believe they shouldn't be able to get married?"

Roman's answer was to abruptly slam the fondant down onto the table, flattening it into a disk with the force of impact. "Because marriage is for boring, normal, stupid, *straight* people. Who needs that?"

"I thought everyone wanted to get married," Justin replied. "You don't? Like, ever?"

"Fuck no! When I was growing up, I used to lie in bed every night, panicked because I thought someday I would have to marry some woman—whom I knew I wouldn't be in love with because I knew that much about myself even then—and try to fake being happy the rest of my life when what I really wanted was dick, and lots of it. Then I finally got to college and realized my dream: that dorm was like a dick buffet."

"You went to a Catholic men's college," Justin said.

"Yep. It had its own seminary. *Sem-in-ary.* You've never seen so many repressed dudes in one place. All I had to do was let one of them know I was 'available,' and pretty soon there was a line down the hall. And the best part? I rowed crew. Strong quads and tight asses as far as the eye could see."

"Wow," Justin said, appalled at his friend's frank account of school spirit. "I had no idea."

"Really? What was college like for you?" Roman asked, picking up the fondant again and tossing it from hand to hand.

"Well, I joined the campus pride group, and we did some political organizing for pro-gay-rights candidates. And I wrote for the campus newspaper—under an assumed name, of course, in case my parents ever saw it. But I covered a lot of important issues for the community."

"The... community?" Roman asked.

"You know, the LGBTQ community."

"And did you actually have sexual relations with any of the members of this community?"

Justin blushed and shrugged awkwardly.

"Seriously? Four years of college and you didn't even get your dick wet?"

"Well, that's a disgusting turn of phrase," Justin replied archly. He shook his head, trying to clear it of what he'd just heard.

"Don't know what you missed, man," Roman said with a leer. "Once you find that out, you're never going to get on the wedding bandwagon again."

"See, I don't get that. Why do you think people shouldn't get married just because you're a complete slut?" Justin's words were sharp, but his tone was friendly.

"Because we're men. Men aren't meant to be tied to one person for life. We evolved to spread our stuff far and wide, not be chained down. And that's the best part about being into guys—we all want the same thing! We can fuck who we want, when we want, and then move on to the next."

"But some people—even gay people—want more than that. You know, love. And commitment and… romance."

At this last word, Roman's face pinched up like he'd bitten a lemon. "The only reason a man ever gets married is because there's something he wants and can't get any other way. It might be money, it might be the most amazing pussy ever, who knows? But he's not doing it because he wants monogamy. It's just not natural. And there's no reason in the world for two guys to get married, unless they've bought into the idea that what they really need to do in order to fit in is to forget that they're men and pretend to be hetero. It's pathetic. Those two we're doing this wedding for? They could be fucking three different guys every night—each. But instead they want to get all dolled up and walk down the aisle just like every stupid normal straight person in the fucking country. They might as well both wear wedding dresses."

"Wow," Justin said at the end of this tirade. "For a slut you're kind of angry about sex."

"You can keep calling me that, but I'll never see it as an insult. It's how a man is supposed to be, dude."

Justin shrugged. "I think we're going to have to agree to disagree on this one." He looked at his long-ago friend for a moment, trying to see the boy he once knew, but he couldn't get a glimpse of him under the hardened surface. He shrugged and gave up. "Since you're here, we should probably talk about the plans for this wedding that you think represents the complete abandonment of masculinity."

"Yeah, lots of pretty blooms and sweet, sweet sugar is going to make it all okay," Roman said with a roll of his eyes. But he pulled a notebook out of his pocket and started riffling through. "Okay, I have their list of preferred varieties, along with some swatches I found that get pretty close to the colors."

"Good. Now, they wanted flowers on the first three tiers of the central cake that would coordinate with the centerpieces—do you have notes on those?"

It was two hours later when they finally set aside their sketches and notes and plans. The shape and scope of the Laurence/Sampson wedding was laid out before them, scattered across the tabletop, and it was nearly complete. There were a few details they needed to consult with the grooms about, but they could start placing orders tomorrow.

"You know," Roman said, surveying the swath of paper, "your dad is pretty lucky to have you working here." He pointed to Justin's sketch of the central cake, a deconstructed grouping of abstract shapes with icing that worked through the tonal range of blues the grooms wanted for their reception. "That's a work of modern art, man. No wonder you guys keep getting spreads in the magazines."

"Shut up," Justin said with a gentle shove on Roman's shoulder. "I'm nowhere near as good as you are. That thing you did with the centerpieces? I've never seen anything like that, and I've been to a few weddings. They're going to be speechless when you bring those in."

"Anything for love, right?" Roman said with a cynical smirk.

"Coffee?" asked Justin, standing and stretching. His shirt rode up over his flat lower belly as he did so, and he caught Roman stealing a quick glance at the pale swath of flesh.

"Got anything stronger?" Roman asked.

"This is a place of business," Justin scolded, then grinned. "A business that just happens to keep supplies for making liqueur-based crèmes and fillings." He walked to a locked cabinet and pulled a key ring from his belt. "What's your pleasure?" he asked as he swung the doors open. "We've got rum, bourbon, and a ton of sweet gaggy stuff that makes a good filling but tastes like gumdrops soaked in kerosene."

"Bourbon it is!" called Roman giddily. He stood and picked up a couple of clean coffee mugs from the counter next to the coffee maker.

Justin poured a healthy splash into each mug, then capped the bottle and set it back on the shelf. As he turned to sit back at the table, Roman snagged the bottle and brought it along. He set it on the table with a thud, startling Justin, who looked at the bottle and then shook his head with a giggle.

"To old friends," Roman said, holding his cup out to Justin.

"Old friends," Justin repeated, touching his cup to Roman's.

Justin took a sip of the liquid and held it in his mouth as if it were a hand grenade; he swallowed it with effort and then panted several times and made a noise like a rusty door swinging open. Roman, meanwhile, simply tossed his entire cupful into his mouth and swallowed it right down. He picked up the bottle and filled his cup nearly half-full. He poured more into Justin's as well—Justin still hadn't caught his breath sufficiently to offer any objection.

They sat and sipped for a few minutes in the silence of the empty kitchen. It was nearing midnight.

"Okay, so here's a question," Justin said, the flush in his cheeks showing how quickly the alcohol was affecting him. "Why did we stop being friends?"

"Are you saying you're not my friend?" Roman said with a wink.

"No, of course not. I just wonder what happened to us. We were totally inseparable until, like, third grade—I don't remember any birthday or Fourth of July or anything when we weren't together—and then all of a sudden, you were gone."

Roman set his cup down. "They sent me to Catholic school, halfway to Springfield. I thought you knew that."

"Well of course I knew that. But it's not like they sent you to Siberia or something. Our families were still living in the same city. Why didn't we see each other anymore?"

"Why do you think that happened?" Roman asked, looking down at his cup.

"I thought you just didn't want to be my friend anymore." Justin's voice sounded almost as sad as he felt speaking those words.

Roman started. He looked up at Justin. "No, that's not it. Not at all."

"Then what happened?" Justin asked in an urgent whisper.

"You really don't remember?"

Justin shook his head.

"Huh." Roman took another pull on his bourbon.

Justin waited, but no more information seemed to be forthcoming. "Roman?" he said softly. "What… what happened to us?"

"You remember Mr. Backus?"

"The art teacher? He was pretty cool."

"Remember when he took us to the Springfield museum to see the Egyptian exhibit?"

Justin furrowed his brow with the effort of remembering. "It was supposed to be mummies and stuff, right?"

"Yep. It was an overnight trip—we took the bus over after school, so we could get to the museum first thing in the morning."

Justin's eyes lit up. "Ah, that's right! They herded us through a McDonald's and then thought somehow we would be able to fall asleep in sleeping bags on a gym floor with kids from three other schools. I remember that now—how that gym smelled, and the weird echoing of the teachers' whispering and pacing around." He stopped and frowned. "That's odd."

"What?"

"I remember the bus ride and the gym, but I don't remember the exhibit—I can't say I remember ever actually seeing a mummy."

"That's because we didn't make it to the museum."

Justin studied Roman's face for a long moment. "Why not?"

Roman looked down at his hands. He took a deep breath, then another.

"What is it?" Justin asked. He put a hand on Roman's arm.

Roman looked at Justin's hand and then closed his eyes as if he couldn't bear the sight of it, the touch of it. "You really don't remember?" He looked quickly at Justin, but then back down to his hand. "It's cruel to make me say it if you do."

"Honest to God, Roman, I have no idea what you're talking about." Justin looked into Roman's face again. "Tell me. Tell me what happened."

"We put our sleeping bags next to each other, of course," Roman began quietly. "Like we always did."

Justin nodded but remained silent.

"In the middle of the night, you woke me up—you were crying and saying you missed your mom."

Justin gave a small chuckle. "It was my first time sleeping anywhere but home or at your house."

"I tried to tell you it was okay, but you were so sad. I...."

"What? What did you do?" Justin asked. "It's okay to tell me— it's not like it's going to hurt anything now."

Roman swallowed hard. "I crawled into your sleeping bag with you."

"Well, that was nice of you. That probably helped a lot."

"It didn't, at least at first. It wasn't until I put my arm around you, and I pulled you tight to me. Then you finally stopped crying. And you fell asleep lying on my chest."

"That's... well, that's just sweet. Thank you."

"If that's all there was, we'd have made it to the museum." Roman stopped for a moment, breathing carefully. "A little later, I think the sun was just starting to come up, we sort of woke each other up—it was pretty tight in that sleeping bag. You were trying to turn over, and I was... well, you kinda were rubbing up against me a little, and I got a stiffy—all four inches of my third-grade dick came springing up. You felt it, like really felt it, and you looked up at me with the widest damn eyes."

Justin's hand came up to cover his mouth. "Oh my God. I remember now. And then—"

"And then I did what any red-blooded boy would do when he's just been caught grinding on his best friend. I kissed you."

Justin's hands whipped up to his ears, as if he were trying to block out the words.

"You remember what happened next, I take it?"

"It was so loud," Justin said, lowering his hands from his ears. "It was so loud."

"That was Mr. Backus, screaming bloody murder at the sight of two third-grade boys making out." Roman tossed back the last of his bourbon, poured more. "Dude had a set of lungs on him. Shrieked like he was getting raped by Nazis."

"Holy fuck. How could I have forgotten that?" Justin said wonderingly.

"Well, in terms of trauma, it's right up there on the list of Worst Things Ever, at least for boys on a field trip. You really don't remember what came next?"

Justin shook his head.

"My dad had to come pick us up. Drove all the way to Springfield on a Friday to retrieve his pervert son."

"I still don't remember everything, but I don't think you were the only pervert in that sleeping bag."

Roman stopped. Stopped talking, stopped breathing.

"What? What is it?" Justin asked, his hand again on Roman's arm.

"I told them… I told them it was… me."

Justin sat back a bit, frowning.

Roman continued. "When my dad came, I told him and Mr. Backus that I had crawled into your sleeping bag and started kissing you. I told them you were asleep and didn't know what I was doing."

Justin gaped at him, mouth slack. "Why would you do that?"

Roman looked him in the eye with an intensity that seemed to startle him. "To protect you. From your dad. From everyone. I did it because I was the dirty one, not you."

"But we kissed each other."

"They didn't know that. And I'm not actually sure you knew that either—not what I knew, about myself. I knew that kissing you was what I wanted, and even once my dad and my mom and God himself had come crashing down on top of me for it, I still knew." Roman paused and caught his breath. "You showed me who I was. I owed you for that."

"I don't know what to say," Justin said, wiping his eyes.

"There's nothing to say. That very afternoon my dad enrolled me at the Catholic boarding school, and I was told in no uncertain terms that I was never to see you again. He said that if I ever laid eyes on you, Satan would know what I did to you, and you would be damned to Hell for eternity."

"He actually told you that?"

Roman nodded.

"And you believed it?" Justin couldn't comprehend the weight that had rested on the nine-year-old shoulders of his friend.

"For a lot of years I did. I was terrified that I might accidentally see you, like at the grocery store or something, and that Satan would jump up right then and drag you down to Hell. I went through adolescence thinking that if I ever kissed anyone, or even felt about them the way I felt about you, Satan would be there. You can see why the idea of getting married was… well, unappealing."

Justin was quiet for a moment. "Thank you," he finally said.

"For what?"

"For growing up so quickly. For protecting me. For… well, thanks. I wish I could repay you for what you did."

"Water under the bridge." Roman finished his third cup of bourbon. "Though I guess there might be something…."

"Name it," Justin said, smiling brightly.

"Kiss me."

"What?"

"Kiss me. Remind me of what started me on my way to being a 'complete slut.'"

"Really?" Justin asked skeptically.

"Really. Just like old times. Just once."

Justin pursed his lips in thought, but then smiled slyly and leaned in to finish the kiss they had started thirteen years before.

CHAPTER FIVE
HEAT IN THE KITCHEN

"AND HE promises this one is different?" Brandt asked.

Donnelly, who had just slipped into bed, read from Bryce's text again. "You will love him. Everything's organic and Zen."

"That doesn't sound like Bryce's voice."

"I edited it a bit," Donnelly said with a shrug. "He actually said 'love love love him,' and after 'Zen' he added 'I fear that means no deodorant, so be warned, darlings.' But I gave you the gist of it."

"It seems almost redundant to say that Bryce may be overcorrecting here."

"We told him we didn't want fireworks and white stallions, so he's not giving us fireworks and white stallions. We must let the master work." Donnelly set his phone on the side table and picked up his reader.

Brandt craned his neck to glimpse the screen. "Aha! I knew it. *Emma.*"

Donnelly fixed him with a withering gaze. "Real men read Jane Austen, love. Get over it."

"Real men, eh?"

Donnelly nodded gravely.

"Prove it," Brandt challenged.

With slow and precise movements, Donnelly set his reader back on the side table. He turned back to his taunting partner with an eyebrow cocked up. "Prove it?"

Brandt nodded calmly, but his heart was racing. Donnelly looked to be the lighter-built man, but he had been a competitive wrestler all through high school and still had fierce moves. In an instant Donnelly was atop him, covering him, owning him. He looked deeply into

Brandt's eyes with an intensity that gave Brandt a shiver down his spine.

"What," Donnelly whispered, "makes a real man?" He ran his stubbled chin along the hollow of Brandt's cheek, nuzzling him with a delicate, abrasive urgency.

"Is it what I'm feeling on my hip right now?" Brandt murmured back. "Because that feels real, and it feels manly, and I think it's starting to drool on my leg."

"That's not what makes a real man." Donnelly's breath was hot and moist as he swept his lips across the strong clavicles and the soft hollow at the base of Brandt's throat.

"What is it?" Brandt's voice was nearly a whine, laced with his need.

"A real man is always in control," Donnelly growled as he kissed his way down Brandt's chest. "A real man never loses his head." He traced his tongue delicately along Brandt's belly, kissing each plated ab muscle, following the path of soft, short hair that led him farther down.

"I like the way this is going," Brandt muttered with a sigh. He could feel the tension draining from his body as his lover tasted him, teased him. But Donnelly stopped short of what Brandt had hoped would be his ultimate destination.

"Now, we're going to see who's the real man—the one who appreciates the gentle humor and wise insights of Jane Austen, or the one who claims as his crowning literary achievement the fact that he has read every issue of *Sports Illustrated* published since he turned eight?"

"Hey, there's some good writing in there," yelped Brandt.

"Please. You just get it for the pictures." He laughed at Brandt's consternation. "But setting that aside, I propose the following challenge. As the test of a real man is his self-control, we will put each other to the acid test."

"And what would that be?" Brandt asked, intrigued despite the recent insult to his reading habits.

Donnelly sat up and reached for the top drawer of his side table. He grabbed a small bottle and held it in his hand. "Here is the contest. We will face each other, and with our hands only—and the contents of this bottle—we will each try to make the other lose control. The first one to come loses his claim to the title of 'real man' for the rest of the evening."

"Meaning what, exactly?" Brandt asked skeptically.

"Simply that he will be at the whim of the other. For, you know, purposes of helping the real man reach... completion." He smiled wickedly at Brandt.

"Fuck yeah, I'm in," Brandt said instantly. "The hardest part of this contest is going to be deciding how I want you to service me afterward."

"Pride goeth, love," tutted Donnelly as he settled into position and popped open the bottle of lubricant. He stretched his legs up over Brandt's so that they were facing each other with direct access to their manly bits. "Ready?"

"You're going to find out how ready," Brandt jeered as he reached for the bottle. He squeezed a large dollop on his palm and rubbed it warm between his hands.

"Go," Donnelly mouthed silently, and with that the men got to work.

Brandt slid his hands along Donnelly's cock, already semihard from their sexy trash-talking. His lubed-up hands crackled as he stroked firmly up and down, and Brandt felt the blood surge into his partner's manhood. It was glossy and slick along its already considerable length, and Brandt paused to swab up the crystal drop that had appeared at the tip. This he rubbed in with swirling strokes of his thumb, knowing that the sudden roughness would shock and thrill his partner. He was rewarded immediately by a sigh of surprised pleasure—he was going to win this.

Donnelly, meanwhile, had reached out and taken gentle hold of Brandt's graceful arc of erect penis. It was hard—it was always hard at a moment's notice, ready for anything. Donnelly held the lube bottle a few inches above the surface of the steely rod of flesh and drizzled a delicate bead of cold liquid along its length. Brandt jumped in shock, but as the shiver worked its way through his body, Donnelly gripped his cock with both hands and began a strong massage that provided a second shock.

Brandt looked with wild eyes at Donnelly and tried to catch his breath. "Fuck," he grunted.

The corner of Donnelly's mouth tucked up in a devilish snarling grin. "Real man," he whispered on a long, slow exhale.

Brandt's response was to play both of his thumbs under the tip of Donnelly's cock, right where the shaft joined the head. He knew his partner was sensitive there, and he applied a stroke that was all business. Donnelly responded by reaching a slippery hand down under Brandt's cock and taking hold of his balls; a few insistent milking motions and Brandt felt himself starting to slip away. He needed to change tactics, get his footing back.

"You know who I saw today?" he said conversationally, as if something had randomly occurred to him.

"Who?" Donnelly asked, playing along with the sudden conceit that they were conversing over tea rather than engaging in competitive mutual masturbation.

"That delivery guy, the new one? He had this huge package—to deliver. It was so hot today that he was wearing a sleeveless shirt and these really tight shorts. It was kind of a good look for him—tight little ass, muscular legs, those big boots. He asked where you were. I think the poor guy looks forward to seeing you. I had to gaze into those big brown eyes, with that lock of golden hair lopping over one of them, and tell him that you were in a meeting and couldn't come out and"—Brandt gave an extra-firm stroke along Donnelly's cock—"play."

"Unnh," breathed Donnelly.

"He looked so disappointed. On his way back to the truck, even his ass seemed sad—just hard muscle, clenching and releasing, clenching and releasing—but no bounce." Brandt made an exaggerated pouty face and then doubled his stroking pace.

Donnelly's eyes rolled back in his head, and he huffed out three quick breaths. Brandt could see his lower abs stand out in stark relief, as if he were trying to hold back his orgasm by force of muscle and will. Finally, he seemed to come back to the present moment, and he fixed Brandt with a steely glare.

"Nice try," he growled. Then he released his grip on Brandt's balls and brought his hand up to his lips. "But now it's time for the boys to pack up their toys and leave the real men to their work." He opened his mouth just enough to allow his middle finger entry, and his lips closed around it as he slid it in. He pulled it slowly out, glossy with his saliva, then slid it back in. He repeated this motion, wetting his finger.

Brandt watched this motion with rapt attention.

Donnelly pulled the finger from his mouth and licked it slowly from knuckle to tip. He made a groaning, growling noise as he did so.

Brandt's stroking slowed as Donnelly's performance overwhelmed him.

Donnelly pulled his tongue away from his finger, a crystalline strand linking them for a drippy moment. He looked deeply into Brandt's eyes and kept locked onto them while his hand dropped back down. Brandt felt the finger slip under his balls, and with the sure aim of the man who knew Brandt's body better than he did himself, Donnelly found his ass. His eyebrow twitched up as he slipped his finger suddenly, rudely, relentlessly into Brandt's most private place.

Brandt gasped, shocked and thrilled with the intrusion. Donnelly crooked his finger, and Brandt felt it grind against his prostate.

"Oh…," he moaned as the sudden electric heat spread through him.

Donnelly's evil grin spread wider as he pressed harder, working Brandt's gland the way a virtuoso fingers the strings of a Stradivarius. Long come-hither strokes interspersed randomly with wild side-to-side flicks and simple, vigorous pressure right on the center of sensation.

Brandt tried to hide the utter demolition of his resistance to Donnelly's expert massage, but he could not mask the jolting pleasure vibrating through him. Donnelly looked down and saw the spurt of clear fluid that his ministrations had forced from deep in Brandt's loins and nodded slowly, as if he knew he had won.

Nothing Brandt could do in his distracted ecstasy was a match for what Donnelly was doing to him. He stroked and tugged, he massaged and tickled. But Donnelly only doubled down on Brandt's prostate, and the outcome was inevitable.

Brandt, faced with overwhelming force, did the only thing he could think of. *Kamikaze*. If he was going to be destroyed, he would take his enemy with him.

"Oh, fuck," he moaned, fluttering his eyes closed. "You always know how to make me… make me…." His voice drifted off as he bit his lip and looked Donnelly in the eye. He raised his voice to a whimper and started to thrust his pelvis in time with the stroking on his cock. "Yes, yes, yes," he chanted. "Take me... take my ass... take everything."

Donnelly's expression was no longer quite so cocky. He was hanging on Brandt's every dirty word.

"All I want is your cock in my ass. When I lose, will you fuck me? I need your hard cock in me... filling me... soaking me with your cum. I want this"—he squeezed and stroked deliberately, slowly—"in me, hard and fast. Take my ass, Gabriel, take my ass just like that first time."

And with that, Brandt knew he had him. But he also knew he could hold out no longer. The surge began, and Brandt gave up and gave himself to it.

"Fuck!" ejaculated Donnelly.

For the next ninety seconds, the two men shuddered and stroked and soaked each other, lacing themselves from hip to throat with streaks of hard-earned white.

Then, finally, their contest was over.

Panting, the men looked at the mess they had created. Donnelly was the first to burst out laughing, followed immediately by Brandt.

"So I guess we'll never know," Brandt said once he had caught his breath.

"Fuck that," Donnelly cried out. "Rematch!"

Brandt looked down at their soaked torsos. "At the risk of sounding less than manly, can we freshen up in the shower first?"

"Oh hell yeah," Donnelly replied. He disentangled his legs from Brandt's and swung his feet to the floor. He stood, then turned back. "And just FYI, real men love that oatmeal exfoliant scrub you got last week."

Brandt sat on the bed a moment longer to watch Donnelly walk from the room, a flawless symphony of muscle and grace. He was very much in love with his real man, he thought, as he rose from the bed to follow.

THEIR KISS lasted longer than they had breath to sustain; it left them panting when they finally broke from each other.

"Fuck," Justin sighed. He shook his head wonderingly at his best childhood friend, whom, he now realized, he hardly knew at all. "That was amaz—"

He was interrupted by Roman's lips pressed to his own. Suddenly Roman's hands were everywhere—clutching at his neck, forcing them more tightly together, then tangling in the hair on the back of his head, and then running down his chest and tugging roughly at the hem of his shirt.

Justin pulled back. "What are you—"

Roman laughed. "What am I doing? I thought it was pretty obvious. Your shirt is between me and something I want, so it has to go."

"This is really… sudden," Justin said.

"Do you want me to stop?" Roman asked in response.

Justin looked at him, up and down. Every boy he had ever felt an attraction to, he now realized, was a pale imitation of the man in front of him now. Roman was so familiar, and yet nothing like anyone in Justin's experience. Sudden desire fought against his native shy reserve, and he felt blood pounding in his temples as they struggled. Then clarity: desire won. "No. I don't," he said quietly. "Don't stop."

Roman's response was to tuck up the corner of his mouth in a sly grin and grasp the hem of Justin's T-shirt once again. Justin lifted his arms to allow Roman to pull it up over his head, but that wasn't what Roman had in mind. The sound of Justin's shirt being torn in half, rent from his body, ripped through the quiet of the late-night kitchen.

Justin's eyes widened in shock. He opened his mouth to speak, but Roman put his fingers against his lips.

"Shhh." Roman kissed him again, pressing him back against the table.

Justin, finally beginning to recover from the surprise of Roman's first kiss, was shocked all over again to feel Roman's sinuous tongue slip between his lips. It came into him, strong and bold and urgent, and he opened to it without thinking. He threw his arms around Roman and held him tight, more tightly than he had ever held another man.

And then, suddenly, Roman was everywhere on him at once—kissing his face, nibbling on his throat, running his lips along Justin's delicate clavicles. When Roman licked at his nipple and then sucked it gently into his mouth, Justin gasped and felt his knees give way. But he didn't fall; Roman held him.

"I've got you," Roman whispered as he slid his body up Justin's.

The friction of Roman's rough shirt against his chest overwhelmed him—it was the most masculine thing he had ever experienced.

Roman looked into his eyes. "You feel it, don't you? You get it now?"

Justin, not sure he fully understood, nodded instinctively.

"This. This is what men do," Roman murmured as he ran his hands down Justin's arms, his fingers tracing the bulges and hollows formed by years of lifting heavy cake pans and endless hours squeezing pastry bags. "This is how men make each other feel."

"I've never...." Justin fell silent, not knowing how to describe what they were doing, what he had never in his life done.

"Never what? Done it in your dad's bakery?" Roman's cocky grin came surging back.

Justin shook his head. "I've never done... anything."

"With a guy?" Roman asked, his eyebrows peaked in surprise.

Justin looked at the ground. "With anyone."

"I don't understand," Roman replied, sounding genuinely puzzled. "Did you not want to?"

"It's not that. I just... never found anyone who wanted to do... who wanted me," Justin said with a shrug.

Roman's mouth dropped open. "Look at you," he whispered. "Look at you." He grabbed a sheet pan from the shelf next to the table and held it up. Its underside, glossy from years of sliding over the lip of the oven, reflected a slightly blurry vision of Justin, shirtless in the dim light of the kitchen.

Justin shook his head miserably at Roman. "No, don't," he pleaded.

"Look," Roman insisted. "You have to look."

Justin reluctantly turned his gaze to the sheet pan. What he saw stunned him. He had long thought of himself as a lanky, pale, somewhat nerdy baker's son, not much to look at. But even this makeshift mirror was able to put the lie to that. The rough devotion of Roman's wandering kisses had flushed his skin with healthy color; the muscles of his chest stood out, strong from weeks of hard labor in the kitchen to compensate for his father's aloofness in the face of the lawsuit. Buoyed by Roman's urging, he stood tall and strong and... handsome. He had never felt handsome in his entire life before this moment.

"See?" Roman said with a smile as he set the pan aside. "You would have had them lining up to take a chance at you." He stepped closer to Justin. "If you'd let them."

Justin looked at him for a long moment, silent. "How'd you do that?"

"What?"

"We haven't seen each other for more than a dozen years, and you walk in here and tell me exactly why I'm alone. Lonely and virginal. What I could never work out on my own, despite all the long nights I spent trying to figure out what was wrong with me. You walk in here, and kiss me, and tell me it's not that no one wanted me, it's that I wouldn't let anybody in." He stopped and caught his breath. "How'd you do that?"

"I know you, Juss."

Justin startled. "You... remember."

Roman smiled. "You never forget your first love, right? I must have said that name to myself a hundred times a day for years and years, like I was casting a spell to get you back."

"And now here we are," Justin said. "I think we have to face the possibility that you are a wizard."

They burst out laughing—Justin had never felt so happy. He had also never felt the warmth in his lower belly that Roman seemed to be inciting.

"Hey, come here," Justin said, taking Roman's hand.

"Where we going?"

"Just come."

Justin led the way down a corridor on the other side of the kitchen and turned into a doorway halfway along. In this room the bakery piled materials to be recycled.

Roman looked around the room and then at the pile of cloth in the middle. "Are those... flour sacks?"

Justin nodded. "Looks like my sustainability initiative is paying off, right?" he said as he pulled Roman into the room and sat down on the empty sacks. He patted the spot next to him, and Roman sat.

"Well, now what?" Roman asked.

Justin answered by placing his hands under Roman's jaw and leaning in close for the most delicate of kisses. He pulled back and smiled. "When I used to dream about my first kiss, that's what it was like," he said. "You made my dream come true."

Roman grinned. "It was in the back of the bakery, on a pile of flour sacks, and it was with a boy?"

"It was with you. That's the most important part. I always imagined it would be you. I just didn't know how to find you. And I didn't know if you would be... you know."

"The kind of boy who kisses boys?" Roman asked with a laugh.

"Exactly."

"Well, now that we've checked off your boyhood romance to-do list, can we move on to what men do?"

Justin, his heart suddenly racing, nodded.

Roman launched himself at Justin with a sudden rapacious zeal, knocking him backward onto the flour sack mattress. He brought their mouths together, but the time for seductive, beckoning kisses was over. He took Justin's lower lip in his teeth and tugged, playfully at first, but with increasing force until Justin cried out from the overwhelming possession Roman was taking of his mouth, of his body. In a flash Roman moved lower, nipping his way down Justin's chest with an erratic intensity. He didn't stop at the nipples this time, though; he continued his descent, over the lightly furred ab muscles just visible underneath the perfect pale skin of Justin's lower belly.

Justin jumped when he felt Roman's hands take hold of his belt buckle. He sat up, instinctively, at the invasive tugging. Roman looked up at him with a crooked grin.

"If you were a woman, I would have to do the PC thing and ask if I have permission to open your pants."

"But you're not going to, are you?" Justin asked breathlessly.

"No, because your dick is going into my mouth and there's nothing you can do about it."

"Oh, fuck," Justin moaned and threw his head back. "You can do anything you want," he whispered.

"I know," Roman whispered back. He worked Justin's belt and then opened the button at the top of his fly.

Justin felt him pull the zipper down slowly. A sudden heat of thrill and danger swept over him from his center, heightened when Roman tugged his jeans down his legs.

"Off with these," Roman said, yanking the jeans down Justin's slender but strong legs.

His shirt was in tatters in the other room; his pants lay crumpled on the floor. Justin had never been so exposed, and the sensation was intoxicating. But of what lay ahead he was truly terrified.

He felt his legs pushed roughly apart, and Roman knelt between them. He brought his face to Justin's boxer briefs, and paused.

Justin could feel hot breath sweeping over his crotch. He had never wanted and feared something so much at the same time. He lay in terror of what Roman was going to do, in desperate need for him to do it.

Roman took in a deep breath. "This," he said, smiling blissfully. "This is what it means to be a man." He rubbed his nose along the contours of Justin's cotton-encased privates.

The contact was electric. No one had ever touched Justin so intimately, and this man was doing it with the casual instinct of a dog nuzzling around for tasty scraps. Finally, he could wait no more. "Please," he whimpered.

"Please what?" Roman asked, playfully.

"Please do it," Justin begged.

"Don't ask for what you want, Juss. A man takes what he needs. Grabs it and makes it his."

Justin was in agony. He needed contact, he needed friction, he needed... Roman. Now.

He set caution—and thought—aside, and he gave himself to his need. With one hand he thrust down the waistband of his briefs; the other he put on the back of Roman's head, and pushed him down until the other man's mouth was pressed against his already rock-hard cock. He ground against Roman, thrust at him until he opened his mouth and Justin's cock slid in.

Justin gasped, his hands flying up away from the place where their bodies met. Roman, however, was unstoppable. He yanked the briefs down, wrapped a fist around the base of Justin's cock, and slurped the entire length of it into his mouth. He sucked and bobbed and moaned until Justin could hardly breathe. He was in free fall, and his only link to sanity was the hard flesh that joined them.

"I… it's… watch out…," Justin babbled, making no sense at all. Roman apparently understood him perfectly.

A few more strokes was all it took. Justin's entire body suddenly went rigid as the orgasm tore through him from head to toe. He had never experienced an orgasm wrought by another person, and now he was having this one forcibly wrenched from him by the vigorous—and, he could almost bring himself to think, manly—force of Roman's athletic ministrations. His fists were tight balls, his breath was shallow, and then… what had previously been only his became Roman's.

If it was the mark of the complete slut that he could take a long-pent-up ejaculation straight down the throat without missing a stroke, Roman had proved himself beyond a shadow of a doubt. He urged every drop out of Justin, absorbed every spasm he could produce.

It was a full two minutes before Justin could even open his eyes. But when he did, he looked down to see a beaming Roman kissing his way from root to tip and back again, a repeating cycle of devotion to Justin's exhausted but still quite firm penis.

"How was it, the first time?" Roman asked.

"It was amazing," Justin sighed.

"Not that you have anything to compare it to."

"Don't need to compare it to anything. That was the most incredible thing anyone's ever done to anyone, and that's a fact." Justin looked down at Roman and put his hands on Roman's shoulders. "Come here," he said softly.

Roman slid up, his fully clothed body contrasting to Justin's fully naked one, and looked Justin in the eyes. "Thank you," he whispered.

"I'm the one who should be thanking you," Justin replied.

Roman shook his head. "I've been dreaming of this my entire life. Thank you for being exactly who I hoped you would be. The one I need."

"For a manly slut you sure talk romantical," Justin said with a giggle.

"You may be the one person in the world who could change me," Roman said.

Looking into his deep green eyes, Justin suddenly knew he could take him at his word. They were each other's dream come true.

IT WAS nearly two o'clock in the morning when Justin opened the back door of the bakery to let Roman slip back out into the alley. They kissed once more at the door, and then Roman stepped out into the dark, quiet streets of the city. He looked back at Justin, who stood looking lovestruck in the doorway. He smiled and blew him a kiss, then walked into the night.

As he reached the end of the alley, he pulled his phone from his jacket pocket. He typed a quick text, hit "send," and then pocketed his phone and strode away.

I'm in.

"YOU'RE SURE this is the place?" Brandt asked Donnelly again.

"This is the address Bryce gave me." He waved his phone in front of Brandt's face.

They were standing before a somewhat tattered bungalow in the oldest part of town—one that had seen gentrification and decline several times over the decades. It was clearly somewhere in the middle at the moment. The block was home to several alternative-medicine practitioners, a pawn shop, some tiny restaurants serving the cuisine of distant lands, and, apparently, a wedding planner. "Organic Unions" the sign above the porch read. It looked like macaroni art. With glitter.

"Hmm," Brandt grunted.

"Shall we?" Donnelly said with a smile that Brandt almost believed was real.

Brandt shrugged and nodded, and they headed up the steps together. There was no doorbell, so Donnelly knocked.

"Enter in joy," a dreamy voice called from within.

Brandt looked at Donnelly, exasperated.

"Dig deep and find your joy, buddy," Donnelly said with a playful warning in his voice. "We're goin' in."

He pushed the door open, and they stepped into an absolutely palpable cloud of incense and patchouli. Donnelly staggered back for a moment but then set his shoulders square and forged ahead. Brandt followed, after ducking back to take a last breath of outside air.

The front room of the house had been converted into a reception area of sorts, furnished with beanbag chairs and tatami mats. Behind a bead curtain, a man sat cross-legged on the floor of an otherwise completely empty room, his open hands resting on his knees, his eyes closed. Brandt and Donnelly stood for a moment in the middle of the front room, not sure if they were supposed to approach the man or sprawl on the floor and wait for a further joyful invitation.

"Please, come," the man said in a slow, drifting voice, without opening his eyes.

Brandt and Donnelly exchanged a look and walked toward the bead curtain. Donnelly reached out and parted the beads, then nodded chivalrously and waved Brandt through.

"Thanks, buddy," Brandt muttered, less than thrilled to be leading the way.

Donnelly followed close behind and came to stand next to Brandt before the meditating man.

"I invite you to sit," the man said, still not opening his eyes.

Brandt's quick scan of the room confirmed that there was no furniture. He looked questioningly at Donnelly, who shrugged helplessly. The men simply sank to their knees, then assumed a cross-legged position themselves.

"Welcome," the man intoned, his eyes finally opening. He looked Donnelly up and down and then did the same to Brandt. He nodded slowly, as if receiving messages from the ether. His gaze drifted to the space between the two men, and he stared in an unfocused but intense way for a long moment. Then he suddenly seemed to return to the moment. "Yes, I see it. Good, good."

Brandt looked at Donnelly, then turned to see if there was something behind him that the man was looking at. Seeing nothing, he came slowly back around.

"What do you see?" Donnelly asked.

This is why he'd be great with kids, Brandt thought. Infinite patience for indulging the silliness of others. As much as he wanted to get the hell out of here, Brandt had to smile to himself, seeing Donnelly's defining kindness at work in the world.

"The mingling of your energies," the man replied, stating this as if it must surely be a regular point of conversation between the two men. "Both strong, powerful—but where they meet, a great calmness, as if their union brought a peace to both that neither imagined they'd ever experience." He sighed and smiled, as if the very sight of the officers' "energies" overlapping made him content.

"That's… interesting," Brandt said cautiously, wanting to avoid causing offense by accidentally revealing his conviction that what the man spoke was utter bullshit.

"I am Seeker," the man said.

"Of course you are," muttered Brandt under his breath.

Donnelly's glare was enough to make him swallow further retorts.

"And you have come to be joined," Seeker continued. He smiled broadly at the two men. "I believe the first step to the union of souls is the purification of the body, but it appears Bryce was right." He looked them up and down again, a little more slowly this time. "Girlfriend said you had it goin' on, and mmm mmm *mmm*!" Suddenly Seeker's eyes snapped wide and he froze, as if realizing he had said that last bit out loud.

Brandt glanced over to Donnelly and saw him trying mightily to keep from bursting out laughing. He looked away quickly to avoid laughing himself.

Seeker took three deep, cleansing breaths and seemed to find his center again. "What are you visioning for the ceremony? Are there cultural rituals or spiritual observances that you are called to make part of your celebration?"

Brandt looked blankly at Seeker, then at Donnelly. He shrugged—to him a wedding was a pretty straightforward affair. The idea of incorporating rituals or observances was mystifying to him. But Donnelly, as usual, knew what to say.

"We don't have a particular religious tradition, so nothing needed there. All we're really looking for is a way for our friends and family to celebrate with us this amazing thing… this miracle that we found each other." He turned to Brandt and smiled.

"I fucking love you," Brandt whispered.

Donnelly leaned across the gap where their energies mingled and kissed him.

"Oh… hot," murmured Seeker. Three more deep, cleansing breaths were evidently required before he could continue. "All right, perhaps we will start with a simple, traditional ceremony and add in any additional elements you wish?"

Donnelly nodded. "I think that would be best."

"Excellent. Now," Seeker said, pulling a notepad out from under the flowing sleeve of his robe, "would you prefer coffee or yogurt?"

"Coffee or yogurt?" Brandt repeated. "For what?"

"For the cleansing before the ceremony, of course. Coffee or yogurt for the enemas?"

Brandt launched to his feet in an instant. "Okay," he announced, his head light from the sudden change in altitude. "I think we're done here."

Donnelly looked up at him, a mixture of shock and relief on his face. He turned to Seeker. "What my fiancé is trying to say is that we're not really sure this is the approach we're most comfortable with. Can we think about it and get back to you?" He smiled charmingly.

"Of course," Seeker replied, apparently unruffled by Brandt's alarm. "One must follow one's own path." He handed them a brochure he pulled from the sleeve of his robe. "Please consider adding one of my signature homeopathic essences to your meditation ritual. Satisfaction guaranteed, and never tested on spirit animals." He gazed placidly at both men. "Go in peace, my brothers. Go in peace." He closed his eyes and assumed the meditation pose in which they had found him when they entered.

Donnelly rose to his feet, more slowly but no less gracefully than had Brandt, and they turned to walk out together. They reached the front door, and as they opened it, Seeker called to them.

"Don't eat the cake," he said in a somber tone, as if delivering prophecy.

Donnelly turned back to him. "I'm sorry, what was that?"

"Wedding cake. Full of chemicals. Turns your aura green, and where does that leave you?" Seeker, having delivered this last bit of wisdom, closed his eyes again and moved no more.

Donnelly and Brandt shared a confused look and made their exit.

CHAPTER SIX
CUPS RUNNETH

IT WAS another late night in the bakery. Justin was once again alone, but this time he wasn't fiddling with accounts or trying to find sustainably sourced sugar. He was waiting for a knock on the back door.

It had been nearly a week since their first meeting—the one that had progressed from wedding planning to Justin losing his virginity. At least he thought that is what had happened; it was kind of hard to tell with guys, he had reflected later. If he were a girl, it wouldn't have counted, but he was not at all interested in doing what would be the most analogous thing to how a girl would lose her virginity. He shuddered a little just to think of it. He was okay with being gay now that he had a sense of what it really felt like to be with a guy, but the idea of something going in *there*? Yeah, that wasn't going to happen.

He stacked the papers in front of him for the seventeenth time, unable to keep his hands from their nervous motion. He had convinced his father that it would be best for just the two of them, himself and Roman, to work on planning the big gay wedding. That would keep the rest of the staff from having to think about it—and most particularly his dad, who still harrumphed angrily when Justin mentioned anything related to it.

Justin had invited Roman over under that pretense, but even as he did so, he knew they were both aware of the real reason for their meeting.

He was stacking the papers again when the knock finally came. He checked through the eyehole, just to be sure, and then unlocked the door. He swung it open and stepped back to allow Roman to come in.

"Hey," he said, knowing as he said it that it was about the most stupid thing he could possibly have said. Roman had been with a lot of guys and probably knew all of the sexy things to say. Stupid! He locked the door and turned around, trying to manage what he hoped was a casual smile.

Roman lunged at him as soon as the door was bolted. He crashed into Justin with a fierce, animal hunger, grabbed his shoulders, and kissed him like his life depended on it.

Justin was shocked. But the heat that radiated from all of the places their bodies were in contact was stronger than any reserve he might have felt, and he closed his eyes and gave himself up to it. He let Roman take what he wanted and was happy to surrender it.

Finally, once time had lost all meaning, Roman pulled back.

"I've been wanting to do that all week," he sighed, flushed with the effort of pinning Justin to the door. "I thought you'd never call. Like you were freaked out about what happened last time."

Justin shook his head. "I was, a little. But not anymore."

"I can see that," Roman growled, reaching out and grabbing a handful of Justin's crotch. "God, you're as boned as I am."

Justin blushed, unused to having his manhood manhandled. He looked down at the clear outline of his erection, then back up to Roman. "I think I need a drink. You?"

"Fuck yeah."

Justin led the way into the main part of the bakery. Roman sat on the same stool as last time, while Justin opened the locked cabinet and pulled out the bourbon.

"Refilled," he said, holding up the nearly full bottle. "One of the perks of being the guy who places the supply orders."

"You can just add booze to the order and no one says anything?" Roman asked, sounding very much like he considered this to be the best deal ever.

"Well, probably not every order. But I needed to get the liqueur that the guys want for the filling in their cake, so I had to place an order with the liquor supply anyway. And with what their special hooch costs, adding a liter of whiskey hardly showed up at all." He poured some bourbon into the coffee cups that Roman had set on the table and turned back to the cabinet.

"What did they want for the cake filling?" Roman asked, lifting his coffee cup to his lips.

Justin turned back to the cabinet and pulled out the bottle. "This." He held aloft a heavy crystal flagon with a band of crystals around the neck and elaborate gold embellishments.

"What's it taste like?" Roman asked in hushed tones.

"I don't know—I haven't tried it. It's supposed to be an orange liqueur, but the bottle was over eight hundred dollars, and that's wholesale. Too much for me to be pouring shots from it. According to their website, it's blended with 150-year-old stuff that they still have sitting around for some reason."

"And that's going into the crème filling for a wedding cake." Roman shook his head. "Seems like such a waste."

"But these guys have the money, so they get what they want." Justin turned to put the bottle back in the cabinet.

"Hey wait—how about if we just take a whiff? See what it smells like? 150-year-old liquor is pretty amazing. Don't you want to find out what it's like?"

Justin paused, looking at the bejeweled bottle and then at his friend. "I guess… it wouldn't hurt just to take a sniff." He set the bottle on the table and loosened the golden clasp that held the cork in the neck of the bottle. It came out with a hushed pop, and then Justin slid the bottle over to Roman. "Be my guest."

Roman gave Justin an excited look and then leaned over the neck of the bottle. He took in a deep breath, and his eyes widened. He turned red and began to cough, turning away from the bottle and clutching his throat.

"Oh my God! Roman! What's wrong?"

"Wa… water," Roman managed to gasp.

Justin dropped the cork on the tabletop and ran to the sink, down at the other end of the kitchen. He grabbed a paper cup, filled it with water, and then ran back to Roman.

"Here," Justin said, handing the cup to his gasping friend.

Roman took a drink, coughed again, and then took another, longer drink. Finally, the flush of color began to fade from this face. He shook his head and wiped his mouth. "Whoa," he said. "That's some strong stuff."

"I'll take your word for it," Justin said as he recorked the bottle and set it back in the cabinet. "I gotta be careful handling that stuff when I make the filling."

"I probably just got too much up my nose at once," Roman said with a laugh. "But at least I have something more appropriate than water to chase it with." He raised his coffee mug of bourbon and took a drink. "Much better."

Justin took a long sip as well, which he tolerated much better than the first time. He hadn't drunk much during college—and bourbon was hardly a drink for amateurs—but he was getting the hang of it.

Roman set his cup down on the table. "So, I'm guessing you didn't ask me here to talk about cakes and flowers," he said with a cocked eyebrow.

Justin blushed again. He wished he could stop doing that.

"I… do you think you might want… I mean, if you wanted to…." Justin drifted off into a confused silence.

Roman smiled slyly. "Are you trying to ask me if I want to do what we did last time?"

"S-s-sort of," Justin replied, stumbling a bit. "I thought maybe this time I could…?"

"Ah, I get it." Roman said with chuckle. "Think you might want to try it yourself, see what it's like?"

Justin, blushing even more intensely, nodded.

"You've come to the right man," Roman said heartily. "I would be honored to serve." He stood up from his stool, and with a quick series of evidently well-practiced moves, he unbuckled his belt, dropped his pants (he wore no underwear), and hopped up onto the table, planting his ass on the butcher-block surface and placing his already semihard penis at Justin's disposal.

"Oh my God," whispered Justin.

"Yeah, I get that a lot," Roman replied, modesty conspicuously absent from his voice. "I'm pretty proud of it."

"No, I mean oh my God that's where we roll out the fondant!"

"What, you think some old wrinkly mother of the bride won't want to taste this?" He wiggled his ass on the table for effect.

"You are such a slut!" Justin cried with a laugh. Then he craned up and kissed Roman's lips. "Thank you. Thank you for being just the slut I needed in my life. And sorry in advance for how clumsy this is going to be."

"I would endure any kind of blowjob for you, buddy."

Justin, never having navigated another man's body, was not at all sure where to place his hands. Or his lips, for that matter. He was convinced that the complex maneuvers of unbuckling a belt—from the outside—would have been beyond him entirely. He was actually quite relieved that Roman had taken care of that part of it.

He kissed Roman's neck, to the collar of his shirt, and ran his hands down farther. The feel of the tight, muscled body underneath the shirt thrilled him, and he instinctively found Roman's nipples, stiffening beneath the fabric. He rubbed them with his thumbs.

"Oh, that feels good," whispered Roman, his head tipping back.

Justin's excitement that he was actually doing this—and doing it right!—led him to bolder moves. He slid down to Roman's lower belly, coming to the place where the hem of the shirt gathered over the base of the strong, imposing erection that jutted straight out into the room.

Justin looked up at Roman, confirming that they were actually going to do this.

"He's all yours, Juss. He's been waiting for you to come back to him all these years."

Justin smiled at this thought and set to the task of getting reacquainted with this old friend of his. He reached out a tentative hand and brushed the hard flesh with his fingertips. It was the first time he had touched a penis other than his own, and he was amazed at how different it felt. Where his own felt soft and smooth, Roman's was hard and mapped with heavy veins running along its length. And it looked enormous.

"Just wrap your hand around it," Roman whispered.

Justin did as Roman ordered, and his fingers almost didn't meet when he had grasped it. "It's so big," he said reverently.

"I've seen bigger," Roman said casually. "Actually, I've done more than see them," he added with a chuckle. "But it is one of the larger ones you're going to see in the wild. I'm just lucky, I guess."

Justin looked more closely at the hard throbbing thing in his hands. "You've never... I mean, no one's ever had this up their.... Have they?"

"You mean have I ever fucked anyone with it?"

Justin nodded.

"Say it," Roman goaded. "You have to be able to say it."

"Have you ever…," Justin began, his voice low. "Have you ever fucked anyone?"

"Very good. You're making progress." Roman looked down at the man who held his cock. "And yes, I've split quite a few guys open. I usually have to go slow, but once they get it in they never want to let it go." Roman smiled dreamily, perhaps reliving some particularly poignant moments of impalement.

"Slut," Justin murmured under his breath, but he smiled up at Roman, still in disbelief that after a life of loneliness, the perfect guy had shown up and plopped his naked ass on Justin's table.

"Now, you're going to want to get the head wet before you put it in your mouth," Roman coached.

Justin nodded and licked his lips. He leaned toward Roman's cock, but instead of licking it he placed the gentlest of kisses at the very tip.

"Oh, fuck," Roman groaned.

Justin smiled and then kissed slowly all around the large mushroom head of Roman's penis. With each playful slurping noise, Roman breathed out heavily and rolled his head from side to side.

"You sure you've never done this before?" Roman asked. "You're kinda driving me crazy teasing like this."

"Beginner's luck," Justin replied. He leaned down once again, and this time his tongue was in manic motion, swirling all over the glans. He hadn't watched much porn, but whenever an attractive guy was getting a blowjob, he paid close attention and knew that a big part of the technique was lots of saliva. He did his best to fully glaze the head of Roman's cock with his spit.

He looked up at Roman for confirmation that he was doing it right, and was delighted to get his answer: a wordless, eager nodding. Roman's endorsement.

Justin opened—wide—and Roman became the first man ever to enter him.

"Ahhh," sighed Roman, an exhalation of purest bliss.

Justin, however, was trying to figure out what to do with the vast, sudden mouthful. He was sure he couldn't get any more of it into his mouth if he tried all night, but he didn't want to let it go either. He moved his head up and down in small strokes, tried to keep his tongue moving, and made every effort to keep his lips wrapped around his teeth. It was kind of like when he had learned to drive a stick-shift—coming into a turn and signaling, downshifting, and not running over the curb all at once. He hoped he was doing it right.

"Fuck, you're a natural," Roman said with a sigh as he watched Justin's tentative bobbing on his cock.

Justin was deeply pleased. Over the years, the very idea of sex had developed into a cloud over him, ominous and mysterious; now he could feel the cloud lifting, replaced with the sunny joy of being so intimately connected to the one person he felt he had ever really loved. He felt his jaw relaxing and was able to make longer transits up and down, slipping more of Roman's hardness into him.

Within a minute or two, Roman started flexing his ass to push his cock upward, as if he wanted to claim more of Justin as his territory. Justin kept up his rhythm and was able to work not only the fat head of Roman's penis into his mouth, but the first inch of shaft as well. But it soon became clear that Roman was not going to fly headlong into orgasm the way Justin had the week before; Justin felt the muscles in his neck start to stiffen with the repetitive movements.

"You know what would make this even better?" Roman murmured.

Justin pulled himself off his cock long enough to answer him. "What?"

"Come on, I'll show you." Roman slipped off the table, then kicked off his shoes and the pants that were gathered around his ankles. He padded around the big table and into the doorway that led to the front of the shop.

"What? Where are you going?" called Justin in an anxious whisper. They were alone in the building, but he still felt the need to whisper, given Roman's scandalous nudity.

But Roman didn't even slow down. He disappeared through the doorway, and Justin had no choice but to follow.

By night the front of the shop was completely dark; streetlights outside shone on an empty sidewalk and deserted avenue, casting their orangey glow onto the floor. Roman hefted himself onto one of the lace-covered tables facing the street and beckoned to Justin with a crook of his finger.

"No! Not here!" Justin whispered urgently. "Get back here—someone's going to see you!"

Roman looked out onto the street placidly. "There's no one out there. And even if there were, it's too dark in here for them to see anything anyway. Come on, it'll be hot."

Justin was mortified at the idea of continuing his carnal education atop one of his grandmother's prized tablecloths, but then he thought of how warm and how hard and how wickedly fun it had been to have Roman's manhood in his mouth, and he gave in. Again.

He walked over to where Roman was perched on a tabletop, and he pulled up a chair as if he were sitting down to a sausage dinner. Roman giggled with delight, and his erection bobbed merrily, having deflated not a bit during the relocation. Justin leaned forward and got back to work. It seemed to him that Roman's cock was even harder than it had been back in the kitchen, and a slickness seemed to be spreading from it as he sucked and swirled on it.

Roman began to moan and writhe, as if facing the street while getting blown was far preferable to getting a blowjob in private. But he still wasn't jumping to the conclusion. Then, suddenly, he jolted upright.

"There's someone out there," he whispered.

Justin sat up and turned slowly around. The street, which had been deserted when they began, was suddenly populated with couples and groups walking past, all in the same direction. "The theatre down the street must have just gotten out," Justin said, thinking of the art house that showed subtitled films until the wee hours. "Shit! Someone's going to see us."

"If we stay still no one will notice we're here," Roman whispered.

It was at this moment that Justin realized he still had his hand wrapped firmly around Roman's cock. He was afraid to move it, so he just left it there.

"Shit—someone's stopping," Justin whispered. A man, looking to be in his late twenties, had paused before the windows of the bakery and was peering through, apparently trying to get a look at the display case within.

"Oh my God, he's looking right at us," whispered Roman.

Justin, frozen with the fear of being discovered, felt the surge in Roman's cock just before he heard the small gasp escape his lips. He turned instinctively back to Roman, just in time to see a jet of white spew forth from his penis. It was followed in rapid succession by a half dozen more spurts, while Roman huffed out tight little breaths of ecstasy. His orgasm was waning by the time the man at the window turned and walked away.

Justin looked at his hand, now covered with Roman's semen, startled. "Oh my God, did you...?"

Roman, panting a bit in the aftermath of his orgasm, laughed raggedly. "I sure as hell did. That was so hot."

"But I wasn't doing anything," Justin replied, amused rather than offended. It fascinated him that Roman had been able to come without any physical stimulation.

"You were holding onto it," Roman wheedled.

Justin looked at him skeptically. Clearly Roman wasn't just slutty; there was a bit of kink in him too. Justin wasn't sure how he felt about this, but there wasn't much time to ponder when there was cum about to drip off his hand onto the tablecloth.

"Shit, we've got to get this cleaned up," he said to Roman, who hopped off the table, his cock still bouncing far out in front of him.

"I got this, bro," he said with a suave nod of his head, and he took Justin's hand in his. He brought it up to his lips, and, as Justin stared at him wide-eyed, he ran his tongue over Justin's knuckles, swabbing up the white with his pink, supple tongue.

"Fuck" was the only word Justin could summon as he felt Roman's tongue slip over his hand.

Roman didn't break eye contact with Justin as he sloppily kissed the cum off Justin's fingertips, finally slipping the wet fingers, one by one, into his mouth for a thorough cleaning. Justin wasn't sure his knees could support him under the weight of this casual obscenity. He stared dumbly as Roman slurped the last evidence of his passion and swallowed it down.

"There," Roman said, his voice low and sultry. "All clean."

"That," Justin panted, "was the hottest thing I've ever seen."

"I'm just getting started. How about we head back and I show you something new?"

"Oh my God, yes," whispered Justin, thrilled to give his consent to acts he knew nothing of. He took Roman's hand and pulled him to the relative privacy of the back of the bakery.

They once again stood before the large table, their half-empty cups of bourbon where they had left them, Roman's pants and shoes on the floor. Roman pulled Justin into a long kiss, which tasted a little different than before, Justin thought with a thrill.

"You. Naked. Now." Roman's commands were staccato and brooked no argument. Justin complied.

He pulled his shirt off over his head (he had worn an old one, in case Roman was in a bodice-ripping mood again) and dropped his pants to his ankles. He heel-toed off his shoes and then yanked off his socks and stepped out of his pants. He stood before Roman in just his briefs.

"I said *naked*," Roman growled impatiently.

Justin, startled by the ferocity of Roman's order, slipped his underwear off and threw them behind him.

"Up on the table," Roman said.

Justin, who didn't even spare a thought as to the disinfectant regime he would need to impose the following morning before any fondant could be rolled out here, hopped up and sat on the table, his legs dangling over the side, his erection poking him in the belly button.

"Turn around," Roman ordered.

Justin considered how he could possibly accomplish this, given that turning around would mean—what? Leaning against the table? He paused for a moment to work out the logistics.

"On your hands and knees."

"Oh," Justin said. It was only when he lifted himself fully onto the table and turned over onto his hands and knees that he considered the position this put him in.

Roman roughly pushed his knees apart, opening him completely. Justin sucked in a nervous breath. Was Roman planning on—what were the words he used? "Splitting him open"? He was about to voice his concern about boundary issues when he felt Roman moving behind him. But he wasn't getting up on the table, so perhaps he was safe?

"Relax," Roman murmured. "I'm not going to fuck you."

"You're not?"

"No. We'd be sanding your claw marks out of the table for days."

"Sorry, I'm just a little nervous."

Roman laughed gently. "I can see that. If your ass were any more clenched it would implode."

"Sorry!" Justin was so embarrassed.

Roman laid his hands on Justin's buttocks and rubbed them gently. "Just relax. You're going to love this."

Justin willed himself to stop breathing hard, to convince himself that he was in good hands. He was completely unprepared for the feel of cold liquid dripping from the small of his back, down between his buttocks. Then he felt Roman's mouth—he was nuzzling and slurping the back of his balls, drinking in the liquid after it had run down through... Justin couldn't even finish the thought.

A pause in the flow of liquid.

"Now this is how a true gentleman drinks his bourbon. Your hot ass beats the hell out of a coffee mug."

More bourbon drizzled down his ass, followed by Roman's insistent, wiggly lapping at the secret skin between Justin's ass and balls. When the flow stopped, Roman surged forward and sucked both of Justin's balls into his mouth, then pulled back, and they reemerged with a slurp. Then he licked his way up from the base of Justin's scrotum, nibbling his way along. He was nearly to Justin's twitchy anus when he lifted his tongue and then continued licking his way up the base of Justin's spine to lap up the bourbon.

Justin was in a frozen frenzy. It wasn't just that he hadn't expected Roman to do this to him—he had simply never imagined that anyone ever did this to anyone. He was relieved that Roman had skipped over his asshole. Really, did anyone ever—

"Unh!" he grunted, shoved forward by the force of Roman crashing his mouth, suddenly, shockingly, right onto his anus.

So, he had his answer. People did do this. At least Roman did. He was actually kissing Justin's ass. The thought was kind of funny, but the feeling was kind of... nice.

And then it happened.

He felt it—Roman's tongue—slither right into his ass.

He tried to lean forward, to get away from this invasion, but Roman's hands were around his hips, and he was held in place with a muscular force he was unable to overcome.

"Oh… God," he grunted, his voice choked with the effort of trying to pull away.

The tongue retreated.

"You okay?" Roman asked, sweetly, as if his tongue hadn't just been up Justin's ass.

"What the fuck are you doing?"

"I'm rimming you. Awesome, isn't it?"

"People do that?"

Roman chuckled. "Oh, yes. People do. Now, take a deep breath and try to relax."

Justin wasn't sure he'd ever relax again. Then he felt Roman's hands, ever on the move, his fingertips venturing into the crack of his wide-spread ass, pulling him even further apart, exposing him horribly. And then he felt the slow, delicate fanning of Roman's breath on his most private place. Suddenly he was calm, feeling that slow cadence, that leisurely flow of respiration. Somehow, it soothed him.

When Roman entered him again, he vowed to count to ten before freaking out. By the time he got to seven, he was starting to feel how the tight ring of muscle was responding to the invasion of Roman's slippery tongue. How that tongue could be thin and pointy, or thick and blunt, sometimes alternating by the second. How it thrashed and plunged, lapped and caressed. Justin lost count. He was about to lose his mind.

Instead of trying to squirm away, he found himself pushing back against Roman, opening to him, arching his back and biting his lip as the sensations surged through him. Roman responded by grunting and pushing harder so that Justin's ass became their site of struggle— Roman to impale more forcefully, Justin to consume him entirely.

Then Justin felt his hand. Roman wrapped his fingers around the head of Justin's cock, which had been oozing a steady stream of fluid since the invasion began. Roman smoothed this slick gel all along his cock and then gripped it firmly. He made a milking motion in time with the thrusting of his tongue, and created a symphony of movement and friction that unstrung Justin completely. His arms collapsed, but his legs were held in place by Roman's hand—and his tongue.

"Oh, fuck," whispered Justin. The circuit between his ass and his cock, something he never knew existed, was electrified by Roman's steady, aggressive rhythm. Burning freezing tingling erupted from his very core, and Justin could only moan as it built up force. He feared it would take him apart; he hungered for the obliteration that this orgasm would bring.

And then he froze. Every muscle in his body locked against his frame, every cell straining for the impending release. He shivered, unable to move, unable to resist the force of Roman who had pitched him into the inferno of this orgasm. By the time he could hear the heavy splatter of his ejaculation raining down onto the tabletop, he could hardly remember a time before this orgasm started. It was unlike anything he had ever known.

Finally, Roman relinquished his grip on Justin's cock and pulled his tongue from its playground. Justin collapsed to the side, breathing like he'd just run a sprint. He hoped he could stay conscious.

He felt Roman's hands, caressing his legs, gently tickling his sides, gradually bringing him back to himself. He breathed a deep, contented sigh.

"You okay?" Roman murmured.

"No," Justin replied dreamily. "I used to wonder what Galileo felt the first time he saw Venus through his telescope. Now I know." He sighed. "If, you know, it was in his butt."

Roman burst out laughing. "Wow. I've been complimented on my technique a few times, but no one's ever said that. Yeah, not once."

Justin joined him in laughing and then slowly sat up and slid off the table. "Well," he said, looking at the tabletop. "This is kind of a mess."

"Totally worth it," Roman said. "To see you experience that for the first time, I would set fire to this place."

"Don't think that'll be necessary. Just some Lysol, I think." He turned and looked at the simply staggering amount that he had ejaculated onto the table. "And maybe a wet/dry vac."

They shared another hearty laugh and then went to get a bucket. They had some cleaning to do. Together.

CHAPTER SEVEN
LOVE AND MARRIAGE

ON A sunny Sunday morning early in the month of May, Brandt and Donnelly walked along their favorite path through the city's largest park, on their way to meet Bryce and Nestor for brunch.

"Did he sound heartbroken that we didn't like any of them?" Brandt asked as they strolled under the shade of the long row of maples.

"Oh, you know Bryce. One minute he's in an operatic frenzy of outraged sensibilities, and the next he's telling you all about this great idea that the angels themselves have just popped into his head."

"I'm just not sure how many more wedding planners I can stand to meet."

"Patience, love."

"Patience I can do. But honestly I've spent longer looking for a wedding planner than I did looking for someone to marry."

"Well, you can't expect someone like me to happen along every time you snap your fingers." Donnelly laughed and kissed him on the cheek.

They crossed the street and entered the restaurant.

"Ethan! Gabriel!" Shirley, their longtime waitress at the diner, greeted them from behind the counter. "I believe your party is waiting for you." She tipped her head toward Bryce and Nestor, who sat in a booth looking around the room from behind their gigantic glamorous sunglasses. They looked like visitors from another planet—a judgmental one.

"That's our party all right," Brandt said, feeling somewhat sheepish. Their sleepy little diner didn't see much in the way of exotic personalities as a rule.

"I'll bring coffee," Shirley replied.

"Bless you," Donnelly called after her.

"Hey, guys," Brandt said as they neared the booth.

Bryce and Nestor turned toward the familiar voice like meerkats in Dolce & Gabbana spectacles.

"Ooh, you're here!" Bryce hooted as he shot to his feet. He delivered a lightning round of air kisses to the cheeks of both Brandt and Donnelly and then sat back down with an exaggerated elegance.

Nestor contented himself with a warm handshake as the officers sat opposite them.

"What a charming little retro diner," Bryce said, taking off his sunglasses and waving them about the room. "It's like a train car that got off on a siding sometime in the 1950s and was recently discovered with everyone's hairstyle completely unchanged."

"Thanks for meeting us here," Donnelly said. "We know it's out of your usual range."

"Oh, pooh," Bryce sniffed. "We are adventurers, happy to get out of our stylish, elegant little rut. Who knew there were places like this, where people wear denim without irony? And bring their children along, just as if they were little people?"

Nestor, who had been engaged in a spirited game of peek-a-boo with a toddler in the next booth, clearly felt the weight of Bryce's judgment and looked down at his hands.

Shirley showed up with two mugs of coffee, which she set in front of Brandt and Donnelly. "Anything for you to drink?" she asked Bryce and Nestor.

"Oh yes—please bring us two mimosas, dear," Bryce answered.

"I'm sorry, we don't serve alcohol," Shirley said, looking mystified.

"Oh," Bryce said, clearly brought up short. "Well then what's the point of having a restaurant at all if—"

"How about two glasses of orange juice?" Brandt interrupted before Bryce could say anything alarming.

"Sure, coming right up," Shirley replied, still studying Bryce and Nestor as she retreated behind the counter.

"Brunch with no mimosas?" Bryce leaned across the table and whispered for the entire restaurant to hear. He looked around in an alcohol-deprived panic. "What hell is this?"

"Calm down, Bryce," Donnelly said, reaching across the table and taking his hand reassuringly. "But we may as well be honest. There's no alcohol, the food isn't organic, and at no point in the meal will a go-go boy dance across our table with the bill clenched between his cheeks."

"Of course not," sniffed Bryce. He reached into his sleeve and pulled out a roll of dollar bills, which he stuffed unceremoniously into a tiny leather clutch.

"The menu is up on the board," Brandt said, pointing above the counter where the specials and other dishes were written in chalk on blackboards.

"How charming," Bryce cried. "I've never eaten in a cafeteria at a steel mill, but now I feel as though I have."

Brandt would perhaps have been a little miffed at these outbursts had he not learned from long experience that the most important thing in Bryce's life was drama, and he would find it wherever he went, even if he had to manufacture it out of whole cloth.

"There is so much meat," Nestor murmured as he scanned the menu boards.

"Well, it is a pretty traditional diner menu," Donnelly said. "They do love their bacon. And sausage. And ham. And steak."

"Well, as we are strangers in a strange land," Bryce said, "I will leave the choice up to you. Please select one of your native foods, and I'm sure I will find it delightful."

Shortly Bryce was looking at a stack of blueberry pancakes with a side of bacon, trying to figure how best to go about introducing it to his mouth. Nestor, meanwhile, dug into his plate of eggs and sausage with great enthusiasm.

"So," Bryce said, having chewed and swallowed his first bite of pancake—ever, from the look on his face—and set down his fork, "Gabriel mentioned that perhaps the first few wedding planners were not to your liking."

Brandt nodded at this understatement and was glad a full mouth relieved him of the obligation to respond immediately.

Donnelly took up the charge. "Lars was a bit… showy? At least for the kind of wedding we're imagining."

"Oh, that's too bad, darling," replied Bryce. "He just called me yesterday and said that he had gotten in some new wedding supplies that he thought you would really like."

"Let me guess—a new laser light show?" Brandt asked.

"Oh, don't be silly. No dear, confetti cannons. He said the new ones can launch a Mylar bundle the size of a baby over 300 feet."

Donnelly laughed. "So that's how they measure confetti? In baby-equivalent units?"

"Apparently," Bryce replied. "He said they would make quite a statement."

Brandt could hold back no longer. "Yes, they would say 'I have too much money to spend on my wedding, so I'm going to celebrate by launching confetti into the next county.'"

"Oh, don't be silly," Bryce said, taking another haphazard stab at his pancakes. "Have you been to the next county? Ick. It's all cows and trees and things."

"It's just that…," Donnelly said diplomatically, "we just don't think we're confetti cannon people. You understand."

"Of course I do, dear. As police officers you have your finger on the pulse of the common man. For that matter, you probably have your hands all over the common man, every day. Ah, public service…." Bryce stared dreamily into the middle distance.

"But we fear you might have overcorrected a little bit when you sent us to Seeker."

"It was the patchouli, wasn't it?" Bryce demanded. "I've told him a hundred times that no one should smell like they haven't showered since the last Grateful Dead concert."

"It wasn't that so much as…." Donnelly frowned, searching for the right words.

"Enemas will not be part of our wedding ritual," Brandt said decisively.

Bryce's eyes widened in horror. "He thought you should"—he made a vigorous thrusting motion with his arm—"at the wedding?"

Brandt and Donnelly nodded.

"Oh, heavens, no!" Bryce cried. "That's something special you save for the wedding night. Maybe two something specials if you've had a sit-down dinner at the reception."

Brandt stifled a groan and took a big swig of coffee to prevent further comment.

"But how was the next one?" Bryce asked. "If you're going to insist on traditional-but-tasteful, she seemed… suitable. Though how a *woman* would know anything about weddings I simply cannot imagine."

Brandt gave a cranky harrumph. "She wanted to drape everything in silk and little white lights, and have us make favors out of mason jars and ribbon. Lots and lots of ribbon. Then she kept going on and on about the 'tablescapes.' Ugh. It would be like getting married on one of those horrible home shows where everything's hot-glued to everything else."

"So she was a no," Donnelly summed up more charitably than Brandt seemed capable of.

Bryce sighed delicately but set his lower lip and tried again. "But the last one—he was just about perfect, wasn't he? Plaid shirt, torn jeans, and he drove a *motorcycle*."

Nestor looked up from his breakfast plate dreamily. "He smell of leather and bad decisions."

"Yes, but he also insisted that we serve only canned beer at the reception to 'keep it real,'" Donnelly replied. "And he used ironic air quotes whenever he said the word 'wedding.' I never knew whether he understood that we wanted to actually come out of the experience, you know, 'married.'" He made ironic air quotes with his fingers when he said this, adopting the pained, knowing look of the tragically hip.

The officers looked across the table at Bryce, winded from recounting their misadventures with wedding planners.

"Why are you smiling?" Brandt asked.

"Because after your days spent wandering in the desert, I am now ready to deliver you to the promised land of wedding planners. I have the perfect, perfect, perfect man for the job."

Donnelly smiled hopefully, but Brandt was less excited. "Honestly, Bryce, I really appreciate all you've done for us, but I'm kind of tired of talking to these insane people. Elopement is looking more and more like a viable option."

Bryce was horrified. "Oh, honey, no! Why would you want to deny your loved ones the chance to gather on your special day and share with each other the joy of seeing the two of you in perfectly tailored tuxedos?"

Brandt opened his mouth to advance the opinion that perhaps the wedding was more about love and commitment than dressing up in a tux, but Bryce was picking up steam and would not brook interruption.

"No, honeys, you will look no further than the man whose wedding plans have become the stuff of legends, the best in the business, the matrimonial magician extraordinaire!"

"That's a pretty big sell, even for you, Bryce," Donnelly replied with a laugh.

"Oh, he is worth every adjective, doll. Now, it is simply impossible to get an audience with him, as he is booked years in advance. I've made an appointment for you to see him on Friday."

"How did you do that, if he's booked years in advance?" Brandt asked suspiciously.

"Well," Bryce replied, delicately smoothing the front of his impeccably fashionable blouse, "it turns out that his office manager and I have some friends in common. I simply arranged a social event that afforded us an opportunity for conversation."

"Friends in common?" Donnelly asked with a raised eyebrow.

"The members of a local rugby team," Bryce answered.

"You're friends with rugby players?" Brandt asked, taken aback by the very idea of Bryce and sports of any kind.

"Oh not the players themselves, dear, no. The *members* of the team. I and a small but dedicated band of athletic supporters provide post-game physical therapy. It helps them relax after smashing all their muscles against all of those muscles of the other team." He sighed. "So many muscles."

"When he say 'members,' he mean penises," Nestor helpfully noted.

"Yes, I think we got that, Nestor, thanks," Brandt replied, shaking his head.

"So," Bryce said brightly, returning to his story, "I simply waited until a moment when neither of us had our mouth full, and I asked him if he might be able to work in a couple of hardworking and gorgeous police officers, and he said he would be happy to." Bryce cleared his throat. "Once I clarified that I meant working you into the calendar for a wedding planning consultation, he was still willing, and so now you have your appointment." He beamed at the officers, clearly pleased with a job well done.

Donnelly raised his coffee mug in salute. "Bryce, you have once again proven that you are not afraid to take one for the team."

"By taking several from the team," Brandt added.

"This is so exciting, my darlings!" Bryce hooted. "I just know it will turn out perfectly."

Donnelly turned to his partner. "Ready to try one more time?"

"After what Bryce put himself through, I think we have to," Brandt replied. "I'm in."

THEY ROLLED up in front of the address Bryce had given them and found themselves looking at a brick storefront in an upscale part of town. The building was clearly a remnant of a previous century, but one that had been carefully restored and modernized with an understated elegance. The sign above the large plate glass window read "wed." in a simple typeface—stylish without being precious.

Brandt, for the first time, was hopeful.

They entered the office and were greeted by a young man about their age who was wearing a tiny headset in one ear. He smiled brightly and motioned for them to sit down as he finished a call.

"Nice place," Donnelly remarked, looking around the reception area.

"Until we step through the door and find him naked, playing bongos, and yelling about how we need to go down the aisle on flaming pogo sticks." Brandt smiled sweetly and picked up a bridal magazine from the coffee table.

"Not sure that's actually worse than the coffee and yogurt enemas." Donnelly chuckled and leaned over to follow along with Brandt's magazine.

"Ethan and Gabriel?" the receptionist called as he walked around the counter to where the men were seated.

"That's us," Brandt answered. He set down the magazine, and they both stood.

"Mr. Dyson will see you now. Come this way." He turned and led them through a large arched doorway into an office that was all exposed brick and skylights.

"Officers Brandt and Donnelly," called the man behind the desk. He practically jogged around the mission-style desk to shake their hands. "So good to finally meet you in person. I'm Wendell."

Brandt and Donnelly shook his hand but exchanged a look of confusion.

"I'm sorry," Brandt said as he and Donnelly took the seats Wendell pointed them to. "Have we…?"

"Oh, no, forgive me," Wendell said as he too took a seat at the large wood conference table that occupied the middle of the room. "I'm just such a fan of your work, it's kind of a thrill to actually have you sitting here in my office."

Donnelly looked just as confused as Brandt. "I don't think I understand. We're not, you know, celebrities or anything."

Wendell laughed. "You are to some of us. That thing up in Woodley a couple of months ago? What an inspiring story—those two kids, the wrestlers? So brave in the face of vicious homophobia. And the picture in the paper of you two spiriting them out of that riot in the school gym! Amazing."

"I had no idea people were following events in Woodley so closely," Donnelly replied.

"Well, when you grow up gay in a small town, you spend a lot of time stuffed into lockers or pulling yourself out of garbage cans. It's just great that you're helping put that right for those who come after. And"—he leaned in a little closer to Brandt and lowered his voice— "I'm kind of a member of your secret fan club."

Brandt was dumbfounded. "My what?"

Wendell kept his voice low. "Your secret fan club. I was one of the lucky few with a subscription to a certain website last year, on which a certain young man named 'Mason' made his… um, video debut?"

Brandt felt the blood drain from his face. He was shocked, not only to have that video mentioned out of the blue, but that a wedding planner, of all people, would think it appropriate to bring up at this moment. He just stared at the man, unable to think of a single thing to say.

"And I'm the lucky one who gets a repeat performance anytime he wants," Donnelly said, beaming at his partner. "I'm sure as hell gonna put a ring on *that*."

Brandt had never loved Donnelly as much as he did at that moment. As always, he made any embarrassment Brandt felt about… well, about anything, just evaporate in the sunshine of his good humor and broad smile. Brandt reached across the table and took Donnelly's hand. "I love you," he mouthed to him.

"All right, so that goes on the to-do list," Wendell said, making a note. "'Become Gabriel Donnelly.' Okay, so now to business. My office manager told me I needed to speak with your assistant—Bryce? Well, he gave me a long and quite colorful story of the wedding planners you've already seen, and I completely understand your frustration. There are some crazies out there. But I think we can get your plan on the right track. And I want you to know that my services won't cost you a thing. Consider it my appreciation for all the good work you're doing for the community."

"Oh, no, we couldn't—" Donnelly objected, but Wendell again held up his hands.

"No argument. Done. Now, tell me what your perfect wedding day looks like, and I will tell you how we can make it happen."

Brandt, unaccustomed to actually being asked what he would like for their wedding, was a bit at a loss. Luckily, Donnelly jumped in to start things off.

"Well," he began, "there's a little church just across from the university campus that might be nice for the ceremony. It was after a service there that I got the crazy idea to propose."

"Excellent! I know the one you mean. Beautiful church. It's cozy, though—how many guests are we thinking about?"

"I don't have much in the way of family, just a couple, but Ethan's whole family tree is going to uproot and make their way here, I'm sure."

Brandt smiled. "Probably twenty-five or thirty relatives plus that many friends?"

Wendell nodded. "So we're looking at no more than a hundred, all told?"

"That sounds about right," Donnelly replied.

"It'll be a perfect fit. Do you have a date in mind?"

"Next June?" Brandt asked hopefully.

"Outstanding. Now how about a reception venue?"

"Someplace beautiful," Donnelly said. "Sit-down dinner, linen tablecloths, champagne, candles." He was warming to his topic now. "A jazz combo, for ambience and dancing, and a terrace for pictures. Something with a bit of grandeur, but not ostentatious."

Wendell's smile had grown while Donnelly waxed on about his vision, and by the end he was positively beaming. "I have just the place." He paused to make a note. "Now, I assume you'll be using Monty's for flowers and Capella for cake?" He looked up and grinned at the officers, then burst out laughing.

"Seriously?" Brandt asked. "How did you know about that?"

"The matrimonial community, even in a city this size, is a tight group. You are legends once again."

"Not sure that those particular businesses would welcome our custom, given the circumstances," Donnelly said.

"Bah. One, it'll be water under the bridge in a year's time. Two, gay money spends just as well as straight money, and they'll never want a repeat of the boycott. Third, they really are the best in the business. I use them all the time. In fact, I have a wedding coming up that I'm using them for—perhaps you've heard of it? The Laurence/Sampson wedding?"

Brandt sat forward in his chair. "You're doing their wedding?"

"Oh yes. And I am certain I can get you an invite so you can see the cake and flowers—and the who's who of society—in person."

"We couldn't crash someone else's wedding," Donnelly cried.

"You wouldn't be crashing. Pete and Greg know full well what you did to help them get their wedding back on track. They'd be thrilled to have you there."

Brandt was trying to work out the ethics of their accepting an invitation in return for doing their job when the receptionist stepped back into the office.

"Wend, Metro Church University is available June 7. Booked it. Yacht Club Lakeview Room and Terrace also available June 7. Booked it. Monty's and Capella both open on the seventh, saved the date with them, consultation ninety days out." He looked up from his tablet. "Anything else?"

"That'll be fine, Tom. Thanks," Wendell said. Tom turned on his heel and walked back to his desk in the reception area.

"How'd he do that?" asked Donnelly in a mystified voice.

"He listens in on the initial meeting so we can have complete notes, and so we can do quick schedule checks. While we were talking he was calling around, so we know where we stand."

"That's amazing," Donnelly said, sitting back in his chair. "Just amazing."

"Well, that gives us our start, gentlemen." He handed them each a card. "Here's a link to our website; just use this code to access your planning portal and you'll see the basics of the day laid out for you. You'll also see a schedule of when decisions need to be made, leading all the way up to the day." He smiled at both of them. "Questions?"

Brandt, a bit whiplashed from the pace of the meeting, shook his head, as did Donnelly.

"Excellent. My number's on the card in case you do have any questions, and we'll see you in a couple of months to talk about colors and menu. Good?"

"Good," Brandt and Donnelly said in unison, unaccustomed to using that word when dealing with a wedding planner.

The men stood, shook hands, and a moment later Brandt and Donnelly were on their way back to their afternoon meetings at work.

"Holy shit, man," Donnelly said as Brandt drove, "we're getting married!"

THE WEEK leading up to the Laurence/Sampson wedding was the busiest of Justin's bakery career. Aside from some salacious text messages exchanged in the run-up to the event, he had little contact with Roman, who was similarly wrapped up in taking delivery of and arranging the exotic blooms he had ordered for the displays.

It was Tuesday of the wedding week that saw Justin making up the crème filling for the cakes. Remembering Roman's distress at inhaling the liqueur, he was very careful handling it as he mixed up the massive quantity required. Having accomplished that, he proceeded to bake, carve, and stack the cake for his ambitious design. Thursday was the highlight of his week, when Roman personally brought over some of the flowers he was using for the arrangements so that Justin could match the fondant colors more precisely.

"You should feel honored," Roman said when he stopped by the bakery—during daylight hours for the first time. Justin had come out to meet him in the alley.

"And why would that be?" Justin asked.

"Because I've never brought a guy flowers before," Roman answered, producing the bouquet from behind his back with a chivalrous flourish.

Justin, terrified that someone might hear, grabbed the flowers from Roman and held them close so that no one else would see. But he was delighted in spite of his embarrassment. "Now you're going to want something from me, aren't you?" Justin said with a wink.

"I've already gotten quite a bit, haven't I?" Roman said with a waggle of his eyebrows. "But, yeah, I'm kind of hoping that you'll feel obligated to let me keep getting it," he growled into Justin's ear.

"Do you think once the BGW is behind us we might… actually go… out?" Justin asked quietly.

"Oh my God, you are so cute," Roman said, nudging Justin with his shoulder. "I'm gonna have a shit-ton of cleanup to do after the wedding—the place is going to be a complete mess once I'm done. But once the pollen settles, I'm all yours." He winked and smiled so sweetly that Justin's knees practically gave way just looking at him.

"Maybe I'll text you Sunday, then?" Justin asked, feeling very much the love-struck schoolgirl.

"If you don't, you'll find me right here waiting to pounce on you," Roman replied. He cast a quick look around and found the alley completely deserted. He leaned in and kissed Justin quickly then stepped back as if to prove he hadn't done anything scandalous in the least.

Justin was indeed scandalized, and deeply thrilled. "Deal. I'll see you at the big event Saturday morning, right? For setup?"

Roman nodded. "I'll be the one with the huge boner every time you walk by." He bowed ridiculously and walked down the alley, pausing several times to look back at Justin, who waved the bouquet at him every time.

"Get a grip, Justin," he scolded himself as he headed back into the bakery. "You're acting like a middle-school girl with her first crush." But no amount of internal scolding could wipe the smile off his face every time he caught sight of the bouquet.

On Saturday morning, the preparations got underway early at the ballroom of the Grand Central Hotel, the city's most glamorous venue. Justin had driven the van carrying the central cake, while two more of the bakery's vans followed him with the guest cakes. There was enough for all eight hundred expected attendees to enjoy a piece or even two.

Justin had been hard at work for two full hours before Roman showed up at 10:00 a.m. with two florist vans. He entered at a sprint, bearing the first of several dozen centerpieces.

"Stand back, bitches—flowers coming through!" he called jovially to Justin as he bustled past.

"Did you sleep late this morning?" Justin called back. "Some of us have been at work for hours."

"Some of us have already had to deck out a hall the size of Notre frickin' Dame, mister," Roman replied. "But I'm sure you've been working really hard on your little dessert." He hooted with laughter and rushed back out to the van to get the next pair of centerpieces. Finally, he brought Justin a crate of blooms specially selected to adorn the various layers of the cake.

Justin continued the painstaking work of making his cake absolutely perfect. He finished a couple of hours before the reception was to begin. Exhausted, he staggered over to where Roman had been sitting and watching him work.

"Locked and loaded?" Roman stretched and yawned. "Been up since four this morning. I'm getting too old for this," he cracked, winking at Justin.

"I hear ya. Nothing like bending over fondant for six hours to make the spine happy."

"Dyson's due here shortly, right?"

"Yep. He's going to do a pass through on his way to the wedding to be sure we've got everything right. Then I need to stick around for another little while to talk to the caterers about how to cut and serve the cake."

Roman glanced over at the extravagantly complicated work of the baker's art. "Where are they going to find caterers with a degree in engineering?"

"Very funny. It's pretty simple, actually, but if they just start hacking at it with a cake knife the whole thing's going to come down."

"Well, I'm just gonna close my eyes until he gets here. Wake me up, okay?"

Justin smiled at his friend, who stretched out on a line of five white chairs set up along the edge of the dance floor.

Wendell Dyson arrived fifteen minutes later and made a whirlwind circuit of the reception hall. "Fabulous, as always, gentlemen," he said once he had reviewed the flowers and the cake. "This will cement the reputation of the new generation at Montgomery and Capella. That," he gestured to the young woman taking pictures of the cake, "is the photographer for *City* magazine. I tipped her off that we were going to see the future of wedding cakes and florals here today, and I think she really likes what she's seeing."

They turned to watch the photographer shoot the product of Justin and Roman's hard work from every conceivable angle.

"Well, congratulations again, gentlemen, and thank you. I know it was a hard decision for you to take on this job, but I think it will pay off well both for you and for our community."

Justin and Roman nodded their thanks, and Dyson hurried off to help Laurence and Sampson prepare to walk down the aisle. Meanwhile, the caterers had been gathering before the cake tables, waiting patiently for the photographer to finish up so that they could contemplate the challenge that lay ahead of them.

"I'd better go," Justin said, tipping his head toward the waitstaff. "Call you tomorrow?"

"You'd damn well better," Roman replied with a laugh. He leaned in close. "I've been drunk off my ass, but I much more enjoyed getting drunk off of yours," he whispered.

Justin gasped and then burst out in giggles at the audacious obscenity. "A slut and a drunk, huh?" he teased. "You're the whole package."

Roman winked and made his exit. Justin walked, exhausted but with work left to do, over to the cake tables to begin his instruction.

A SHORT distance away, the ceremony was getting underway at the ornate theatre on the campus of the university. Both grooms were alumni, and the university was, like all state institutions, diligently following the state law when it came to marriage equality. Large enough to hold convocations and commencements, the capacious building had been decked out with a staggering number of Roman's distinctive arrangements along the aisle and at the dais that had been set up at the front of the room. In the balcony, a full orchestra played a selection of classical pieces while the guests filed in.

"It's beautiful, isn't it?" Donnelly said to Brandt as they waited for an usher to see them to a seat.

Brandt looked around the space. "I never thought I'd be in here again after graduation," he replied. "It's kind of huge for a wedding, isn't it?"

"I don't think we even know this many people," Donnelly said as they were conducted down the aisle to their seats. "And look at all the cameras." He pointed to a row of video cameras arrayed along each side of the auditorium, pointing at the dais. "Every television station has a camera, plus CNN. Is that the Spanish-language station? Wow."

"I imagine the governor is pretty happy right now, with all of this coverage," Brandt said as they took their seats.

"Yeah, he looks pretty happy," Donnelly said, pointing to the front row, where the governor and his wife sat awaiting the start of the ceremony.

"Kind of gives you hope that our fair state has finally resolved its issues with marriage equality."

Donnelly turned to look at him with a hint of a smile. "Does that mean we're out of a job?"

"I don't think that this one happy couple is going to make places like Woodley suddenly embrace the rainbow. But it can't hurt." He gave his partner a kiss on the cheek.

As the ceremony began, Brandt watched with a new perspective—that of groom-to-be. He had been to weddings before, and even in a few over the last couple of years as his college friends began to get married, but this was the first time he'd watched it in the knowledge that he would be up there himself in the not-too-distant future. It both fascinated and terrified him. As he looked at Donnelly, he could see traces of the same complex of emotions on his face. Brandt took his hand and held it tight throughout the ceremony.

"Good God, they're a handsome couple," Donnelly remarked as the newly married grooms made their way up the aisle to the triumphant accompaniment of the orchestra.

"No argument there," Brandt replied. "But seeing you in morning dress would be…."

"Yes?" Donnelly prompted.

"Sorry, got a little lightheaded with the blood suddenly surging to my dick," Brandt murmured.

Donnelly grinned at him. "How am I going to make it through the reception without ripping your clothes off?"

"You should at least wait until we get home. Wouldn't want to cause a disturbance while they're cutting the cake."

ROMAN PARKED the floral van in the middle of a dark block of shuttered storefronts. He stepped out, casting a quick look up and down the deserted street, and then he turned and walked briskly, cutting through two alleys, avoiding streetlights. When he arrived at an unmarked door, he turned to scan the sidewalk behind him before knocking.

The door swung open, and he entered.

Marcus sat at the folding table that was the only furniture on this level of the flat. He pecked languidly at the keyboard of his laptop and in no way acknowledged Roman's entrance. The man who had opened the door stepped back into the small kitchen at the back of the house, from which emanated the angry sound of news channel pundits at war with each other on some hot-button issue.

Marcus suddenly slammed his laptop shut, got to his feet, and crossed the empty room in three long strides. He stood in front of Roman, half a head taller and at least forty pounds heavier, all of it muscle and anger.

He cocked his head at Roman. Roman nodded and lowered his gaze.

Marcus brought his hand up to stroke Roman's cheek. Roman looked up, then smiled and tipped his head into the large, powerful hand that caressed him. As suddenly as it had risen, the hand dropped away, and Marcus jerked his head at the stairway. Roman immediately turned and mounted the stairs, Marcus following close behind.

At the top of the stairs, Roman turned and entered the room on the right side of the hall. This room had three large windows that looked out onto the street, and it too was empty. Except, that is, for a single piece of furniture. It stood almost waist-high and resembled an old-fashioned gymnastics vaulting horse. But it was covered in smooth black leather and had metal-and-leather attachments at various points.

Marcus jerked his head toward the bondage horse, and Roman quickly stripped off his clothing. Naked, he walked to the device and stood at the narrow end closest to the windows. Marcus came up behind him and pushed him forward so that he fell onto the top of the horse, his feet barely touching the ground. Marcus leaned down and clamped his ankles with leather cuffs attached to the frame several inches above the ground. Roman could no longer touch the floor, even with his toes. His hands were similarly bound to the legs on the other end. Then a belt was fastened around his waist, binding him tightly to the surface of the horse. With his ankles wide apart and his torso immobilized, Roman was completely in Marcus's power.

Marcus approached the other end of the horse, where Roman's head hung over the end. He lifted his head at the sound of a zipper being lowered slowly. Marcus pushed his pants to his knees and shuffled forward, presenting his cock to Roman. Roman looked at the massive tool before him and opened his mouth. Marcus sighed when the head entered Roman's mouth, and then he pushed forward and kept pushing. Roman gagged and struggled, but Marcus kept pushing. It wasn't until Roman's face was nearly purple that he pulled back, and when his cock slid out of Roman's mouth, long strings of saliva came choking out. Marcus's penis had been as large as Roman's when it went down his throat; now, it was even longer and thicker.

Marcus's grin grew into a grimace as he walked around the horse again, leaving Roman gasping for air. He kicked off his pants, placed himself behind the bound man, and used his thumbs to spread open Roman's anus until it gaped, red and twitching at him. He spat roughly, a glob of white spittle landing directly on Roman's asshole, and then he jammed his right thumb inside, right up to the knuckle. Roman jolted, but could not move away from the invasion, even if he wanted to. Marcus spat again and jammed his left thumb in beside the right one. He pushed them in and out several times, and then he grunted with the effort of prying them apart. Roman gasped as the ring of muscle was spread open, which seemed to drive Marcus on; the corded muscles of his arms stood out in relief as he wrenched Roman open still further.

Then, abruptly, he pulled both thumbs out and watched with a bored expression as the muscles tried to close the distended gap he had forced open. He pulled a condom out of his shirt pocket and, with some effort, managed to stretch it over his enormous erection. He approached Roman again.

Marcus placed the head of his cock against Roman's anus, just now returning to its previous size, and he again spat. That was all the lubrication Roman was going to get. Marcus shoved viciously and ran the entire length of his cock into Roman, grunting with the effort. Roman cried out, but Marcus grabbed his mouth from behind and clamped it shut. He began a pummeling rhythm of thrusts, crashing into Roman's body over and over again.

It was nearly twenty minutes later that Marcus's pounding began to quicken, his breath to shorten. Roman, by this time, was simply slumped over the horse, offering no resistance or reaction to Marcus's abuse. With a growl like a furious grizzly, Marcus jerked spasmodically into Roman for another full minute.

Finally, he slumped and took a deep breath. He pulled out of Roman with a jerk, then yanked off the condom and tossed it aside; it splattered heavily into the corner of the room. Marcus pulled his pants on and tied his bootlaces. Making a desultory circuit of the equipment, he released the restraints and then exited the room without looking back.

Roman slowly got up from his prone position, stretching his arms and legs and arching his back, twisting gently side to side. He stood at the end of the horse for a moment, then dropped to his knees and leaned forward to lick up the semen he had deposited there during Marcus's assault.

After he had cleaned it all, he stood and dressed himself, then walked gingerly back downstairs and out of the flat without a word to anyone. Once he was on the sidewalk, he looked up at the late afternoon sun and smiled.

CHAPTER EIGHT
FLOWERS AND CAKE TO DIE FOR

BRANDT AND Donnelly walked up the aisle with the other guests and drove the short distance to the hotel for the reception. Soon they were in the foyer of the grand ballroom, partaking of a cocktail at the bar set up to lubricate the wedding guests. The doors opened precisely on time, and the guests flowed into the dramatically lit space, overflowing with the lush arrangements Roman had worked on for weeks.

"I gotta see this cake," Donnelly said, pulling Brandt's arm to guide him over to the tables bearing the confectionary genius of the young Capella. They stood before the monument to matrimonial excess, agape.

"That's just.... Wow," Brandt exclaimed, trying to take it all in. "How did he even do that?"

"I have no idea, but I'm pretty sure I want him to do ours," Donnelly replied. "It would be smaller, of course—this thing looks like it could feed everyone Laurence and Sampson have ever met."

A hush fell over the room, and all eyes turned to the doorway, where the happy couple themselves were making their entrance to surging applause. They were beaming, smiling and laughing, and handshaking their way across the room until they suddenly veered over to stand before the cake. Brandt and Donnelly stepped aside, but Peter Laurence recognized them and extended a hand, smiling broadly.

"So glad you could make it," he said over the hubbub of the joyous room. He nodded to the cake. "You made this all possible. Thank you."

"We were just doing our jobs," Brandt said, which was his usual response to such praise. "Thank you for inviting us."

"Enjoy the party," Laurence said as his new husband tugged him off to greet another group of guests elsewhere in the room.

"Why don't you find a place to sit," Donnelly said, "and I'll grab a waiter."

Brandt raised an eyebrow.

"To get some of those amazing-looking appetizers! Though," he said, casting a glance at the cadre of sharp-jawed cater-waiters working the room, "I think our Bryce would wholeheartedly approve of all these dishes." He winked at Brandt and then headed off to hunt and gather.

The dinner was served, the speeches made, and much champagne uncorked as the evening glittered on. There was a lull as the tables were cleared for the serving of the cake, and Brandt took the opportunity to stretch his legs a bit by walking back to the bar for a mineral water. He had stopped to admire one of the floral arrangements when he noticed it: something smelled odd. He stepped closer to the flowers, and the smell increased, but he couldn't place it. He figured it was one of the more exotic blooms included in the arrangement and returned to the table with his mineral water.

The grooms cut into the layer of the cake reserved just for them, and despite the nontraditional nature of their union they yielded to tradition when it came to wedding cake: they each managed to smash it all over each other's faces, resulting in the raucous laughter of all in attendance. Then the caterers descended on the cake complex and began the complicated work of dismembering it into plate-sized pieces for eight hundred guests.

Then, that smell again. Brandt sniffed the air, trying to determine where it was coming from. "Do you smell that?" he asked Donnelly.

"Smell what?"

"I don't know. Something smells… off. I noticed it before, over by the bar, but now I'm smelling it again, and it's stronger."

Donnelly took a deep breath through his nose. "Uh-huh," he grunted. "It's something chemical. Bleach?"

Brandt slapped the table. "Ammonia. That's what it is. They must be cleaning something in another room. I hope they finish up soon—it's enough to make my eyes water."

But at that moment, the cake arrived, and conversation at the table turned immediately to an appraisal of its artistry in fondant texture and color, as well as the merits of the cake itself. Brandt, however, set down his fork before even taking a bite; the smell was getting stronger.

Donnelly looked up, his first bite of cake halfway to his mouth. "You okay?" he asked.

"It's getting worse. I'm going to go see if I can figure out where it's coming from."

"I'll come with you. I just had a flashback to Seeker telling us not to eat the cake. I wouldn't want to have to spend the rest of the evening with a green aura." He laughed and got to his feet to follow Brandt.

"Here's where I smelled it first," Brandt said when they reached the door to the foyer. He pulled Donnelly over to the flower arrangement, and they both took a sniff that almost sent them reeling.

"Holy crap, what is that?" Donnelly gasped.

"Definitely ammonia," Brandt replied. "And it's definitely coming from this arrangement. Someone must have dumped something in here. Help me move this out to the foyer."

They lifted the large vase, carried it through the door, and placed it near the bar. Their eyes were watering by the time they set it down.

"You should call someone and have them dispose of this before it makes people sick," Brandt advised the bartender. "Something must have gotten into it by accident." The bartender nodded and picked up the phone.

"Care for a breath of fresh air?" Brandt asked Donnelly.

"Yes, please," he replied.

They found a nearby door that led to a terrace overlooking the hotel's courtyard. The evening was clear and warm, and a few deep breaths soothed their lungs and eyes after the irritation of the ammonia.

"It's beautiful, isn't it?" Donnelly asked, looking at the stars.

Brandt laced his fingers into Donnelly's and stood close. "Anywhere you are is beautiful to me," he whispered.

"I love that you still sweet talk me, even when you know you can have me anytime you want," Donnelly murmured back, nuzzling Brandt's neck with tiny, teasing kisses.

"We should get back," Brandt said after a few more leisurely moments of making out under the stars. "Wouldn't want to miss the dance."

"Why, Mister Brandt," Donnelly said, in his best Jane Austen voice, "You are so forward! I'll give you one dance, but you must promise me on your honor as a gentleman that you will take me home in your carriage afterward. And then pound my ass until I beg for mercy." He finished by batting his eyes coquettishly.

"Holy fuck, you are the sexiest man alive," Brandt said, then kissed him with a vigor that would have made Miss Austen reach for the smelling salts.

The men composed themselves after their heated flirtation on the terrace and opened the door to return to the reception. What they found on the other side of the door, however, was a war zone.

The first sign of trouble was that the foyer was now filled with people, all of whom seemed to be gasping for air. The stench of ammonia was overwhelming, and it nearly knocked Brandt and Donnelly back as they stepped into the chaotic scene. Then the retching began.

An elderly guest, who was steadying herself by holding the arm of one of the groomsmen, suddenly pitched forward and vomited out everything she had eaten for what appeared to be the last six weeks. The force of it sent her reeling backward so hard that the groomsman was almost unable to keep her from crashing to the floor. He held on but then was seized with the same affliction as his elderly charge, and emptied his guts onto the floor as well.

And the dominoes fell.

Almost instantly, an emetic wave tore through the assembled crowd, and the menu that was the result of months of careful planning by the grooms and their chefs was hurled back out the mouth of every guest. This was not the exhausted regurgitation of the lifelong drunk, nor the gentle oozing of the newborn; this was projectile pandemonium.

"9-1-1 dispatch, this is Officer Donnelly, state police, badge one-one-three-four. Suspected mass poisoning, Grand Central Hotel, main ballroom. I can see at least one hundred people, all projectile vomiting. Overpowering odor of ammonia. Send everyone." He pocketed his phone and looked to Brandt.

"Triage here, I'll take the ballroom?" Brandt said, already in motion.

Donnelly nodded and set his jaw as he prepared to wade into the mess.

Brandt skirted the worst of the destruction on his way to the ballroom doors, but what he found inside was no better. It seemed that all of the guests, not just the ones who had fled the ammonia odor, had succumbed to whatever was causing all the barfing.

Brandt caught sight of the grooms, who were racing about the room trying to comfort the afflicted. They didn't seem to be affected themselves, however, which struck Brandt as odd. But his top priority was to find those most in need of medical attention so that he could identify them to the first EMTs to arrive. Which he hoped would happen soon, given the severity of the situation. Brandt was thankful that his iron stomach seemed to be holding out—though it was being sorely tested by the rising stench and splatter of every other guest falling victim to the illness, or whatever it was.

He had identified several elderly and very young guests who would need immediate attention and had tried to group them and recruit some of the hardier guests to watch over them until the ambulances arrived. The governor's wife came to help, while the governor himself was draped over a chair rebuffing the efforts of his assistant to evacuate him from the ballroom.

It seemed like an eternity, but no more than five minutes after Donnelly's call the first responders arrived. When they entered the ballroom, Brandt waved his badge in their direction and they came to him. He pointed out the weakest victims, on whom they immediately began to work. More EMTs arrived over the course of the next few minutes, followed twenty minutes later by reinforcements called in from hospitals in the farther reaches of the metropolitan area.

After about an hour of triage and maintaining order as best he could, Brandt was approached by Dr. Neill, the city's director of public health, and Dr. Robertson from the state task force on infectious diseases. The call about a mass poisoning, Brandt knew, would have triggered the state's terrorism action plan and the dispatch of high-ranking officials to the scene. Dr. Neill asked Brandt to tell her as much as he knew of what had happened.

"I smelled ammonia. It seemed to be coming from one of the floral arrangements, but I couldn't identify a source. My partner and I stepped outside for a moment for a breath of fresh air, and when we returned the smell was much stronger, and then everyone started hucking up their guts. That's not a normal reaction to ammonia, is it?"

The public health director shook her head. "The stuff stinks at around five parts per million, and you'd need a hundred times that to get any kind of respiratory reaction. Even then, projectile vomiting is not likely, and certainly not on this scale." She looked around the room at the scene of devastation. "I'd also rule out airborne pathogens. Nothing could work this quickly and universally. Agree?" She raised her eyebrows to Robertson, who nodded his assent.

"So what would do this?" Brandt asked.

"An emetic," Robertson replied. "A strong one, delivered to all of the guests at once, it seems. Did they serve a set menu, or did different people eat different things?"

"There were some appetizers—too many for me to try all of them. The main course had three options: filet, salmon, and something vegetarian. Not sure if the sides were different for each."

"How about drinks?" Robertson asked. "A champagne toast, perhaps?"

"There were several of those, but our table had at least two people who didn't drink alcohol; one of them brought a ginger ale from the bar, and the other just drank water all night."

"Sounds like too many bases to cover if someone wanted to introduce an emetic," Robertson said. "What does that leave?"

"You are such *men*," Neill said, exasperation in her voice. "We're at a wedding. What does every single person at a wedding eat?"

"We didn't eat the cake," Brandt cried. "I was smelling ammonia and wanted to get some fresh air, so we got up and walked outside."

"And your partner, the one who's running the field hospital out in the lobby?" Neill asked.

"He is?" Brandt asked.

"Like he's conducting an orchestra," she replied. "I've never seen anything like it. Think he'd come work for us? I've seen military med stations that weren't run as efficiently."

"That's my guy," Brandt sighed with a smile.

Dr. Neill nodded, her eyes showing she understood exactly what Brandt meant.

"But did he eat any cake?" Robertson demanded, bringing the conversation back around to the immediate situation.

"No. He was worried it might... oh, this is going to sound silly. But someone told him a few weeks ago not to eat the cake."

Neill startled. "Do you think this person knew something about a plot of some kind?"

"Doubtful. The warning was that it would turn his aura green." Brandt looked around the room. "Though given the way everyone is looking green, I'll make sure we talk with the fortune teller again—just to be sure we cover all the bases."

Robertson nodded and scanned the room. "Are those the grooms?" he asked, pointing to Laurence and Sampson, who were still apologizing to every guest and trying to make those awaiting evacuation as comfortable as possible. "They didn't eat any cake?"

"They did that silly thing where they pretend to feed each other but mash it into each other's faces," Brandt said, his disdain for that particular tradition coming through clearly. "I don't know if they actually ate any."

"Can't imagine they eat much cake as a rule," Neill said. "You don't keep in that kind of shape by having dessert."

"I know, right?" Brandt muttered to her. It was the first light moment since the barfing began, and he was greatly relieved to share a chuckle with the good doctor.

"I can run a quick assay on the cake—I brought a field kit," Robertson said. "All signs point to ipecac, though."

"I didn't think people used that anymore," Brandt replied.

"We don't recommend it for poisoning—haven't for the last decade," Neill explained. "But it's still available, mostly for homeopathic treatment, though the concentration is much lower. And there may be some leftover stock of the juice in pharmacies or distributor warehouses."

"If someone were to get enough of it and cook off the other constituents of the syrup, they might be able to get it to a concentration that would be effective," Robertson said. "But at that concentration we're dealing with a poison, not just an emetic."

"How does the ammonia odor fit into this?" Brandt asked.

Both physicians shrugged.

"I can't see how it would be related, if ipecac is what we're dealing with here," Robertson said.

"I'm going to go take another look at the floral arrangements," Brandt said. "Keep me posted on the cake?"

Robertson nodded and walked in the direction of the cake table.

Brandt noticed that most of the floral centerpieces had been moved off the tables and placed against the walls of the ballroom. As he approached the largest grouping of them, he saw someone he recognized.

"Walters—good to see you, man. Sorry to ruin your Saturday night."

"All part of the glamor of being on the force. Chris and I were just watching a movie and eating leftovers anyway."

"Gabriel's sister has sure domesticated you," Brandt replied with a chuckle.

"She must have learned it from how her brother has you whipped," Walters shot back jovially. "But in a room full of barf, how are you two the only men standing?"

"Didn't eat the cake, apparently. They're testing it now. But the ammonia smell still bothers me—any ideas?"

"It seems strongest here by the flowers," Walters said. He put latex gloves on and hefted one of the heavy floor vases onto the nearest table. He handed Brandt a pair of gloves as well. "Let's take a look." He pulled the stems and greens out of the vase, laying them out one by one on the tabletop. He looked at each one, and shook his head repeatedly.

"Not finding anything?" Brandt asked as he too examined the flowers.

"Nope," Walters replied, feeling around the inside of the wide, low vase. "Wait, got something."

Brandt dropped the bloom he was holding and peered into the vase with Walters. "What is it?"

"Something… gooey," Walters said, pulling a gelatinous mass from the water. He looked closely at it, then brought it to his nose. He sniffed delicately and then thrust it away from his face. "That's the stuff. Ammonia in a gel cap."

"What does that mean?" Brandt asked, sniffing the goo for himself and grimacing at the irritating stench.

"It means that someone tossed gelatin capsules full of ammonia into the floral arrangements. Once they dissolved, they released the ammonia, and bam—stink time."

"But most of the flowers were on the tables. Someone walking through the room plopping capsules into the vases would have been noticed, don't you think?"

Walters shook his head. "These are pharma capsules. They're meant to dissolve after someone swallows them. They require a warm, acid environment to break down the gelatin. The water in these vases is cold, so it would have taken hours for them to release the ammonia."

"But there's no acid in a flower vase," Brandt said.

"There usually is," Walters replied. "Most floral preservatives are acidic, like lemon juice or vinegar. The commercial ones can be pretty strong."

Brandt pondered this for a moment. "So the ammonia gel caps were like a time bomb, waiting to go off."

"That's about it. This much ammonia would just be annoying, though. It's not enough to do any physical harm. Looks more like a prank than an attack of some kind."

"Some prank," Brandt remarked, looking out at the ballroom, which was finally emptying of people.

"Officer Brandt?" Robertson called from the cake table.

Brandt jogged over, eager to find out what the doctor had discovered. Robertson and Neill were standing before an array of field testing equipment in which they had dissolved samples of the wedding cake.

"Found something?" Brandt asked as he approached the table.

"The cake tests positive for alkaloids consistent with ipecac juice," Robertson said.

"But there's more," Neill said, motioning Brandt to come closer. "I tested the parts of the cake separately. This"—she held up a tube and shook it—"is the sample of icing. See how there's no precipitate?"

Brandt looked; the tube contained only clear liquid. He nodded.

"I also tested the piped decorations, and this one is the cake itself—still no precipitate. But this one is the filling." She held up a test tube in which a grainy layer could be seen at the bottom. "There's your ipecac. We tested filling samples from a dozen pieces of cake, all from different areas. Same thing."

Robertson chimed in. "And that means—"

"That whoever contaminated the cake did it at the bakery," Brandt said. "If they had applied it after it was finished, it would be on the icing. If they injected it somehow, it wouldn't be present in every piece."

"I think you should have a word with the baker," Robertson said. "He seems to have poisoned his own cake."

"A cake he made under legal threat," Neill added, eyebrows raised at Brandt.

Brandt nodded gravely. This did not look good for Capella, nor for Montgomery, for that matter, who seemed to have followed the same strategy. He would need to pay both a visit, right away.

"Hey, how are things in here?"

Brandt finally heard the voice he'd been waiting to hear since the whole mess began. Donnelly was standing behind him, and Brandt turned around and took in the sight. His tie was gone, as was his jacket, and his brand-new stiff white shirt was a Jackson Pollock of regurgitated blue fondant. Brandt didn't care a bit. He lunged at Donnelly and kissed him fiercely.

The good doctors Neill and Robertson stepped aside so as to leave the troopers some privacy for their reunion.

"I hear you ran the show out there," Brandt said, beaming at Donnelly.

"I got the same story about you. From the governor and his wife, no less. They made you out to be some superhuman hybrid of Florence Nightingale and the Terminator."

"Everyone safely out?"

"Just the crime scene folks left now, and a bunch of uniforms starting to write up reports. The grooms were going to cancel their honeymoon and spend the night making rounds of all of the area hospitals, apologizing to their friends and family, but their parents stopped heaving long enough to convince them to get out of here." Donnelly shook his head at his partner. "Not the best way to start married life, huh?"

"I think it's going to take them a while to get over what we've witnessed here," Brandt said sympathetically, but shook it off and got back to work. "The chief got here about a half hour ago. I need to bring him up to speed on what we've found. Then we can get going."

"Awesome," Donnelly said with an exhausted smile. "I need a shower, and then another shower, and then to sleep until Monday afternoon."

"Or—and I'm just thinking out loud here, see what you think—how about we go right now and ask the good people at Montgomery and Capella why they tried to poison everyone at the wedding?"

Donnelly's eyes widened with surprise. "What the—"

"I'll explain on the way."

AS THEY drove up to Cakes by Capella, Brandt and Donnelly were surprised to see lights on in the back of the shop. They had assumed they would need to track down the Capellas at home, as it was now almost ten in the evening, but since the bakery was closer to the hotel, they started here. They parked in front, space being ample this late.

"Ready?" Brandt asked.

"I guess so," Donnelly said, his voice still hinting of his exhaustion. "I'm just really glad you'd already packed our gym stuff in the car for tomorrow's workout. I have never been so glad to take off a shirt in my life." Donnelly, like Brandt, was now attired in the après-workout T-shirt and khakis that they had intended to wear to the diner.

"It will make an interesting story for the dry cleaner. Or maybe we should just give up and burn it."

"And risk making our auras green from frosting fumes? The very idea." Donnelly laughed and stepped out of the car.

Brandt walked around from the driver's side of the car to the door of the bakery. He knocked and waited a moment, but there was no movement within. He knocked more loudly, and called "Police!" but there was still no response.

"Let's try the back door," Donnelly suggested. "I think there's an alley that runs behind."

They walked the short distance to the corner and then around the side of the building and finally into the alley. Two sets of locked doors and dark windows corresponded to the stores next to the bakery, and then they came to a door with a feeble light shining through the transom above. A faded "Capella" shone in red paint under the light of Donnelly's flashlight.

Brandt knocked loudly on the solid steel door. A light above the door switched on, blinding them for a moment with its sudden brightness.

"Who is it?" a voice called from within.

"State police," Brandt replied, shouting to be heard through the door. He held his badge up so that it would be visible through the peephole.

A lock slid, then another, and then the door swung out toward them. "Oh, it's you," Justin Capella said, his voice full of relief. "Come on in."

He stood to the side and admitted the officers and then pulled the door shut and locked it again. "Come into the bakery," he said, leading them to the large central room with its vast butcher-block table. "What can I do for you?"

"We've just come from the Laurence/Sampson wedding," Donnelly began. "Have you seen the news?"

"No, I've been getting prepped for the coming week. Now that almost all of the cancellations have been canceled, we're going to be pretty slammed." He stopped and looked at the grim faces of the officers. "What… happened?"

"The guests were poisoned." Brandt meant to shock him by using that word, and it worked.

Justin practically left the ground he jolted so hard. "Poisoned? Oh my God."

"It gets worse," Donnelly said. "Tests run at the scene indicate pretty clearly that the source of the poison was your cake."

Justin froze, color draining from his face. His mouth moved, but he couldn't make a sound. Suddenly he bolted; Brandt was only steps behind him, thinking he might be trying to escape, but he was only running to the sink to throw up—which he did, three times, noisily and until tears ran down his face. Brandt walked back to Donnelly to await Justin's recovery.

It was nearly five minutes later that Justin walked back to where they stood. "Is anyone…," he said, still trying to catch his breath, "Did anyone die?"

"No," Donnelly answered. "Not yet, anyway."

"Oh my God, oh my God, oh my God," Justin murmured as he sat down on a stool. "How did this happen?" His eyes were pleading. "How?"

"We think it was ipecac," Brandt said. "There was enough in the cake to sicken everyone who ate it—even just a bite or two."

"So someone poisoned the cake?" Justin said, looking at Brandt with wide eyes. "Why would someone do that?"

"We don't know. Maybe someone who didn't want the wedding to happen in the first place did it just to lash out."

Justin's eyes bugged out. "You don't think that someone in the bakery might have…?"

"I'm not accusing anyone, but it would be the most logical explanation. Everyone knows that your father was adamantly opposed to participating in the wedding."

"My father would never do that, no matter how he felt about it," Justin said, offense edging into his voice. "And anyway I did the cake personally. He wasn't even around most of last week. I mixed, baked, decorated, and assembled that cake myself, except for the parts that were too heavy for me to lift on my own."

"Any new suppliers for ingredients?" Donnelly asked. "Anything in that cake that was new or unusual?"

Justin shook his head. "I've been changing suppliers for some things, but not in the last week. Everything that went into that cake has gone into a half dozen other cakes, and no one's gotten sick from those. Someone must have found a way to put the poison in after I delivered the cake. Maybe someone at the hotel?"

"No, that couldn't have happened," Brandt replied.

Justin turned to him quizzically. "What makes you so certain?"

"The poison was in the filling of the cake."

Justin stopped cold. "It was in the filling?"

"It's the only part of the cake that tested positive," Brandt answered. "Every piece they tested showed the same thing."

"Then I know what happened," Justin said.

Brandt shook his head, sure he had misheard. "You know what happened?"

Justin walked over to the special ingredients cabinet, unlocked it, and pulled out the now-empty bottle of liqueur. "This," he said simply, setting the ornate bottle on the table.

"What is this?" Donnelly asked, looking at the bottle and then up at Justin.

"The liqueur that they had me order for the filling. I'd never used it before, and it's really strong. I needed to use it all for the filling, but you can have the bottle. The stuff was supposed to be 150 years old or something, so maybe it went bad and made everyone sick."

Donnelly picked up the bottle and held it up to the light. "There are a few drops left—maybe it's enough to test."

"At least it gives us a working theory," Brandt said. "But it would help us out a lot if you could think of anyone with access to the cake who would have a reason to want to sabotage the wedding. Just in case the liqueur proves not to be the problem."

Justin shook his head. "I didn't really let it out of my sight," he said, shaking his head. "I've been working late every night, and I'm the first one here in the morning. No one besides myself and my dad has a key to the building."

"And you're certain about your father?" Donnelly asked.

"Our paths hardly crossed this week. I don't think he was anywhere near the cake. And before you try to come up with a subtle way to ask, no, I didn't have an objection to working on the wedding. I'm actually really happy that my design got to be a part of it. At least until the whole poisoning thing." He looked over at the scheduling wall, and its many colored sticky notes. "I hope it wasn't the cake. I dread having to take those orders back off the wall."

"Well, thank you for your time," Brandt said. "We'll be in touch when we have the results of the tests on the bottle. And, please, text me right away if you can think of anything that might help us figure out what happened."

"I will, believe me," Justin said, escorting them to the back door. "The sooner we clear this up the better."

Brandt and Donnelly walked back around to their car.

"What did you think?" Brandt asked when they had settled into their seats.

"I believe him," Donnelly said. "If he had poisoned the cake, he would be ready for questions about it. I think he was genuinely mortified to hear that his cake had ruined the wedding. You can't really fake that much barfing." His face turned queasy. "I'm kind of an expert on barfing now."

"I'm with you on that," Brandt said with a shudder. "But we can't rule out someone else who works there trying to get revenge by contaminating the filling. We'll know more once we get the bottle tested. For now, though, I think Justin is pretty low on the suspect list."

"Now let's go see what our Mr. Junior Montgomery has to say about the adulteration of his floral arrangements."

As successful as their visit to Justin had been, they were to be disappointed in their attempt to talk with any of the Montgomery family. There was no one at the shop several blocks from the bakery, and when they arrived at the Montgomery house, no one answered the door. They left messages on every phone whose number they could associate with the Montgomery family and then returned home.

On the way, as Donnelly drove, Brandt called Dr. Neill.

"Sorry to wake you, Doctor, but we may have found out how the cake filling got tainted. The baker used a somewhat exotic liqueur to flavor it, and we have the bottle. I think there's enough left for you to test."

"I should look at it right away," she replied. "Can you bring it to my lab first thing tomorrow morning? Say, at eight?"

"Yes, we can. You're in the city administration building?"

"Yes, and call me when you get there—on Sunday I'll need to open the door for you."

"We'll see you tomorrow morning."

Brandt ended the call and smiled brightly at Donnelly. "So now you don't have to worry about sleeping late on a Sunday."

Donnelly didn't seem to share Brandt's sunny assessment. "Did I mention I stopped counting when the tenth person threw up on me? Not near me, not in front of me, *on* me." He heaved a great sigh. "All I want is a hot bath, a cold beer, and a long talk with my pillow about how I haven't been spending enough time with him lately."

"Okay, here's my counteroffer," Brandt replied. "A hot bath, a cold beer, and a special 'good morning' blowjob to wake you up in time to be at the city department of public health by eight."

Donnelly cast him a sidelong long. "You mean, *special* special? Where you—"

"Yep."

"And then you—"

"Uh-huh."

"And then you do that thing to my—"

"Oh yes. That will get extra special attention."

Donnelly nodded calmly, but Brandt saw that his knuckles were white as he gripped the steering wheel. Got him.

"Here," Donnelly said as he handed Brandt his phone.

"What's this for?"

"Set my alarm for six. You're going to need a good solid hour."

THE COVERAGE of the wedding disaster geared up early Sunday morning. The city's daily newspaper had held its front section for photos from the ceremony, but that had to be put to bed well before the reception got underway. By dawn, social media and Internet boards were crackling with photos of the city's elite barfing spectacularly.

Brandt browsed on his tablet while brushing his teeth. After viewing what seemed like the hundredth candid video, he pulled the toothbrush and spat into the sink. "Who would have thought that someone could be throwing up and still hold a camera to capture other people throwing up?" he called to Donnelly through the clouds of steam emanating from the shower.

"Hmm...," Donnelly called back, still in the loopy aftermath of Brandt's special wake-up maneuvers.

"Hey, you're in this one!" Brandt exclaimed, and thrust the tablet toward the shower.

"Ugh, I remember him," Donnelly replied. "Guy must have had curry for lunch." He turned back to the shower to begin scrubbing again.

"Wrap it up in there, buddy," Brandt said with a chuckle. "We gotta get moving if we're going to be there at eight."

Donnelly muttered something into the water that he would probably prefer Brandt not hear clearly anyway.

Just before eight they rolled into the mostly empty parking lot at the metro building. Brandt called Dr. Neill, and she met them at the side door near the compressed gas tanks and emergency generators.

"Good morning, Officers," she said with a smile. "Thanks for coming this early. The city's homeland security protocol sets tight deadlines for us to report on cases in which so many people are affected, and I'd rather have more periods than question marks when I meet with the task force tomorrow morning."

Brandt handed her the heavy bottle. "This is what flavored the filling."

She regarded the bejeweled crystal vessel with a raised eyebrow. "Not much for subtlety, are they? Well, you can come up if you like—it will take just a couple of minutes to run the assay and see if we get the same alkaloid profile as we did last night on the cake filling."

Brandt and Donnelly accompanied Dr. Neill in the elevator up to her lab, and within ten minutes, she brandished a test tube triumphantly at them.

"Looks like we found the source of the ipecac," she said, holding up a test tube full of clouded liquid to the light.

Brandt peered at the glass cylinder. "What are the odds that this very expensive and rare liqueur happened to be tainted with a very strong dose of ipecac?"

Neill narrowed her eyes in thought. "Thing is, if someone were to drink this straight, or even mixed in a cocktail, this concentration of ipecac would likely be deadly. An overdose of ipecac syrup is rarely fatal, because it's vomited up before it can reach toxic levels in the body. But this is far, far more concentrated than the syrup. This kind of contamination would be disastrous for the distiller, besides the fact that accidental ipecac contamination has never occurred that I know of, and the chance of it is even lower now that commercial production of the syrup has stopped." She stopped and pondered the bottle for a moment. "No, the contamination had to have occurred after it was opened. It's the only thing that makes sense."

"Thank you, Doctor." Brandt turned to Donnelly. "I guess we need to pay another visit to our baker."

Donnelly nodded his assent. They left Neill to the writing of her report and headed down to their car. As Donnelly drove, Brandt called Justin and asked him to meet them at the bakery. Justin, worry evident in his voice, agreed.

"Try Montgomery Floral one more time on the way there?" Donnelly asked.

"Sure. Maybe we'll get all of our answers in one morning."

"And then pancakes," Donnelly said with a pout. "You said there'd be pancakes."

"First we unravel the criminal enterprise; then we have pancakes. You are such a baby."

"Humph."

Montgomery Floral looked as deserted as it had the night before, so when Brandt knocked he was surprised to hear movement inside. Roman peered out from the back of the shop and, seeing who was at the door, walked over and let the officers in.

"Can I help you?" he asked once they had stepped into the still and silent front room of the shop.

"Roman, we're here to talk to you about the Laurence/Sampson wedding," Brandt began. "Are you aware of what happened at the reception last night?"

"Well, I should hope that no one could stop talking about the centerpieces, but I assume you didn't come over here on a Sunday morning to congratulate me on my work."

"I'm afraid not. Were you aware that gelatin capsules were placed in the vases? When the capsules dissolved a noxious gas was released into the ballroom."

Roman looked confused. "We don't use gelatin capsules here, so I don't know why they would be in the arrangements. Did you talk to the hotel people? Did they put them in there?"

"No one knows when they were dropped, or who put them there," Brandt replied. "But it is possible that they were placed in the flower arrangements before they were delivered to the hotel."

"Are you saying that someone in my shop did it?" Roman looked skeptical.

"As I said, it's possible," Brandt said diplomatically. "It's common knowledge that your dad didn't want to be involved in the wedding in the first place; do you think someone might have done it as a prank, or to send a message about being forced to do the wedding?"

"I did the centerpieces myself, start to finish. I ordered the blooms, I chose the vases, I did the arrangements. No one else from the shop got near them, except when they were delivered. But I never let them out of my sight until the wedding planner showed up and approved them. Then I and my entire crew left. It had to have been later."

"So you don't believe that anyone else in the shop could have done it?"

"I'm sure of that. We don't even use ammonia in the shop."

Donnelly put his hand on Brandt's arm. "Roman, do you think you might be able to come with us to Cakes by Capella? We're meeting Justin there in a few minutes, and I think it might be useful to have your input as well."

Roman seemed surprised by the request but agreed. "I'll go lock up, and I'll meet you at your car in a couple," he said with a smile.

Brandt and Donnelly went back out to the car to wait.

"Why did you ask him to come along?" Brandt asked once they were in the car.

"Because he knows more than he's telling."

"How do you know that?"

"He said that they don't use ammonia in the shop."

Brandt nodded.

"You hadn't said that the gel caps contained ammonia."

Brandt sucked in a surprised breath.

"Knowing that, I wanted to see how he reacts when we tell Justin the results of the test on the liqueur bottle. See if something shakes loose."

Brandt shook his head. "You are brilliant."

"You were the one doing the questioning," Donnelly replied. "I was just doing the listening."

The back door of the car opened, and Roman stepped in. "Thanks for waiting."

"No problem. Glad you could come," Brandt replied. He pulled smoothly away from the curb and set out on the two-minute drive to Cakes by Capella.

Justin met them at the front door of the shop.

"Roman," Justin said, his surprise—and delight—evident. "I didn't know you were coming."

"Just trying to help get this all figured out," he said, smiling.

Justin guided them through the precious shop to the kitchen. "Coffee?" he asked, gesturing to a full pot.

"Thank you, that would be great," Brandt answered.

Donnelly gratefully accepted a cup as well and closed his eyes as he sipped. "That's the stuff," he murmured. "You make some pretty great coffee, Justin."

"It's kind of important when you're running a bakery," Justin replied with a flattered smile. "We're often several pots in before the sun comes up." He took a long swig himself. "Now, you said you had the results of the tests on the liqueur bottle?"

Brandt set his cup down on the butcher-block tabletop. "It tested positive."

Justin's face fell; he'd clearly been hoping that the test would show that the ipecac had come from a source outside the bakery. But then he brightened a bit. "So I guess you're going to talk to the distiller about how it got contaminated?"

"This isn't something that would accidentally happen," Brandt replied. "It's not like it went 'off' and made people sick. The poison was put into the liqueur intentionally, and it looks like it happened here."

Donnelly stepped forward. "The bottle came sealed, right?"

"It had a wax band around the gold clasp at the top," Justin replied.

"And you were the one who broke the seal?"

Justin nodded.

"And did anyone have access to it after you opened it?"

"No. I kept it locked in the cabinet over here, and I'm the only one with a key."

"Doesn't your dad have one?" Brandt asked.

Justin shook his head. "His broke off in the lock a couple of weeks ago. I had to have it replaced, and he said as long as I had one he didn't need to carry another key around."

Donnelly looked at the locked cabinet, then back at Justin. "And when you were making the filling, was anyone else around who might have been able to get into the bottle?"

"I really don't think so. I kept it in the cabinet until I needed it because I kept having nightmares about dropping it and having an eight-hundred-dollar puddle on the floor. I mixed the other filling ingredients, walked over to the cabinet, unlocked it, and then poured the entire bottle into the mixer. That's it."

"Now, Justin, I want you to think carefully," Brandt asked slowly and calmly. "Did anyone else have access to the bottle at any point after you broke the seal, but before you poured it into the mixer?"

Justin shook his head.

"Even just for a second or two? Just to take a little taste, or even smell it?"

Justin froze. His eyes widened slightly, and he seemed to suck in a little gasping breath. But then he blinked and shook his head again. "No, no one touched it but me." He turned his back to the officers and refilled his coffee cup.

Brandt looked at him quietly for a moment, trying to figure out what that startled reaction was all about. "So," he said to Roman and Justin, who were standing together by the coffee maker, "we have a lot of unanswered questions about how both the flowers and the cake came to sicken several hundred people at a wedding that neither of your companies wanted to participate in."

"I know it looks bad, but—" Justin blurted, but Brandt held up a hand.

"If this was intended as a prank, or a way to embarrass the people who filed the lawsuit, it has gone pretty seriously off the rails. Because of the number of people affected, the homeland security task force is going to take this up tomorrow, and that means that there are going to be a lot more people asking a lot more questions—hard questions—in the coming days. We've just been trying to get the basics figured out, and that's why we haven't arrested anyone, or taken you in for formal questioning. But the people who show up here tomorrow won't be as gentle."

Brandt intended to continue, but at that moment both his phone and Donnelly's sounded their dispatch tone, the one only used for urgent messages.

"I got it," Donnelly said, and put his phone to his ear. "Donnelly. Oh? Yeah, put him through." He shot Brandt a confused look and pointed to his phone, shaking his head. "Yes, Mr. Sampson, it's Gabriel Donnelly. I'm surprised to hear from you, sir, on your honeymoon." Donnelly fell silent. His eyes widened. "Oh, I'm so sorry. When did— do they know what—yes, yes I understand. We're doing everything we can to find out what happened. I'm so sorry." He took the phone from his ear and pocketed it.

"What happened?" Brandt asked.

Donnelly swallowed hard and took a halting breath.

"Peter Laurence is dead."

CHAPTER NINE
VOWS AND OATHS

BRANDT AND Donnelly left immediately, heading back toward the metro building to inform Dr. Neill about the death of Peter Laurence.

"Did he say anything about what happened?" Brandt asked. They had rushed out of the bakery so quickly he hadn't had a chance to get any additional information from Donnelly. "And why call us?"

"All he said was that he collapsed during the night. They don't know what happened. I think he called us because he knew we were there, and it might help the investigation." Donnelly put his hand on Brandt's leg. "He sounded so sad and so... shocked."

"Easy to see why. And on their wedding night! I just can't believe it."

They drove in silence for a few minutes.

"I wonder if this has anything to do with the cake and flowers," Donnelly said as he looked out the window.

"The docs were pretty sure that the levels of ammonia released would only be annoying, not dangerous. But Neill keeps referring to ipecac as a poison, so there may be something there."

"But you said they didn't seem to be affected by the cake. And a lot of the guests ended up going to the hospital, at least to get rehydrated. But Laurence and Sampson were able to go on their honeymoon."

"Maybe he just reacted differently to the ipecac. Like an allergic reaction or something?"

Donnelly shook his head slowly. "Just so sad."

Dr. Neill met them at the parking lot entrance again. They accompanied her back to the office next to her lab, where they sat around a small table.

"So, what's this new development?" Neill asked, pouring herself a cup of tea. She offered the pot to them, but both men declined.

"Peter Laurence died this morning," Donnelly replied.

Neill set her cup onto its saucer with a clatter. She held her hand to her mouth for a moment as she composed herself. "What happened?"

"We don't know," Brandt replied. "Greg Sampson called just a few minutes ago to tell us."

"Do you know where they were honeymooning?" she asked.

Brandt turned to Donnelly. "Didn't the paper this morning say something about where they were going?"

"Taylors Beach," Donnelly said definitively. Then to Brandt he murmured, a little sheepishly, "Keeping a list of possible honeymoon locations."

"They would have taken him to Springfield. Let me do a little checking." Neill picked up her phone and flicked briskly, then held it to her ear. "Dr. Snyder. It's Parker Neill. I'm sorry to bother you on a Sunday, but we have a situation here—yes, that's the one. I've just found out that one of the grooms, Peter Laurence, has died." She listened for a moment. "We don't know yet. That's why I'm calling. Can you find out which hospital he was taken to? I have some questions that relate to our investigation into the poisoning. Yes, this number would be best. Thanks, Jack." She lowered the phone to the desk. "Public health directors are a pretty tight-knit bunch. It's faster than going through official channels for getting information across state lines. Jack's great—I'm sure he'll find out soon."

"I didn't think Laurence had any of the cake, but I might have been wrong," Brandt said.

"He certainly wasn't affected the way the others were," Neill agreed.

"What would ipecac poisoning look like?" Brandt asked.

"Hard to say," Neill replied. "The major impact would likely be myocarditis. But that's a difficult one to diagnose, at least until the autopsy."

"Myocarditis? Inflammation of the… heart?" Donnelly asked.

Neill nodded. "The muscle tissue, specifically. That's what makes it hard to diagnose, because you have to do a biopsy to be sure."

Her phone rang. She looked at the display before putting it to her ear. "Jack, thanks so much for calling me back. Uh-huh. Got it. Thanks so much. Say hi to Grace for me. Bye-bye."

She set the phone down. "Peter Laurence was taken to St. Andrew's. Dr. Snyder told them to expect my call." Flipping open her laptop, she typed rapidly for a moment and then picked up her phone and dialed a number. "Patient information, please." She paused, drumming her fingers on the desk. "This is Dr. Parker Neill. I'm calling to inquire about a patient, Peter Laurence." She made a quizzical face, as if she had heard something that surprised her. "Yes, I know that. I'd like to speak to the attending physician please. I'm investigating a possible poisoning. Yes, I'll hold."

She held the phone away from her face for a moment. "She sounded exasperated, and said, 'again?' when I asked about Laurence. I don't seem to be the first person calling about him."

"Hello?" she said into the phone. "This is Dr. Neill, who is this please? ... I'm sorry, I asked for the attending physician for Peter Laurence. I have two state police officers here with me, and we need to speak to the doctor. You can check with Dr. Jackson Snyder at public health if you need to. Thank you."

"That was the hospital attorney," she explained. "Either someone dialed the wrong extension, or the hospital doesn't want people asking questions."

Brandt glanced at Donnelly, trying to sort it all out. At every turn things kept getting stranger.

"Ah, yes. Doctor... Gupta, you said? This is Dr. Neill. We have a potential mass poisoning here that may have affected Peter Laurence. What can you tell me about him?"

JUSTIN CLOSED and locked the door as the officers drove away. He walked back into the kitchen to find Roman sitting stiffly at the big table, looking at his hands. Justin came up behind and wrapped his arms around him. He pressed his cheek against Roman's shoulder and breathed deeply, taking in the safety of his scent. Before he even realized it, he was crying.

"I just can't believe it," he said softly.

"Justin," Roman whispered. "Someone died. Oh my God."

"I might as well close the bakery now. My dad's going to hate me."

Roman turned around suddenly and clasped Justin's shoulders with his hands. "It wasn't your fault," he said slowly and seriously. "You didn't do anything wrong."

"I don't think that the police believe me. I could tell they thought I might be lying when they were asking all of those questions."

"You *were* lying."

Justin looked up, eyes wide. "What? Why would you say that?"

"You lied for me," Roman said. He blinked hard and squeezed out the tears from his eyes.

"They didn't need to know about that. What does it matter if you smelled it? It's not like that's going to make any difference in the investigation."

"Justin, I'm sorry." Roman sobbed, unable to continue speaking. He stood suddenly and rushed to the back door. "I'm so sorry." He flung the door open and ran out.

"Roman? Roman, wait!" Justin called after him, but by the time he reached the doorway to the alley, Roman was gone.

BRANDT WAS able to glean very little information from hearing only one side of the medical conversation that took place over the next five minutes. He and Donnelly waited patiently for Neill to finish.

"Thank you, Dr. Gupta," Neill said into the phone. She set it on the desk and shook her head. "There's a lot going on here. Let's start with the medical stuff. He was brought in at 3:30 a.m., unconscious. Mr. Sampson said that Laurence had woken suddenly about half an hour before, clutching his chest and gasping for air. He lost consciousness after a minute or so, and Sampson called 9-1-1. They tried to revive him at the hospital, but he never regained consciousness. He died at seven thirty this morning as they were prepping him for more imaging."

"What do they think caused it?" Brandt asked.

"All signs point to a cardiac problem. They were attempting to rule out aortic dissection when he arrested."

Donnelly shifted uncomfortably in his chair. "So, it could be myocarditis?"

Neill nodded. "At this point they can't rule it out. Not until the autopsy."

"You said you were going to start with the medical stuff," Donnelly prompted. "What other 'stuff' was there?"

"Apparently the hospital wouldn't allow Sampson to accompany Laurence into the ICU. They said that only family could be present."

"But they were married," Donnelly blurted, disbelief in his voice.

"And they were in a state that doesn't allow gay marriage," Neill replied. "They wouldn't recognize his right to be there."

Donnelly slumped back, mouth hanging open. "But they can't just decide to disregard someone's marital status!"

"They couldn't do that here," Brandt said, anger rising in his chest. "But since gay marriage isn't legal there, they don't have to recognize it."

"Gupta said that he tried to keep Sampson informed while they worked on Laurence, but then the hospital attorney got involved and said he couldn't even do that."

"Seems like Sampson would have a few attorneys of his own in the fight," Donnelly observed. "What with Laurence being a partner at onc of the biggest firms in the state."

"Maybe that's why the folks at the hospital were on edge," Brandt said. He got to his feet. "Thanks very much, Dr. Neill. We're going to head back to have another conversation with the baker and florist. This new development may encourage them to remember some details they hadn't before."

"I'll let you know if I hear anything more from the hospital, though I assume we won't get an autopsy underway until Mr. Sampson manages to get the body released. Who knows how long that will take."

Brandt and Donnelly nodded grimly and headed back to the parking lot.

JUSTIN AGAIN met the troopers at the front door of the shop. He stood aside and let them enter, then shut and locked the door behind them.

"Are you okay?" Donnelly asked him. "You look like you've been crying."

Justin shook his head miserably and led them back to the kitchen.

"Where's Roman?" Brandt asked as they entered. "I thought he was going to wait for us to come back."

"He was really upset by that Laurence guy dying. We both were. He said he… needed to get some fresh air, clear his head."

Donnelly nodded, but Brandt could tell he did so to encourage Justin to keep talking, not because he believed what he was saying. "And how are you doing with it?"

Justin fairly collapsed onto a stool. "This is the end," he said simply. "Three generations of Capellas built this business and kept it going through good times and bad, and it will end with me."

"If you didn't do anything wrong, there's no reason why this has to mean the end of the bakery," Donnelly said, his voice consoling. "We just need to figure out what happened, and once the explanation comes out, everyone will forget all about it."

"A guy died," Justin said, agonized. "A guy died after eating my cake. I'll never forget that, and no one else will either."

"Actually, we don't think he ate any of the cake," Brandt said. "We were at the reception, and they just pretended to feed each other the cake so they could smash it all over each other's faces. I never saw them eat it. They didn't seem to be feeling any effects, anyway."

Justin looked up, a glimmer of hope in his eyes. "You mean it might not have been the cake that did it?"

"I wish I could tell you for certain," Brandt replied. "We don't know for sure what happened, and we won't know until the autopsy is done. He may have eaten some cake and not been affected in the same way as everyone else. Or he didn't eat any, and something completely unrelated happened to him. We just don't know."

Donnelly's phone buzzed with a new text message, and he pulled out his phone to read it. "We'll know pretty soon, though," he said. "That was the coroner's office. The hospital in Springfield has released the body, after the governor got involved. They'll have him here by this evening, and they're planning the autopsy immediately."

"They do autopsies on Sunday nights?" Justin asked.

"When they involve high-profile people who may or may not be the first fatality of a mass poisoning, yes, they do."

"Wow," Justin sighed, slumping again.

Donnelly put a hand on the young man's shoulder. "Until we know what happened, there's no use getting upset," he said soothingly. "Why don't you go get some rest, and we'll let you know if we find out anything significant. And if you happen to remember anything, no matter how insignificant, that you haven't told us, please, get in touch right away, okay?"

Justin nodded, clearly trying to buck himself up. And not succeeding at it.

As the troopers got back into their car, Donnelly looked at Brandt tiredly. "Can we get something to eat now? It's almost noon and the maple syrup level in my blood is dangerously low."

Brandt chuckled. "Might as well. Nothing for us to do until the autopsy results come in."

At eight in the morning—a Monday morning, as Donnelly had pointed out several times already—the officers were back at their desks awaiting the arrival of Gregory Sampson. The results of the autopsy weren't due back for several hours, so why Sampson wanted to meet with them was unclear. But he had said he needed to talk with them, and so here they were.

"Ethan, you have a visitor," the officer at the front desk said as she walked into the area that housed their desks and those of several other officers and detectives.

Brandt stood and was shocked to see not the tall, dramatic presence of Gregory Sampson, but instead the slumped shoulders of a very distraught Roman Montgomery.

"Roman, what are you doing here?" Brandt asked, prompting Donnelly to pop up from his desk as well.

"Can I...." He paused to wait for the front-desk officer to leave the room. "Can I talk to you for a minute?"

"Sure," Brandt said, pulling up a chair to his desk. "Have a seat."

"Can I get you some coffee or something?" Donnelly asked. "You look like you haven't slept much."

"No thanks—my stomach couldn't take it. And I haven't slept much. Actually, not at all."

"Then why don't you tell us what's up?" Brandt asked, sitting next to Roman at his desk.

"Ethan, Gregory Sampson's here," the desk officer interrupted once again.

"Can you go settle him into the conference room, and I'll be right there?" Brandt asked Donnelly. Then he turned back to Roman. "What you have to say is very important to me, Roman," he said with deliberate seriousness. "But I need to go talk to Mr. Sampson right now. Is that okay? Can you wait here for a little bit until I get back? If you need anything, just ask Carole at the front desk."

Roman nodded and stuck his hands in the pocket of his hoodie.

Brandt joined Donnelly and Sampson in the conference room. "Mr. Sampson, I am so sorry for your loss," he said, extending his hand.

Sampson's normally ice-blue eyes were red, and he looked haggard. "Thank you," he said, his voice rough.

Brandt sat at the table where Sampson and Donnelly were already seated.

"Now, Mr. Sampson, how can we help you?" Donnelly asked.

"Greg, please call me Greg," Sampson replied. He took a deep breath and blew it out slowly. "Peter and I never got a chance to properly thank you two for what you did for us. You accomplished what a lawsuit couldn't: you got our wedding back on track, and it was beautiful. Until…." His voice failed, and he sighed deeply.

"Greg, you have my assurance that we will find out what happened," Brandt said softly. "And we will bring those responsible to justice."

"I would trade all the justice in the world for one more day with the man I married," Sampson said. Then he shook his head and seemed to try to find his center again. "But that's not why I've come. I wanted to tell you what happened."

"Dr. Neill told us what she got from the doctor at St. Andrew's," Donnelly said. "You don't need to put yourself through that again on our account."

Sampson shook his head. "I'm not talking about what happened to him physically. I hope we'll have some answers on that today. But I wanted you to know what happened to me… to us."

Donnelly nodded encouragingly.

"Once most of our poor wedding guests were safely off to the hospital, we decided we might as well do what our parents urged us to do and leave on our honeymoon as we'd planned. Though all we did was check on people on our phones the entire drive to Taylors Beach. Three hours of apologizing to everyone, feeling just horrible about what happened. I kept thinking, this has got to be the worst honeymoon ever." He chuckled grimly. "Those were the beginning of the last hours I would spend with him.

"Peter's family had vacationed at Taylors Beach every year when he was growing up, and he was so looking forward to showing it to me. He had rented a beautiful villa right on the shore, and we pulled up just after one in the morning. The staff had heard what we'd been through, and they were wonderful. Within ten minutes we were sitting on the bed, sipping champagne and laughing for the first time since the cake was cut. Peter was like that; he could look adversity right in the eye until adversity blinked. Anyway, we were exhausted, but it was our wedding night, and we...." He looked down, his shoulders shaking with silent sobs.

Donnelly handed him a box of tissues. He took two and held them to his eyes for a long moment.

"I was lying next to him. The entire bedroom was open to the night, sheers blowing in a gentle breeze, waves crashing on the beach. I lay there with my head on his chest, listening to that great heart beating, thinking how lucky I am. I was born to a single mom who worked two jobs just to keep food on our table, and here I am with the man of my dreams on my wedding night, listening to the surf in a bedroom larger than the apartment I grew up in. I think I had just drifted off when Peter jolted. It was like someone had punched him in the chest. He gasped, and it was like he was suffocating. He flailed around, and he turned the most horrible purple in the face, veins standing out on his neck. I felt all over him, looking for a wound or something. I mean, if someone is in that much distress, there's got to be blood somewhere. But there was nothing.

"I held him, tried to get him to respond or do something other than gasp and struggle. I said his name over and over again, but it's like he didn't even see me. His eyes were wide and glassy and unfocused. It's like he could see Death already, coming for him."

Sampson closed his eyes and heaved a long sigh.

"That was the last time I held him."

Donnelly cried out and instantly stifled his reaction with his hand. He looked at Brandt, eyes full of tears, his face bereft. Brandt put his hand on Donnelly's knee and tried to convey with his eyes how deeply this was affecting him as well.

"I picked up my phone and called 9-1-1. The operator asked all kinds of questions, and I did my best to answer them. Peter struggled less and less wildly as the minutes passed, as if the life were draining out of him. The ambulance got there quickly, or at least that's what they told me later. It seemed like an hour, but they said they were there four minutes after getting the call. They worked on him a few minutes on the bed, shoving a tube down his throat and hooking him up to all kinds of monitors. Aside from a few questions that the 9-1-1 operator had already asked me, they didn't really take much notice of me. They wheeled him out to the ambulance, and I threw on my clothes and followed. The doors swung shut before I could get in, though, and I pounded on the back of the ambulance until they opened the doors again. The EMT said something about not expecting me to come along, and I told him that I wasn't about to let my husband be taken to the hospital without me. He just looked at me for a couple of seconds and then turned back to the monitors. It was like I wasn't even there during the whole ride to the hospital.

"The closest trauma center to Taylors Beach was St. Andrew's, on the outskirts of Springfield. They were able to get him there in under twenty minutes, and they took him right in. I couldn't go with him because he was swarmed with an entire trauma team. They told me to sit in the waiting room, so I did, and I started calling our families to tell them what was going on. I couldn't reach most people, since they were probably also either at the hospital or sleeping off the wedding cake. After a half hour of not giving me any news about his condition, finally his doctor came out to see me. He told me they were working on him, trying to stabilize him, and they thought it was something with his heart. The doctor got paged back into trauma before I could ask if I could see him, so I went to the nurse on duty. She told me only family was allowed in the ER, and if I were a family member, I could go right in and be there with him. I told her I was his husband, and… I could see it on her face. The way she looked at me, I just knew... I was actually carrying a copy of our marriage license. For some reason I thought to grab it out of Peter's bag while they were putting him on the stretcher. I tried to show it to her, but she wouldn't even look at it."

"Did she understand that you were showing her a marriage certificate?" Brandt asked, astounded.

Sampson nodded. "She knew what it was. She just didn't care. And then it got worse. The doctor came back out to update me on what they had been able to rule out, and she came over to him and said I wasn't family. He just sort of glared at her and finished talking to me, then went back into the ER. He came back out a little while later, but the nurse had apparently called the hospital's legal department, and an administrator headed him off and took him down the hall for a conversation. After that, he never came back.

"I called Peter's partners at the law firm, but most of them were recovering from the reception, and I could only reach one of them. She didn't come to the wedding because she's due to deliver twins next week. There wasn't much she could do from here, though she woke up about half a dozen lawyers in Springfield who lit up the switchboard. The hospital just kept saying that their policy is that only family is allowed into the ER or the ICU, where they had moved him by that point. The fact that we were married made no difference at all. The lawyers did everything they could, even waking up a judge at five in the morning to get an injunction or whatever you get when you force someone to do something they don't want to do.

"But by that point it didn't matter anymore. He was already gone. I was there, a hundred feet away, but I might as well have been on the moon. I never got to see him again. My...." He choked back a sob. "My husband died alone. He died without anyone to hold his hand or to cry over him. He died surrounded by no one who loved him, or who even knew him at all. No one to say his name or comfort him. He was my husband, and he died alone." Sampson broke down completely, sobbing into the tissues he had wadded and unwadded a dozen times while he told his story.

"I'm sorry," he managed to say through his tears.

Donnelly rose and walked to the other side of the table. He sat next to Sampson and put his arm around him. "It's okay," he whispered.

Sampson turned his face to Donnelly's shoulder and sobbed into it, filling the room with his deep, resonant keening. Tears poured down Donnelly's cheeks as he held the other man and rubbed a hand up and down his back. Brandt could only watch, crying himself but unsure how he could help any more than his emotionally adept partner was able to.

After five excruciating minutes, the cadence of Sampson's grief slowed, and he fell silent. Donnelly released his hold, and Sampson sat back in his chair, seemingly beyond embarrassment that the raw wound of bereavement had reduced him to tears and the sheltering embrace of a man he hardly knew.

"Thank you, Gabriel," Sampson said softly, putting his hand on Donnelly's damp shoulder. "I appreciate your…." At a loss, he looked across the table at Brandt. "You're a lucky man."

"That's the truest thing anyone could say of me," Brandt said, wiping his eyes with a tissue.

Sampson took a deep breath and exhaled exhaustedly. "So that's the story. Since you two are the public face of the Section 28 issue, I thought you should know what happens in a place where equal rights aren't the law. I wanted you to know that while everyone makes a big deal about cakes and flowers and all of the pomp and circumstance, what really matters about being married isn't the wedding. It's what comes after. The life you lead together. Marriage equality isn't about having an equal chance to get married; it's about gay marriage actually being equal to straight marriage. Marriage means that you are there for each other, and that everyone recognizes that. The marriage certificate I have in my pocket looks the same as one that unites a man and a woman, but it doesn't work the same. People don't have to acknowledge it. My marriage, Officers, my marriage wasn't the equal of anyone's marriage. When I needed it most, it wasn't worth the paper it was printed on. Peter fought for years to be treated like a citizen, with rights equal to any other citizen's. He won. He got married. And he died alone. All alone." Sampson closed his eyes and held his head in his hands.

"I am so sorry, Greg," Donnelly said, for what seemed like the dozenth time, but Brandt could think of no better words himself. "If there's anything we can do…."

Sampson opened his eyes slowly and rubbed them with exhausted motions of his shaking hands. "You two are doing great work, and I just wanted you to know that there's much more to be done. It's not a matter of what you can do for me. It's what I can do with you. Peter wasn't one to ever take injustice sitting down, and I'm going to honor him by standing up now. I've resigned from Channel 3. I'm going to take some time to pull myself together, and then I'm going to take on the cause of making sure that what happened to me and Peter never happens again. I'm going to start a foundation in Peter's name, and that's going to be my mission in life: my remembrance of him. I'd like to be able to work with you on that mission. We can make a difference, and that's what Peter would have wanted."

"We would be honored to work with you, Greg," Brandt said, deeply impressed at the determination evident in Sampson's manner.

Sampson stood slowly and rubbed his face with the air of a man much older than he was. "I guess I'll go camp out at the coroner's office. Peter's family is here, except for his mom, who's still in the hospital. I don't know what to say to them, to make it okay…," he said, his voice trailing off miserably.

"Sometimes," Donnelly said, "you don't need to say anything. It's enough to be there with each other. They'll understand that."

"Thank you… thank you so much," Sampson said warmly, shaking Donnelly's hand. He shook Brandt's as well, and walked, unsteadily at first, but then with surer steps, out of the room.

"Oh my God," Brandt said once he had left. "I—"

"Shh," Donnelly interrupted, pulling Brandt into his arms. "Just hold me for a minute, okay?" He sobbed softly into his partner's shoulder, and Brandt dampened his in return.

Finally, they were able to take a deep breath and release their hold on each other. They walked from the conference room back to their desks, to find Roman still in the chair where they had left him when Sampson arrived.

"Roman?" Brandt said, keeping his voice steady with great effort.

Roman looked up at him, tears streaming down his face.

"What's wrong?" Donnelly asked.

Roman tried several times to make an answer, but no sound would issue from his mouth. Finally he took a deep breath and was able to begin. "I heard him," he said. "I heard him tell you what happened."

Brandt sat next to Roman and put a hand on his arm. "I know. It upset me too."

"No, that's not it," Roman said, his voice barely audible. He cleared his throat and steadied himself with a couple of quick breaths. "It's more than that."

"What is more than that?" Donnelly asked.

"It was my fault," Roman said, looking at the carpet. Then he looked right into Donnelly's face. "It was me. I did it."

BRANDT WAS stunned. At first he was certain he had misunderstood what Roman had said. "Roman, we don't know what happened to Laurence. It might have been completely unrelated to what happened at the wedding. Just because you worked on the wedding doesn't mean you're to blame for what went wrong."

"No, you don't get it," Roman said, tears still flowing freely from his eyes. "I did it. The stuff in the filling. The ammonia in the flowers. That was me. I just didn't know it was going to be this bad. I'm so sorry." He reverted to sobbing again.

Brandt turned to Donnelly, completely baffled. Donnelly shrugged in response.

"Why don't you tell us what happened," Donnelly prompted.

Roman took a deep breath. "I just want to say at the beginning that I never intended for anyone to get hurt. This was just supposed to be a kind of protest, just to make a statement."

"About gay marriage?" Brandt asked.

Roman nodded.

"Because of the lawsuit?"

"No. It wasn't that. And my dad had nothing to do with it, and Justin had nothing to do with it. This wasn't about that at all."

"I don't get this," Donnelly said, his voice wavering with emotion. "You burst into tears because of what Sampson went through, but now you're saying you're against gay marriage? Against it strongly enough to sicken several hundred people? That's how much you hate the idea of two men together?"

Roman shook his head. "That's not it at all. I've got nothing against—look, I'm gay, okay?"

Brandt sat back in his chair, shocked. Donnelly simply blinked and shook his head in confusion.

"I don't understand any of this," Brandt said, his frazzled nerves starting to get the better of his professionalism. "What you're saying makes no sense."

"It's not that I don't think guys should be able to get married—I just don't think they should *want* to get married. All they're doing is pretending to be just like hetero couples, and it's stupid. Men should be men."

"What the fuck is that supposed to mean?" exploded Donnelly. His jaw was set and he looked ready to spring at the young man.

"You two are a couple, aren't you?"

"Our personal life has nothing to do with—"

"Yes, it does. Look at the two of you. You are men, strong and capable. And when I insult you—accidentally, by the way, sorry—you look like you're going to punch me rather than go off and cry about it. I can't see you two getting married, because neither of you is the girl in this relationship. But everyone who went to that wedding on Saturday saw those two guys and wondered which one was the wife. And that's how they would see you. Because that's what a wedding means to them. But what would it mean to you? What did it mean to those guys when they needed it? Nothing. It didn't do anything for them. They did the big hetero ritual, and pretended to be just like the normals, and in the end it brought them nothing. Nothing. They sold themselves out for equality, and the fuckers in power pretended to give it to them. But you heard him—he had the piece of paper, and his 'husband' died alone." Roman fell silent, breathing hard after his rant.

Brandt stared stony-faced at the young man. In his exhausted and muddled state, he could almost see his point—what had Laurence and Sampson actually gained? But he couldn't let his face reveal that.

"Whatever your opinion on gay marriage, what you did endangered a lot of people, and may have killed one—maybe more. Where did you get the ipecac?"

"The what?" Roman asked.

"The ipecac. The poison you put in the cake filling?"

"Oh, that's what that was."

Donnelly leaned in again. "You had no idea what you were putting in the cake filling?"

Roman shook his head. "He didn't tell me what it was."

"Who didn't tell you what it was?" Donnelly asked, his patience again wearing thin. "Justin? Was it Justin who put you up to it?"

Roman's face was suddenly serious. "Justin had nothing to do with this. I told you. Nothing."

"Then where did it come from?" Brandt snapped.

Roman took a deep breath. "Marcus. Marcus Verona."

"Who is that?" Donnelly demanded.

"He's a guy I met a couple of months ago. At a club. We started talking about gay marriage one night, and it turned out we believed the same things. And then when he found out that I would be working on the big wedding, he said it was a chance to make a political statement. He came up with the whole plan. He gave me the stuff to put in the cake, and in the flowers."

"And you just did it?" Brandt said, unable to keep the taunt out of his voice.

Roman nodded.

"Why? Why would you do that?"

"Marcus can be very… persuasive," Roman said, shifting uneasily in his chair.

"Did he threaten you?" Donnelly asked, his voice softening for the first time.

"Sort of."

"How could he 'sort of' threaten you?"

Roman sighed, as if giving up his struggle to keep any part of his actions private. "He's a really aggressive guy, and he has really aggressive friends. But it's not what he threatened to do to me, as much as what he threatened to… stop doing."

Brandt sat back in his chair and squinted at Roman. He raised his eyebrows and made a "come on, out with it" motion with his hand.

"He… I mean, we…," Roman stumbled.

"Are you and Marcus… intimate?" Donnelly asked.

Roman nodded and looked at the floor.

"Did he assault you?"

Roman shook his head. "He can be really rough, but… I guess I found out that I… kind of… like it a little rough."

"Oh my God," Brandt muttered, rubbing his brow with his hand. It wasn't yet nine o'clock on a Monday morning, and he was already exhausted.

"Look, I know this sounds weird, but with Marcus it's simple: he takes what he wants, and I give it to him. We don't mess around with any of the emotional stuff; we just meet each other's needs. Like men should."

"I don't need to hear any more about your sex life," Brandt said abruptly. "I just need to know where you got the stuff, and how you got it into the filling of the cake."

"Marcus gave me a vial, said I should find a way to get it into the cake. I went to visit Justin a couple of times, and when he showed me the liqueur bottle, I saw my chance. I asked him if I could smell it. After I did, I pretended to choke on it, and when he ran to get me some water, I dumped the vial into the bottle."

"Justin said that no one had a chance to add anything to the bottle," Brandt protested. "He said no one even smelled it."

Roman looked him in the eye. "He lied. He lied to protect me. He had no idea what I did, but he didn't want you to even think I had anything to do with poisoning the cake. So he covered for me." He sighed sadly and looked down. "I've known Justin about all my life, and I've never known him to lie. Never. Not until yesterday, and he only did it to protect me. He didn't even know what he was protecting me from."

"What he ended up protecting you from is looking like a manslaughter charge. You better hope no one else at that wedding dies."

"That's why I'm telling you this. I was on board for a prank, but I had no idea that what Marcus gave me would end up hurting anyone. He said it would just make them barf, and that it would be funny. And that the ammonia would throw people off, keep them from trying to pin all the blame on the cake. Once I found out that guy died, I knew I had to come tell you what happened."

Brandt was about to point out to Roman that his intention counted for exactly nothing, given the results of his action, but his phone's text sound interrupted him. He pulled his phone out and read. Then he handed the phone to Donnelly.

"Looks like you're off the hook for manslaughter," Brandt said, no cheer in his voice. "Peter Laurence died of an aortic dissection—the main artery from his heart basically ripped open. Had nothing to do with the poison in the cake—he tested negative for ipecac alkaloids. They think it was just a congenital weakness in the artery wall."

Roman heaved a sigh of relief.

"You're not out of the woods yet, my friend," Brandt said warningly. "There are still charges that are certainly going to be brought against you for what you've done."

"What if I told you that Marcus has plans to do this again?" Roman asked.

"Are you telling us that he's going to try to disrupt more weddings?" Donnelly replied.

Roman nodded. "This was kind of a trial run, I think. If it seemed like it worked, he was going to keep doing it. And barfing is going to seem pretty mild compared to some of the stuff he talked about."

"Why should we believe you?" Donnelly demanded. "It sounds like you're trying to throw your fuck-buddy under the bus to save yourself."

"I can get him to talk about it—I can record him talking about his plans."

Brandt and Donnelly exchanged a look.

"You can throw the book at me, but he'll still be out there, plotting to do this again, only worse. Or you can cut me a break, and I'll deliver him to you."

Brandt considered the options. "I can't make that kind of deal," Brandt said. "I need to talk to the DA first. And, just to let you know where you stand, the DA who's handling this case was at the wedding. He may not have a very good first impression of you."

Roman shrugged weakly. "That's a chance I'm going to have to take."

Brandt turned to Donnelly. "How about I go meet with Phillips, and you stay here with our Mr. Montgomery? Just to be sure we can find him if Phillips decides to charge him right away."

Roman flinched at this, which was what Brandt intended.

"Sounds good," Donnelly replied. "And tell Phillips I hope he's feeling better. He was throwing up so hard at the reception I thought he was going to turn his stomach inside out."

Brandt stuck his tongue out and made his best nauseated face. "Yeah, I don't think I'll mention that last part." He stood and walked out of the office to seek out the DA.

CHAPTER TEN
DOUBLE AGENT

IT TOOK Brandt a full hour to convince the DA to hold off on charges in a case that was coming to dominate the public's attention. Many prominent citizens were calling for an aggressive investigation, including several who themselves had suffered through the worst of the emetic symptoms. But with the chief's help, Brandt won the argument and also got the agreement of the coroner's office to hold back the results of the Laurence autopsy for forty-eight hours. The cause of Laurence's death was important leverage, Brandt thought grimly. The cop in him had overtaken the human, but it was for the right reason, or at least that's what he told himself.

He returned to his desk to find Roman asleep in the chair and Donnelly nearby, at his own desk, typing. Brandt walked over to stand behind his partner.

"Down for the count, huh?" he asked, nodding in Roman's direction.

"Yep. He fought it for a while, but he really seemed exhausted. I almost feel sorry for him. I guess people always look innocent when they're asleep." Donnelly swiveled in his chair to face Brandt. "Get it all set with Phillips?"

Brandt nodded. "Took long enough. He really wants to charge someone—anyone—so his phone will stop ringing and people will stop posting angry messages to Facebook about how no one's doing anything. But the chief backed me up, and the fact that he's on the homeland security task force they're convening this afternoon will provide some cover." He looked over at Roman. "That kid is a piece of work, huh?"

"I can't really figure him out," Donnelly replied. "I don't think I've ever met anyone who was both gay and adamantly opposed to gay marriage. I get that marriage isn't for everyone, but that's true of straight people too. How you go from there to poisoning people… that's the part I just don't get."

"I know you're going to think I'm getting soft, but I'm starting to think he's just a kid who got caught up in something that spun out of control. Like this Marcus guy kind of wound him up, and he went along to keep seeing him."

"The things people do for love," Donnelly said with a knowing chuckle. "Or for manly, manly sex. As the case may be." He winked at Brandt and smiled.

Brandt joined him in a chuckle, but then was right back to business. "We got the green light for this, but they made it pretty clear that we have forty-eight hours and not a second more." He glanced over at Roman again. "We need to get Sleeping Beauty over there into action right away. Nap time's over."

Donnelly rose and walked over to Roman. He nudged him on the shoulder gently, and the young man started awake.

"We need to get a plan together," Donnelly said gently.

Roman nodded. "Can I get that cup of coffee now?" he asked, wiping the grogginess from his face with his hand.

"Sure," Donnelly said, and walked over to the coffee pot. He poured a mug and handed it to Roman.

"Thanks." He took a deep sip. "I'm really sorry if what I said before offended you," he said, the drowsiness starting to clear. "I think some bad experiences have kind of soured me on the whole social-acceptance thing."

"After what happened to Greg, I have to admit I see your point," Donnelly said. "I don't agree with you that gay couples shouldn't marry, but it's really clear that having a wedding doesn't mean that everything's equal and the struggle's over."

"Not that the struggle for equality should ever include large-scale food contamination," Brandt added. He was somewhat surprised that his partner was being so placid about Roman's antimarriage views. But he had to admit that what happened to Greg Sampson had opened his eyes to some uncomfortable realities as well.

"Yeah, that was a bad idea," Roman agreed. "But I really had no idea that Marcus would do something so dangerous."

"You said that he had other plans in the works," Brandt asked. "What can you tell us about those?"

Roman set his coffee cup down. "Well, it seems like all the publicity about gay marriage over the last couple of months really set him off. He said that if it looked like disrupting the big wedding would discourage others from getting married, he was going to do more of them, but with stronger chemicals in the flowers. I told him that I wouldn't do it again—I didn't want anyone to get hurt. But he was also talking about other stuff, like rigging chandeliers to fall, or for limousines to crash. It got really scary."

"Do you think you could make him talk about those plans," Donnelly asked, "so we can use it in court? Would you be comfortable wearing a wire?"

"I don't think a wire would work," Roman replied.

"Why not?"

Roman studied the carpet for a moment. "Because when I'm in the same room with Marcus, I'm generally... naked."

"Ah, that is a problem," Donnelly replied carefully.

Brandt was deep in thought—there had to be a way to make this work. "Where do you normally meet him?" he asked.

"At his place, over in the Heights. That's the only place I've ever been with him."

"One of those brownstone-style places?"

Roman nodded.

"What are you thinking?" Donnelly asked.

"Those old places were built to last—solid double-brick walls. No way to listen from next door. But most of them have never been renovated, and that means single-pane glass. We could set up across the street with a parabolic mic and have a pretty good chance of picking up conversation, assuming that you can get him talking near the windows."

Roman chuckled. "Yeah, his place is definitely one of the nonrenovated ones." He thought for a minute, then, somewhat reluctantly, began to speak again. "I could be sure he's near the window, but it would be a kind of ugly recording."

"What do mean, ugly?" Donnelly asked.

Roman blushed and looked away for a moment. "There's a room on the second floor where we usually... meet. It's near the window, but we don't normally do a lot of talking while we're there."

"So we'd be recording you having sex with the guy while you try to make him talk about the crimes he's planning?" Brandt summed up, an exasperated brutality sneaking into his voice.

"It's more than that," Roman said quietly. He looked up at the officers, who were looking baffled at him. "It gets kind of... rough."

"Does he hurt you?" Donnelly asked, putting a hand on Roman's arm.

"Sometimes it hurts, but not in a bad way." Roman shrugged. "It's just what we do—it's not rape or anything. It's just kind of rough. That's the way he likes it, so I play along, making it seem like he's really hurting me. Just don't freak out and come in with guns drawn or anything, because if I don't make it sound like it hurts, he'll know something's up. But I'm okay—this ain't my first rodeo."

"The chief is going to hate this," Brandt muttered.

"The transcript is all that matters," Donnelly said. "We'll just gloss over anything that's too graphic by saying 'unidentified noises' or 'sounds of struggle,' something like that."

Brandt thought for a moment, trying to find other ways to get the information they needed. But with the clock running, they needed to move quickly. "All right. Here's what we're going to do. Gabriel, you grab Walters and have him pull a parabolic kit together, then get the address from Roman and see if there's a place across the street we can squat. Roman, I want you to talk to one of our informant counselors on how to interact with Marcus—we need a clean statement from him, and she can help you figure out how to get it. I'll go see Phillips about getting the surveillance warrant. We'll meet back here in an hour and get sorted. Good?"

The other two men nodded, and they set out to set their trap.

EVEN IN the middle of the afternoon, the Heights neighborhood was not a terribly safe place to be. From their vantage point on the third floor of a vacant brownstone across the street from Marcus's hovel, Brandt and Donnelly watched an endless parade of dejected, drugged-out, and generally forsaken people wander aimlessly by on the sidewalk below.

They'd been here for nearly two hours to be sure they had everything ready. It had taken most of the day to plan out the operation, as even in a neighborhood as neglected as this one, sudden activity in an abandoned building would arouse suspicion. The listening equipment had been delivered by a pest control company whose presence in this old building would be routine. Walters, dressed as one of the bug poisoners, stayed behind in his green coveralls, which sported a colorful image of a dead cockroach across the back. Donnelly had arrived ten minutes later, dressed as one of the lost souls of the street, perhaps trying to locate the place where he bought drugs once upon a time. Finally, just as the sun was disappearing behind the buildings, Brandt had marched into the building in a suit, carrying a briefcase, as if looking to take advantage of the "for sale" sign that was posted, hopelessly, in the front window. Their elaborate fakery was likely lost upon an audience of passersby deeply involved in their own dismal circumstances, but it was executed flawlessly.

"He should be along in a minute," Donnelly said as Brandt fidgeted restlessly, pacing up and down the length of the room.

The few streetlights that worked were just flickering to life as Roman appeared at the corner, several houses away from Marcus's. Walters switched on his equipment, the three-foot-wide parabolic microphone and the digital recording equipment. The men retreated to a smaller room toward the back of the house where they wouldn't be seen through the windows as darkness fell on the street.

Roman knocked at the door, and Walters switched on a monitor speaker so Brandt and Donnelly could hear the conversation across the street.

The door swung open with an angry creak.

"Oh, it's you," Roman said, sounding surprised.

"I sent him on an errand" came a deep voice through the monitor.

Roman stepped through the door, which slammed shut behind him. All three men watching from across the street jumped at the thunderous noise.

"Sorry," Walters said, spinning his dials. "I'll crank it back up once they start talking."

The voices were muffled, but they could still make out the words.

"What's got you so sad?" Marcus said, the taunt in his voice clear even through the distortion.

"Did you hear what happened to the guy who got married?" Roman asked. "Laurence?"

Marcus gave a nasty chuckle. "Yeah. Couldn't have planned it better myself."

"He's dead, Marcus. That's not what I signed up for."

"Ooh, is wittle Roman afwaid? Because the pwetty bwide went and died?" Marcus expectorated a mirthless laugh. "Look, I made a poem about it."

"They'll find out what killed him. And then we're going to jail," Roman said angrily.

"They got nothing on us," Marcus retorted. "Well, they got nothing on me. You—*and your boyfriend*—now, that's a different story."

"You keep your hands off him." Roman's voice was deadly.

Donnelly shot Brandt a glance. "He mention a boyfriend to you?"

Brandt shook his head, still listening intently.

"I'll put my hands on whatever I want to put my hands on," Marcus growled, and there was a sound of some scuffling. "You like that?"

"You know I do," Roman said, rather woodenly to Brandt's ear. But Marcus didn't seem to notice, or if he did notice, he didn't care.

"Let's go upstairs," he said, the invitation sounding like a command in his snarling voice.

"Wait," Roman said. "You said that the wedding we did was just the opening act. What else do you have planned?"

"I'm planning to bone you to within an inch of your life, that's what I have planned."

"But what else are you going to do? Are you going to use the same stuff, or something stronger?"

"My plans are my plans, you little shit. Now get upstairs. If I have to carry you up there you aren't gonna be able to walk back down."

There were heavy treads on a staircase that sounded as though its best days were long behind it and then footsteps across another floor.

"You better be naked in ten seconds."

They could hear shuffling, and even the sound of Roman's clothes hitting the floor. Walters's mic was working better than they'd dared to hope. But they hadn't gotten anything they could actually use.

"Get up on there," Marcus growled.

Brandt looked at Donnelly, puzzled. Donnelly shrugged. Then they heard some odd creaking noises—not like the stairs or floorboards, something different. The sound of chain, though, came through clearly. Donnelly's face turned to one of alarm.

"Gotta make sure you're on there nice and tight," Marcus said, a ridiculous sing-song note in his deep, angry voice.

They could hear grunting, as if he were working hard at whatever he was tightening.

"There," he said, apparently satisfied with his craftsmanship. "No way you're getting loose from that."

"So now will you tell me what you have planned?" Roman asked.

"You gotta admit, he's working really hard to get him to talk," Donnelly said.

"But I'm starting to think he's not the talkative type," Brandt replied.

"I'll tell you what I have planned for you. And for your boyfriend." Marcus made a noise that could have been mistaken for a laugh, if he were a person capable of showing emotion. "Now, you know I've never been one for foreplay." More laughter, even rougher and more ghoulish now. "But today I want to be sure you're in the right mood. So how about this: I know you went to the police."

"Fuck!" blurted Brandt, slamming his fist onto his knee.

"Do we go in, arrest him before he hurts Roman?" Donnelly asked.

"For what? He hasn't done anything. Yet. I just hope he doesn't."

There was panic edging into Roman's voice. "I… I wanted to find out what happened to that guy who died. I didn't tell them anything— why would I? I'm the one who did it. Why would I tell them that? I'm not stupid."

"We can agree to disagree on that one," Marcus said, his voice devoid of emotion. "But I think it's a funny coincidence that you were with the cops yesterday and all this morning, and then out of the blue, you want to meet with me. Kind of a funny coincidence, don't you think? And yes, you little shit, I've been watching you."

"What, you think I'm working for the police now? That's crazy. I just wanted to find out what was going on. Don't you think it would have been even more suspicious if I didn't talk to them at all? I was just playing the game, Marcus. Just protecting us. Protecting you."

"I think I can take care of myself, Roman. And that's what I'm going to do. Now, first, I need to be sure you're not working for the police. You're not wearing a wire, are you?"

"Where would I put a wire?" Roman's voice was growing steadily higher.

"Oh, I don't know," Marcus said. "There are places."

Roman grunted. "Ow, stop it! Do you really think I have a tape recorder up my ass?"

"I don't know. Why don't you tell me."

"I don't have a tape recorder up my ass."

"I wish I could believe you, Roman, I really do. But when you went to the police you betrayed my trust. So now I have to see for myself. Now, this might be a bit… uncomfortable."

"Ouch—you're hurting me. Stop it."

"Oh, I am so sorry. I didn't mean to hurt you. Here, let me put a little of this on my fingers." There was a pause during which Brandt couldn't make out any identifiable sound. "There. That's better. I'm still going to have to push pretty hard, though. I am *so* sorry about that."

Roman's scream filled the room. Donnelly was on his feet in an instant, but Brandt grabbed his arm. The screaming died off after an agonizing moment, replaced by frenzied sobbing.

"I guess you were telling the truth," Marcus said. "I had to be sure, you understand, and the only way to really check was to get my whole hand in there. Actually, my whole fist—I really needed to be thorough."

"Oh my God," Donnelly moaned, clearly distraught.

"Keep it together, Officer Donnelly," Brandt warned. He was desperate to break into that room and save Roman from that beast, but that's not what they were here for.

"Now, I'm going to fuck you—not that you're worth fucking anymore. That asshole is almost turned inside out right now, you really should see it. But for old time's sake, why the hell not. One last fuck."

"Last... fuck?" Roman asked, his voice broken.

"Not for me, of course. I have a long line of fucks ahead of me. No, this is your last fuck."

"What does that mean?" Roman asked, panic replacing pain in his voice.

"It means that once I'm done here, I'm moving on."

Marcus grunted loudly, and Roman cried out. The grunting and pained moaning continued wordlessly for five endless minutes while Donnelly sat listening with his jaw set and Brandt tried to imagine a calm, peaceful meadow in which Marcus Verona would be trampled to death by bison.

Finally, Marcus's animal noises grew to a crescendo, and the mighty rhythm of slapping and creaking slowed to a stop. There was some shuffling in the room and some quiet crying.

"Now, as I said, I'm moving on. I don't need you anymore, and I don't need this place. But that's the nice thing about this neighborhood—these old houses burn down all the time, and no one bothers to really look into it. Unfortunately for you, the fire started in the kitchen—or, it'll start in the kitchen once I set it—and that means it'll take a while. You better hope the smoke gets you, because burning is a fucking awful way to go." There was a loud kissing noise, then a moment of silence. "Sorry it had to end this way. You were a good fuck."

Donnelly pulled out his phone and cast Brandt a questioning look. Brandt nodded emphatically. Donnelly dialed.

"Oh, and in case you're worried about your boyfriend, don't. My business partner is paying him a visit right about now, and after we're done here, I'm going to have a little chat with him. Make sure that he's out of the way for good."

"Dispatch, this is Donnelly. We need fire and medical right now!"

"Go!" Brandt yelled, and Donnelly bolted after him. They ran down the stairs and across the street, but found the front door of the house bolted. Brandt threw himself against it twice, but it wouldn't give.

"I see flames!" Donnelly shouted, pointing through the front window of the house. "One... two... three!" he counted down, and both men hit the door with all the force they could muster. It gave way.

They tumbled into the empty front room of the house. Donnelly sprang to his feet and sprinted up the stairs. Brandt moved to the back of the house and found that the kitchen was completely engulfed in flames. Marcus was nowhere to be seen—he must have escaped through the back door after setting the blaze. Brandt could smell kerosene or some other accelerant and knew the entire house was going to go up quickly.

"We gotta go!" he shouted as he shot up the stairs. He ran into the front room, where Donnelly was unbuckling the restraints that held Roman to the bondage horse. "Are you okay?" he asked Roman. "Can you walk?"

Roman slid weakly to his feet and stood unsteadily. The flames were licking at the staircase. The three men stood at the top and tried to judge the safest route down.

"Stick close to the wall," Brandt instructed. "I'll go first. Don't let go of my hand."

They joined hands and started down the stairs at as brisk a pace as they could manage. The heat was overwhelming, and the house was beginning to groan ominously as the heat rose, testing the structural strength of the century-old construction. Once they hit the ground, they dashed for the door and out into the evening. The smoke rising from the house and the flames lighting up the street were beginning to attract attention, and the first sirens could be heard wailing as they rounded the corner.

"I have to go," Roman shouted over the noise of the approaching fire equipment as he finished pulling his clothes on.

"What you have to do is be seen by the EMTs," Donnelly replied. "Ethan, go wave down that ambulance."

A fire/rescue truck was roaring toward the scene. Brandt stepped into the middle of the street and held his badge aloft, waving toward the sidewalk where Donnelly stood with Roman. Then a crashing sound erupted from the burning house—the second floor collapsed onto the first, blowing out the windows and sending flame and smoke roiling out onto the sidewalk. Donnelly and Roman were thrown into the street. Firefighters pushed around them, trying to get their equipment into new positions to fight the blaze, and for a moment Brandt could find neither of them in the chaos. Finally, when the EMTs waded into the mess, they were able to pull Donnelly out. He got to his feet, panting, covered in soot.

"Where's Roman?" Brandt demanded. He spun around, searching for signs of the young man.

"I had his arm, but we were both knocked back pretty hard," Donnelly said, panting and coughing. "I lost my grip."

"You okay?" Brandt asked, putting his arm around his partner.

"Yeah. Nothing like rolling around on the pavement to loosen those tired muscles."

They searched the scene from one end to another but could not find Roman. It wasn't until Walters joined them that they discovered what had happened.

"I was looking out the window across the street when that collapse happened," he told them. "As soon as the smoke cleared I saw Roman running up the street. He took off in the confusion and no one noticed. I tried to yell to you, but you couldn't hear me—and you ran out without picking up your walkie-talkies," he added, scold in his voice.

Brandt turned to Donnelly. "Where do you think he's going?"

"He thinks he can save his boyfriend from Marcus," Donnelly replied. "We just need to figure out who that is. That's where Roman will be."

JUSTIN WOKE up slumped over the butcher-block table, a pool of blood starting to congeal on its surface, stuck to his cheek. The room was blurry, and he rubbed his eyes to clear his vision. This proved a double-edged sword; his vision cleared, but he also discovered that his bone above his right eye was, if not broken, then certainly badly bruised. A quick inventory of his bodily parts revealed similar bad news: he was covered in scrapes and bruises and was bleeding from several of them. His head pounded as if it were being beaten by the biggest wooden spoon in the kitchen.

"What the fuck...," he muttered, spraying a fine mist of spittle and blood across the table. He wiped his mouth with the hem of his T-shirt. "Shit," he said with a sigh.

The guy was huge, he remembered through a cloud. He shook his head and tried to clear the fog.

A banging on the back door. He had looked through the viewer, but it was dark. More banging, then whoever it was yelled that Roman had sent him. Justin unlocked the door, and the man rushed in, sending him sprawling backward onto the floor. He picked him up by grabbing him roughly under the arms and carried him into the kitchen, throwing him backward against the big table.

"You been talking to the cops," he said, his voice deep and rough.

"About what? What are you doing here?" Justin asked. His voice sounded weak and reedy in comparison with the man facing him, who seemed twice his size.

"I have a simple instruction for you. You listening?"

Justin didn't respond, and the man gave his arm a painful twist. "Yes," he gasped.

"Good. From now on, you don't say nothin' to the cops. You got that? You don't know nothin' about them faggots and their poison cake, right?"

"But I don't know anything about it," Justin said.

"That's what I wanted to hear. Now I'm just going to make sure you remember it." He sneered at Justin, then pulled back a huge clenched fist. "Oh, and one more thing: if you ever talk to the cops again, I'll be back to remind you. And your family, too."

Then all Justin remembered was an enveloping red cloud.

He wasn't sure how much time had passed. Without thinking, he got up (in the process discovering that his legs had also come in for some bruising), walked to the sink, and began running water onto a rag. He wiped his face, viewing the damage in the shard of mirror that one of the more vain cake decorators had placed on the small shelf above the sink. Then he rinsed the blood out of the rag and returned to the table to try to wipe up the blood pooled on its surface. It left a crisp crimson outline on the table, one that would probably require sanding to efface. He was scrubbing with cleanser when he heard it.

"Justin?"

He wasn't sure—that couldn't be—was it? He dropped his rag and walked toward the door. Roman was standing in the doorway as if he were afraid to enter.

"Oh my God, Juss!" he cried, rushing at Justin with his arms open. "Oh thank God I got here in time." He gripped Justin tightly and panted into his shoulder, sounding like he was beating back sobs.

Justin, bewildered by Roman's sudden appearance, was completely baffled by this statement. "I would have preferred you here about a half hour ago, I think," he managed, with a small laugh.

"Come here and let me look at you," Roman said, taking Justin by the arm and leading him into the kitchen. He traced his fingers lightly over Justin's right eye and sucked in his breath with a wince. "I am so sorry," he whispered.

Justin felt a hundred times better now that Roman was here with him. "I'm sure this happens to wedding bakers all the time," he joked.

"Justin, I have to tell you something."

BRANDT AND Donnelly tried to piece together any clues Roman might have dropped as to the identity of his boyfriend.

"Did he say anything to you at the station this morning?" Brandt asked. "While I was meeting with the chief and the DA?"

Donnelly shook his head. "He was still pretty torn up about what Greg had been through. Didn't say much."

Brandt furrowed his brow. "Marcus said the boyfriend was his second problem. That means it must be someone who knows about the wedding plot. Who would that be?"

Donnelly and Brandt seemed to come to the same answer at the same instant. "Justin!" they said in unison.

"Where did you park?" Donnelly asked. He'd shaken off the shock of being thrown in the street, and a fiery determination lit his eyes.

"About three blocks over. Come on!"

They ran up the street, hoping they had the right destination in mind, hoping they would get there in time.

"IT WAS me," Roman said.

"What was you?" Justin asked. This wasn't the first time Roman had said something like this, and Justin still didn't know what to make of it.

"You're going to hate me." Roman looked down, his voice dismal.

"I could never hate you. You disappeared from my life, but I never stopped thinking about you. Now that I have you back, I'm never going to let you go. No matter what happens, no matter what you did."

"You don't understand."

"Tell me. Tell me what you did that was so bad."

Roman swallowed hard. "I put the stuff in the cake filling."

Justin's face paled, and he drew a pained breath of shock. "What?" His voice was hollow.

"I put the stuff in the fancy bottle when you let me smell it. It was me."

Justin fumbled behind him for the stool and plopped on it with a thud. "I don't... why would...?" he muttered, unable to fully understand what Roman was telling him.

"I am so sorry. I didn't think it would be this bad. I really didn't know what I was doing."

"Then how did you do it?"

"Someone gave me the stuff, told me what to do."

"Who? Who would want to put both of us out of business?" Justin's voice was stronger now, but no less aggrieved. "Who would want to make all those people sick? Who would want to kill that poor man?"

"I met this guy at a club one night, and we got to talking about gay people getting married—he thought it was really funny that I do flowers for weddings when I'm not sure gay people should be rushing out to get hitched. He came up with the idea—told me it would just be a prank, just to let people know they shouldn't be doing it."

"Doing what?"

Roman heaved an uncertain breath. "Helping gay people get married. Going to gay weddings. The whole gay marriage thing."

"And you went along with this because you feel that way too?"

Roman nodded, clearly ashamed to admit what he had done. "I did. I don't anymore. I was there when Mr. Sampson told Gabriel and Ethan about what happened to Mr. Laurence. It was awful, Justin." Roman sat on a stool, looking like he was trying to catch his breath. "I had this idea that marriage was just a way to imitate straight people—to pretend to be socially acceptable. I didn't want that, after what happened to me."

Justin was confused. "You lost me. What happened to you to make you think that gay people shouldn't get married?"

"They took me away from you, just because I finally got up the nerve to kiss you. You have no idea how long I'd been waiting to do that, Juss. Every time we had a sleepover I would try to work up the courage to tell you, or to show you, what I felt for you. But I just couldn't. Not until that night on the field trip. And then… they took me away. What I got for the next decade was a daily lecture on how my life would only be fulfilling when I married a nice girl. Then whatever perverted demon that had possessed me in that dark school gymnasium would finally be defeated, and I would be straight and normal. It took me a long time to get over all of that, to become my own person, to be okay with who I was. My parents could take me away from you, but I could still find my way back to you someday. Marriage, though—that would mean I could never go back, never find you again. It became my greatest enemy."

"But it doesn't have to be that way. Now that everyone can get married, it won't be."

"Tell that to Greg Sampson. He got married, and his 'husband' died alone. We're not there yet, and to pretend we are just doesn't make sense."

Justin shook his head sadly. "Roman, I get that marriage is a weapon that they beat you up with, but what you've done is going to end my family's company, and yours too. Did you really think this stunt was going to make a difference?"

"I didn't mean for this to happen. He said that people would just get a little sick, and it would make the news, and people would start talking about how gay marriage wasn't such a good idea. He was very persuasive. He went on about how gay men should be men, and not pretend to be straight."

"And you just went along with that?" Justin studied Roman's face more closely. "Let me guess. He has a huge dick, right?"

"That's not…," Roman stumbled. "He's… what he and I…." His denials trailed off. Then he simply nodded.

Justin stared hard at his friend. "You need to go."

"Justin—"

"No. You need to go. Just go." Justin got up and pointed to the back door, which was still standing ajar. "I need some time to get this all figured out. Too much has happened too quickly for me to just be okay with this."

Roman, tears rolling down his cheeks, turned to leave.

They heard a car squeal into the alley and skid to a halt. A door shut, and heavy footsteps approached the bakery.

"WHAT'S THE quickest way there?" Donnelly shouted as he pointed the cruiser away from the curb and roared down the street.

"Take Seventh Avenue. It has a bus lane down the middle that should be clear at this hour," Brandt replied. He radioed for backup at the Capella bakery, but dispatch reported back that every available officer was helping with the evacuation of a block in the Heights, and it would be at least fifteen minutes before any units could respond.

"It's just us, buddy," Brandt said. "Drive like hell." Brandt pulled his service weapon out of its holster and checked the magazine. He did the same for Donnelly's as the cruiser weaved through the traffic in the center of the city. "Locked and loaded. Let's hope we don't have to use them."

"This Marcus guy just tried to burn down a house to get rid of Roman. I don't like shooting people, but I think I can make an exception for him."

"I'm with you," Brandt said grimly. "I just hope we can get there in time."

MARCUS PUSHED the door open and stomped into the kitchen.

"What the fuck?" he shouted, apparently unsettled at seeing Roman uncharred.

"You stay the hell away from him," Roman growled, his voice low.

"Roman, who's this?" Justin asked, sensing the danger that was clearly rising in the room.

"No one," Roman said bitterly. Then he looked Marcus in the eye. "Now you get the fuck out of here."

Marcus seemed to recover his footing. A snakelike smile spread across his face. "I don't know how you did it, but you did. Good for you. And good for me, because you're both here, and I can do this all at once."

"Fuck off, Marcus. There's nothing left you can do to me. Why don't you just get the fuck out of here while you can."

"While I can? Ooh, brave talk from the faggot. I'm really scared."

"Roman?" Justin pleaded. He had watched his friend change from contrition to monstrous anger in a flash and had no idea why.

But Roman didn't answer him. "You're calling me a faggot?" Roman retorted to Marcus. "You're the one who's been balls-deep in my ass twice a week. I think that makes you a faggot too."

"Shut up!" Marcus bellowed. "That's what's wrong with you faggots. You never fucking stop talking."

Marcus's sudden defensive anger seemed to strengthen Roman, and it changed Justin's perception of the entire situation. This admittedly enormous man had barged into his place of business—his birthright—and started abusing his friend. His... lover. That shit, Justin decided, was going to stop right now.

"Roman?" Justin's voice was no longer pleading, but rather smooth and conversational. "Aren't you going to introduce me to your friend? The faggot?" He bit off this last phrase with a sudden venom in his voice that quite pleased him to hear.

"Roman, tell your precious little flower to shut the fuck up."

Justin stepped over to stand next to Roman, shoulder to shoulder, facing Marcus down. "Get the fuck out of my kitchen," he said slowly.

Marcus's serpentine smile stayed in place, an oily grin that took on greater malevolence the longer it lasted. "We have some business to finish." He looked Justin up and down. "I see my associate introduced himself to you. That's nothing compared to what I'm going to do."

"You," Roman said, his voice murderous, "keep your fucking hands off him."

Marcus's grin disappeared. "I will touch what I want to touch," he hissed. He reached out a hand, bringing it up to Justin's cheek.

Before his hand made contact, however, Roman grabbed his wrist and slammed his arm down. Marcus's response was instantaneous: his other hand, balled into a fist, flew up and smashed into the side of Roman's head. Roman crumpled from the force of the blow, dropping to his knees and then flopping over to the side, dazed.

Marcus stepped over the motionless body at his feet, advancing on Justin. "Roman didn't tell you about me? About his good friend Marcus? I don't know how he could have forgotten to mention me. After all, we're such close friends." Justin was backed up against the big table now, but Marcus kept coming at him. "Such close friends. So close that I don't think his ass will ever go back to normal size." He leaned in close, whispering his venom into Justin's ear. "He begged for me to fuck him, and I did. He cried like a little bitch the first time, said I was tearing him open. Begged me to stop. But I knew what he really wanted. I just pushed harder and faster and fucked him until he fucking passed out."

Justin was leaning backward over the table now, unable to move away any further.

"You want to know what it feels like, faggot? You want to be torn open by my big fuckin' dick?"

"Get away from him." Roman's voice was a little groggy, but unmistakably serious.

Marcus sighed dramatically. "I'll be right back," he whispered sweetly into Justin's face. "There's someone I have to kill." He stood and turned around to face Roman.

If he expected to find a bruised and feeble man facing him, he was mistaken. What he saw was a furious and determined Roman staring at him with wild eyes. What he didn't see was the heavy copper pan that Justin used for caramelizing sugar as it whipped around from where Roman had been holding it behind his back. It clanged across Marcus's skull with a hollow, metallic crack.

Marcus staggered back, and Justin just had time to slip out of his way as he slammed into the table. Roman swung again, but this time Marcus grabbed his arm and twisted it horribly around. The pan dropped to the floor, as did Roman, screaming at the wrenching of his arm. Marcus kicked him viciously in the ribs and shoved him back toward the alley door.

"I am fucking done with you," Marcus snarled. He reached under his jacket, around the back of his waist, and pulled out a gun. He aimed this at Roman's head. "Now, this is going to be a bit messy," Marcus said coolly. "But don't you worry about that, Roman. I'll have your boyfriend here mop up your brains from his pretty kitchen. But," he said, "who's going to mop up his? Hmm. Oh well. Once I fuck him, I'm not gonna care too much."

"I'll fucking kill you," Roman growled, but he didn't seem able to rise from the floor this time.

"No, I'll fucking kill you," Marcus retorted, and he raised his gun. He took aim at Roman's head and pulled the trigger.

It was a clean kill shot. Or, it would have been, had something not blocked its path.

That something was Justin.

He threw himself in front of Marcus's gun, taking the shot point blank just below his left shoulder. He felt like he had been punched, hard, and then he felt a flash of heat. He crumpled to the floor, hoping that shock would set in quickly because it hurt like nothing he'd ever experienced. He looked up at Marcus and realized that he was not afraid anymore. Maybe shock was setting in after all. His left arm didn't seem to be working, but with his right he found Roman's hand and squeezed it.

"Isn't that sweet," Marcus said. "Trying to protect your slut boyfriend. Just makes it easier for me, now that you're both on the floor." He took aim again. "Bye, now."

The shot seemed to Justin to be much louder than the first. He closed his eyes but didn't feel the punch this time. In fact, he didn't feel anything. That meant... Roman. Overwhelming loss joined the throbbing pain in his chest as he squeezed the hand he held, half expecting it to already be growing cold. But Roman squeezed back. Justin opened his eyes and saw a surprised look on Marcus's face. And a deep crimson spot spreading from his right shoulder. The hand holding the gun dropped to his side as he looked down at the rapidly growing bloodstain. He tried to raise the gun again, but then a voice— or was it two?—shouted "Drop it! Police!" He looked at the source of the order, a puzzled expression on his face, but he didn't drop the gun. He raised it, with great effort, and pointed it again at Roman. Two more shots rang out, and Marcus flew backward onto the table. He slumped to the floor, two spots of red blossoming into one on his chest.

The last thing Justin saw was Donnelly leaping over him to take Marcus's gun.

Chapter Eleven
Pox on Both

EVERYONE RESPONDS differently to the pressured stillness of a hospital waiting room. Some jabber endlessly, as if their small talk were a litany of prayer. Others cannot listen, seeming to believe on some level that they must not be distracted from their desperate effort to keep a loved one alive by sheer force of will. Some pace, some stare vacantly out the window. Some prefer to stay away entirely.

The waiting room outside the trauma surgery in the wee hours of a dark Tuesday morning hosted all types. Brandt paced up and down the shiny hallway, apparently committing the names and faces of decades of hospital administrators to memory. Donnelly sat and played hand after silent hand of gin rummy with Justin's grandmother—neither keeping score. Justin's mother talked nonstop on the phone, updating a family tree whose roots and branches seemed to span the country.

"Here," Brandt said to Donnelly, handing him a cup of coffee.

"Thanks, but that's the fourth cup you've brought me in two hours. Even I have limits, Ethan."

"Walking to the cafeteria gives me something to do," Brandt replied with a sigh. "They also have cookies. Want a cookie? I'll bring you a cookie." He strode off, full of purpose, not waiting for an answer.

Donnelly shook his head as he watched Brandt's shadow retreat down the corridor.

"Don't be too hard on him," Justin's grandmother said quietly, without taking her eyes off her cards. "When men don't know what to do, they try to provide for the ones they love. And he does love you." She smiled sweetly as she looked up at Donnelly. "Gin, dear." She laid her cards down on the small end table they were using for their game.

"Nana Capella, I'm surprised at you," Donnelly replied in an awkward whisper, a blush coming into his cheeks.

"Oh, foo," she replied, in the way old ladies beyond the age of caring about decorum do. "It's sweet the way he dotes on you, and I see how you look at him. It's the same way I used to look at Justin's grandfather—wondering what's going on inside that big old heart of his." She shuffled and dealt with a cardsharp's limberness of wrist.

Donnelly smiled at his opponent. "I take it you don't agree with your son's stance on gay marriage?"

She shook her head dismissively. "Life is too short to spend my time judging how other people find happiness. I had fifty-five good years with my husband; why would I want to deny anyone else that chance? I hope you get that many years with your man, dear." She sorted her cards. "May I ask you a question?"

"Of course."

"Were you there when my grandson was shot?"

"I was," Donnelly replied. "We got there just as it happened, thank God. I drove like a madman to get there, and we were almost too late."

"You saw it? You saw what happened?"

Donnelly nodded. "The man with the gun had apparently knocked Roman to the ground, and was aiming his gun at Roman's head. Just at the moment he pulled the trigger, Justin leapt in front of him—he came out of nowhere. The gun went off before I could even get in the doorway."

"Justin got shot protecting Roman?"

"It was the bravest thing I think I've ever seen," Donnelly said.

"My little Justin," she whispered.

"Your little Justin saved Roman's life. I honestly didn't think he could survive a point-blank impact like that. I think that's what the man who shot him was counting on, because he pointed the gun at Roman again."

"That horrible man," Nana Capella said, her cards drooping to the side. "What did you do?"

"I shot him," Donnelly said simply. "It happened so fast, I didn't even have time to tell him to drop the gun—I just pulled the trigger and hoped I was quicker than he was."

Justin's grandmother gasped.

"We shoot to disarm if we can, so I aimed for the shoulder. His arm dropped to his side, and Ethan and I moved into the kitchen. But he managed to lift the gun again, and aimed it at Roman, so we both fired."

"And he dropped the gun?"

Donnelly looked into Nana Capella's eyes. "I wasn't aiming to disarm him anymore. The medical examiner who got to the scene after the ambulances left said that our bullets were side by side in his heart. He was dead before he hit the floor." He looked back down at his cards.

She put a hand on his, gently. "Thank you," she whispered. She met his gaze for a long moment, then went back to her cards. She laid one down on the table, then looked back at him with a raised eyebrow. "I guess your Ethan's found a pretty good man too," she said with a hint of a smile.

Donnelly smiled back, the blush returning to his cheek again.

"Mr. and Mrs. Capella?" The surgeon padded into the room, still wearing a surgical cap and blue covers on his white clogs. He came and sat between the baker and his wife.

"Is he okay?" Capella asked, his voice hoarse.

"The bullet entered just above and to the left of his heart, and it fragmented when it struck a rib. Parts of it lodged in the pectoral muscle, but a few small pieces lacerated his pulmonary artery—that's what moves blood into the lungs to pick up oxygen. It was damaged in several places; he lost a lot of blood internally. We were able to remove the fragments and repair the artery, but with all of the internal bleeding, we think his brain may have been deprived of oxygen for some time at the scene. We're going to keep him sedated for twenty-four to forty-eight hours, to give the repairs time to start healing. Once he's out of sedation, we'll be able to tell whether there's been any brain impairment."

Mrs. Capella blinked at the surgeon. "Will my son be okay?" she asked, as if the surgeon hadn't heard the question when her husband asked it a moment ago.

"Recovery from traumatic injury is a difficult thing to predict, Mrs. Capella. I am confident that we were able to repair the damage to his heart. We simply don't know enough at this point what the effect on his brain will be. I'm sorry I can't tell you anything more definite right now."

Capella nodded vaguely, while his wife simply sobbed into a tissue.

The doctor stood to go. "We'll be moving him to the CCU shortly. You'll be able to see him then, but know that he won't be able to respond to you for a day or two."

"Thank you, Doctor," Capella said, clearly struggling to regain his composure.

Brandt, who had been standing in the entrance to the waiting area while the surgeon spoke, came to Donnelly's side. "So, some good news, right?"

Donnelly nodded. "Let's hope there's more to come." He looked down at his cards. "Well, Nana Capella, I guess we should get going. We'll check back in tomorrow on Justin's progress."

She extended her hand. "Very nice to meet you, Gabriel," she said, and she shook Brandt's hand as well. "And you too, Ethan. You saved my grandson's life, and I will never forget that."

"We look forward to seeing him up and about again," Brandt said.

He and Donnelly had just turned down the corridor from the waiting room when Roman came around the corner. He froze when he saw the officers, his face a kaleidoscope of conflicting emotions: fear, shame, relief, joy, worry. Instantly there were tears in his eyes as he walked slowly toward the men.

"Roman, how are you?" Donnelly asked. He seemed unprepared for Roman to launch himself forward, tackling the trooper into a full-body hug.

"You saved my life," Roman whispered. "You saved his life. I can't... I can't thank you enough." He broke into sobs on Donnelly's shoulder. His grip slackened after a full minute of this, but only so that he could reach out and grab Brandt into his hug.

"Are you okay?" Brandt asked once Roman's embrace had relaxed slightly.

"I'm fine. A little bit of bruising, some of it in an area that shouldn't ever have bruises," he replied with a game smile. "But nothing serious. I came to see how Justin is doing."

"The surgeon was just here," Donnelly said. "They took care of the bullet, but he was low on oxygen for a few minutes before the ambulance got there. They'll know tomorrow or the next day if that's going to cause him problems."

"Is the family in there?" Roman asked.

Brandt nodded.

"I'll go in once my parents get here. They want to see how Justin is too."

His parents rounded the corner at that moment, Mr. Montgomery holding his wife's arm as they walked down the corridor. They clearly had had a rough night—she looked bone weary, his jaw was set grimly. But they both seemed a bit relieved when they saw their son and how much his mood had brightened in the presence of Brandt and Donnelly.

"Officers," Mr. Montgomery said, not in greeting but rather acknowledgment.

"Mr. Montgomery, Mrs. Montgomery," Brandt said in a formal tone.

"Roman says that we have you to thank for saving his life," Montgomery said. "I guess that's only fitting, as you were the ones who caused it to be endangered in the first place. First forcing us to do that wedding and then using him as bait. You ought to be ashamed."

Brandt was clearly taken aback, but his face instantly reset into professional bearing. "It's been a long night, Mr. Montgomery. I'm glad that Roman's okay."

Mr. Montgomery gave a dismissive grunt and continued walking down the hall.

"I should go," Roman said. "My parents and the Capellas don't exactly get along. I don't want them making a scene while we wait for news about Justin."

Roman hurried down the hall, and the officers watched him go.

"I hope he's going to be okay," Donnelly said.

"I hope they all will," Brandt replied.

Donnelly nodded. "Nana Capella seems to be the only one with her head on straight."

Brandt looked at his watch. "It's probably going to be daylight already. What a night."

"Can we get some sleep now?" Donnelly asked with a yawn.

"How about a power nap? I need to debrief the chief about what happened last night, but I can probably put that off until noon."

Donnelly consulted his watch. "I guess a few hours is better than none. I'll come back and check on Justin when you go in for your meetings." He looked up at Brandt. "But seriously, we'd better be naked and snoring in ten minutes."

"Then I'd better get you home before you give someone a heart attack by stripping down and falling asleep right here in the hospital," Brandt said with a tired laugh as they resumed their walk to the exit.

BACK IN the waiting room, the arrival of the Montgomery family caused an immediate stiffening in the spines of the Capella clan. All eyes were averted while the Montgomery parents tried to find seats as far away as possible from the Capellas. It was a small room, however, and the farthest seat still seemed uncomfortably close.

Roman made the first move. "Mr. Capella?"

Capella looked up from his magazine—the same one he hadn't been reading for two hours now—and grunted before looking back down.

"Mr. Capella, I'm so sorry about Justin."

Capella pretended not to hear anyone speaking to him.

"He saved my life, Mr. Capella. I would be dead right now if it weren't for Justin. You should be proud of him."

Capella looked up slowly, squinting critically at Roman for a long moment. When he spoke, it was in a low growl that no one else in the room could hear. "Young man, I grew up in that bakery. My son grew up in that bakery. And in all that time we have never had trouble like this. Until now. Until you. You show up and suddenly people are getting sick and dying. My son is lying in a hospital right now because of you." Capella looked hatefully into Roman's face. "You will never set foot in my bakery again. You will never—*never*—see my son again. Take your perversion and your filth and get out of my sight."

Roman, stricken, stepped back from Capella, looking as if he'd been slapped. He sat in the nearest chair, which happened to be the one vacated by Donnelly.

Nana Capella looked at him with a sideward glance for a time, and then she patted him on the knee. "I'd like some coffee, young man. Do you think you could walk with me?" she said, seeming much older and frailer than when she had been playing cards.

Roman nodded and got to his feet, then offered his arm to her. She rose gracefully, then seemed to remember that she had asked for his assistance and took a little half step to one side. He steadied her, then, with a stronger grip on her arm, walked with her out of the waiting area and down the corridor. They walked along for a minute or so in silence, following signs and arrows.

"It's a terrible thing that happened," she said, as they waited for an elevator to take them up to the cafeteria.

Roman nodded glumly. "Terrible things are the only things that have happened to me lately," he replied.

She nodded sympathetically.

"Officer Gabriel told me what Justin did," she said in a conversational tone that did not accord with the dramatic act she referred to.

"I owe him my life," Roman said solemnly.

She looked at him critically for a moment. "He must love you very much."

Roman's cheeks reddened, and he took an unsteady step before recovering. They entered the cafeteria. Roman bought a cup of coffee for each of them, and they sat at a little table by the window. The sunrise made the entire sky pink.

"Can I ask you something quite rude?" she said after sipping her coffee.

"I can't imagine you being rude," he answered. "I learned which fork to use at your table, and I can't recall anyone ever being rude in your presence, much less you."

She smiled. "Those were happy times," she said wistfully, and looked for a moment at the sky, beginning to golden as the sun rose higher. "I will preface my rude question with a statement: I know full well what happened between you and Justin in grammar school. My foolish son thinks I don't, and we've never talked about it. But I have my ways of knowing. You must be aware of that first of all. Now, my question. What happened back then between you and Justin… well, that was real, wasn't it?"

Roman gaped at the old woman, his breath knocked out of him by the bluntness of her question. But then he looked at his hands, fidgeting, and spoke softly. "It was for me."

She put her hand on his. "It was for him too," she said whispered. "He jumped in front of a man with a gun, Roman. To save you. Love is the only thing that would make someone do that." She looked him in the eye, unblinking in her honesty. "Love."

The tears sprang into his eyes, and he didn't move to blot them. They ran down his cheeks, and still he sat motionless, hanging on her words like a drowning man would a life preserver.

"I don't deserve him," he finally croaked. "He risked his life to save me, and all I've done is cause him trouble."

"Now, you poke under the surface of anyone's love and you'll find trouble," the old woman said with a brisk chuckle. "Why, my beloved husband did things no man would be proud of. In the army— Korea, it was. There's something else no one thinks I found out about, but I did. We were always honest with each other. I forgave him everything he did because I loved him, and I knew that deep down he was a good and honest man who had made some mistakes, and he made good when he could. Everyone deserves that chance. Everyone."

Roman squeezed his eyes shut to force out the tears that were filling them.

"Now, I know my grandson. I know he's not like his father, and I thank God every day that that's the case. He knows how to forgive. And he loves you. When you were taken away from him, he knew he couldn't talk to his parents about it, so he came to me. After school just about every day. I'd make him some cookies and sweet tea, and we would talk about, oh, everything. But mostly we talked about you. Then, as he got older, and the wound started to heal over, he talked about a lot of things, but he never talked about anyone the way he talked about you. He's been so lonely. I had hoped that if he got away from home and had some time to figure some things out, he might find somebody. But four years at college didn't do it—didn't dim the memory of his first best friend and all you meant to him. I was so happy when I found out you two were going to be working on the wedding. I couldn't say anything about it to anyone, of course, because we're all supposed to abhor the very idea of two men being happy together, but I was happy for you and Justin. It's just awful what happened last night, but soon all that will all be behind you. Trust me— I'm old, and that makes me smart about this kind of thing."

"Nana Capella, I don't know how to thank you. You have no idea how good it feels to finally be understood by someone. It seems like no one else is even listening."

"They don't want to listen, because they are afraid that what they will hear might disturb what they already think they know. People don't hate other people because they think they are different; they hate because they are afraid they'll discover we are all the same. If we accept that other people are like us, then we don't have any special claim on happiness, or love, or money, or whatever is important to us. So we build up divisions where there were none, and hatreds rise from the gulf of difference that we imagine separates us."

"You are the wisest person I know," Roman said reverently.

"Oh, foo," she said with a laugh. "I'm just the oldest person you know." She knocked back the last of the coffee in her cup. "Now we should get back to those dolts in the waiting room and see if there's any trouble we can kick up."

She got to her feet with a giddy giggle and walked energetically out of the cafeteria. Roman had to hustle to catch up with her.

Back in the waiting area, the Capellas and the Montgomerys had maintained their distance, occupying the antipodes. Mr. Capella still stared at the same magazine, at the same page; Mrs. Capella had apparently run through her entire phonebook and sat glaring at her phone as if willing it to ring. Mrs. Montgomery sat with her eyes closed, her lips moving prayerfully. Mr. Montgomery just stared with an unexplained intensity at the wall above the Capellas' heads.

"Well, isn't this a cozy little cabal?" Nana Capella remarked as she and Roman entered the room.

Eight eyes glowered at the new arrivals, then immediately returned to their previous occupations. She and Roman took seats in the middle of the room, and they sat silently for a few minutes, until a woman in scrubs entered the waiting area.

"Mr. and Mrs. Capella?" she asked and then walked toward the Capellas when they raised their hands. "I'll be coordinating your son's care in the critical care unit. He has been moved from surgical recovery into the CCU, and you'll be able to see him shortly. A nurse will come in a few minutes to bring you to the CCU family room, and you can wait there until he's settled. Do you have any questions for me?"

The Capellas shook their heads, clearly overwhelmed by their sleepless night in the hospital. "Thank you," Mrs. Capella managed before clutching a tissue to her mouth.

The CCU doctor nodded and walked briskly from the room.

"At least we'll get to see him soon, dear," Nana Capella said to Roman, a little more loudly than she needed to.

Roman smiled as if he wished her words would make it true, but there was a doubtful cast to his expression.

"The hell you will," Capella snarled.

Roman closed his eyes and took a deep breath. Nana Capella put her hand on his knee.

"Robert," she said, in the kind but stern manner of a schoolmarm, "we are all worried about Justin. There's no reason why we all can't go see him. Even if he's not awake, he will know we're there. It will be the best thing for him."

"The people who love him will be there, Mother," Capella replied venomously. "The person who brought a murderer into our own kitchen to shoot my son will not be there."

"You know how closely the boys have been working together," she said. "Justin would want to see him. He should be there."

"So he can climb in the bed with him? So he can force his filth and perversion on my son again?" Capella's voice was rising in anger. "So he can try to make my son into a... *faggot*?" He hurled this last word like a spear.

Montgomery was on his feet before Capella had finished enunciating his hate. "Don't you *ever* say such a thing about my son," he hissed, his arm raised, his finger pointed at Capella across the room.

Capella rose to his feet. "Get the hell out of here," he barked.

Roman started to stand as well, but Nana Capella held firm to his leg, and he sat back down. She looked at him and shook her head once, slowly.

"We are here because our sons have been through something terrible, and we're concerned about Justin. We have every right to be here."

"You keep your faggot son away from my boy!" Capella shouted.

"Don't call him that," Montgomery said, biting off each word with a slow menace.

"He hasn't changed since third grade," Capella said, advancing across the room toward Montgomery. "Nothing you have done has helped. Religious school, seminary, college, none of it fixed him. He will never be normal. You keep him away from my son."

Montgomery blinked hard. Roman winced at him, clearly dreading what might come out of his father's mouth next.

"No," he said simply. "My son hasn't changed." He shifted his weight from side to side, cleared his throat. "And there's no reason why he should."

Roman gasped. Nana Capella patted his knee reassuringly.

"I will not sit by and listen to you call him horrible names. He's not the way I wanted him to be, not the way I tried to make him. But that's his right, now that he's a man."

"Dad?" Roman said, his voice small.

"It's okay, Son," Montgomery replied. He walked to where Roman sat and put his hand on his son's shoulder.

"Well isn't that sweet," Capella jeered. "But just because you're fine with your son's perversion doesn't mean that the rest of us are. Some people still have values, and I make no apology for sticking with them." He turned around and said to his wife, "Come on, let's go find a nurse to take us to Justin."

The Capellas stormed from the room.

Roman looked up at his father. "Dad, how did you—"

"How did I know?" Montgomery interrupted gently. "Roman, I'm a florist. It's not like I've never met any gay people."

"And you're okay with it? With… me?"

"You will always be my son. Do I wish you were straight? Of course I do. I wanted you to meet a nice girl, have a big church wedding, lots of kids to carry on the business." He had a faraway look for a moment, but then snapped back to the present. "But that's not my choice to make, is it?"

Roman had tears in his eyes as he stood and embraced his father. Nana Capella watched with joy—and some dabbing of her eyes. Mrs. Montgomery still sat with her eyes closed, in some happy place far away from the hospital.

"You should get some rest," Montgomery said to his son. "Let's get you home."

"No, Dad," Roman replied, clearly pleased at the display of paternal concern. "I need to stay here for Justin."

Montgomery held his son by the shoulders, at arm's length, surveying his face. He nodded as if he saw what he needed to see. "Let me at least buy you breakfast. You need to keep your strength up if you're going to be sitting a vigil."

Roman turned to Nana Capella. "Will you join us?" he asked, holding out his hand.

"I would be delighted to," she said, rising elegantly. "But only if you let me treat you. It's the least I can do to make up for the brutish behavior of my benighted son."

The trio walked from the room, leaving Mrs. Montgomery to awaken upon her return from her happy place, alone in a room finally at peace.

CHAPTER TWELVE
VISITATION

THE FIRST thing Brandt felt was the light tickle of fingertips. They ran across his shoulders, down his back, and over the tops of his buttocks. Then the circuit repeated, with slight variations, until his entire back had been graced with their gentle attention.

"Mmmm," he said. "That's nice."

"I'm just checking to make sure you're still there," Donnelly whispered.

Brandt rolled over onto his back. "Where else would I be?"

Donnelly, propped up on one elbow, shrugged. "I just keep thinking about how lucky I am. What happened to Greg… I just can't imagine. Can't imagine losing you like that."

Brandt rolled over onto his side so he could look Donnelly in the eyes; he put his arm around him for good measure. "You will never lose me."

Donnelly smiled sweetly but shook his head. "That's what Peter and Greg thought, I'm sure."

Brandt was silent for a moment. "But what happened to Peter was just a freak thing. It was like a time bomb in his chest, and it could just as easily have gone off when he was twelve… or a hundred and twelve. You can't really worry about stuff like that. It'll make you crazy."

"I will always worry. That's the cloudy lining in the silver of being in love. I can't imagine my life without you, but if something like that does happen someday, I want us to be together. I wouldn't be as sad about it if we could at least face it together."

"The time we've spent apart from each other over the last almost three years probably amounts to less than any couple we know. If something wanted to kill you, it would pretty much have to get through me first, because I'm always here."

"I know. It just makes me think about the whole getting married thing. That's one of the things that marriage is supposed to do for you: ensure that when bad things happen, you aren't alone. And it just makes me crazy how it ended for them."

Brandt thought about this for a minute; then the idea came to him. "How about this: as soon as we get this thing with Roman and Justin taken care of, we go see a lawyer and get a power of attorney to tide us over until we get married. Something that either of us could use to get to the other, no matter what?"

Donnelly beamed. "That's the most romantic thing I think you've ever said to me." He kissed Brandt on the nose.

"Really? I mention a legal document and that's what gets you going? Good God, Gabriel—we're old."

"I'll remind you that I still have more than two years to go before I turn thirty."

"That's right, old man. You'll get there way before I do."

"A year and a half hardly counts as 'way before.'"

"Waaaay before."

"Young man, I think I will have to give you a tongue lashing."

"Oh, fuck yeah," Brandt moaned. He kissed Donnelly, their tongues finding each other and sparring for dominance. The contest lasted several long, sloppy minutes.

They were interrupted by Brandt's alarm going off, telling them that they needed to get up and hit the shower if Brandt was going to make his meeting with the chief. He reached over to smack at his phone, and Donnelly spooned up behind him and wrapped him in his arms.

"I could stay like this all day," Brandt murmured, snuggling deeper into Donnelly's embrace.

"Me too," Donnelly whispered in response, his lips brushing the short, velvety hairs at the base of Brandt's head. "Do we have to get up?"

Brandt chuckled. "Feels to me like somebody's already up." He gave his hips a little wiggle and felt Donnelly's erection slide between his buttocks.

"Oh, bloody hell," Donnelly groaned as his cock slipped through Brandt's legs and nestled up under his balls.

"Is that what they say in your Jane Austen novels when someone slips a boner in?" Brandt teased.

"Haven't gotten to that part of the book yet, I guess," Donnelly replied as he started to nudge his erection back and forth.

Without a word, Brandt reached to his nightstand and pulled a small bottle of lube from his top drawer. He popped it open with one hand and slid it below the covers. Blindly, he squirted some lube onto Donnelly's invading prick and slid a sloppy hand between his legs to slick up the entire works.

Donnelly gasped. "So, that's not a 'no' I'm hearing, then?"

"I am all 'yes' this morning, big guy," Brandt replied, squeezing his legs together for a little extra friction. The heat and pressure of Donnelly thrusting against his balls and the sensitive skin beneath them rose, bringing his pulse up as well.

The lube had worked its way down between Brandt's legs, spurring Donnelly to more urgent motion. Brandt reached down and grabbed at the head of his partner's cock as it emerged and then withdrew, gently forcing his balls to part and then reunite with each thrust. He gave it a twisting tug every time he could get his slippery fingers on it, and Donnelly's breath caught every time he did.

Donnelly kissed all along Brandt's neck in rhythm with his thrusting and then brought his hand around to tweak Brandt's already stiff nipples. He knew full well the effect this would have, and Brandt responded by arching his back and moaning into the pillow.

Brandt knew when the head of Donnelly's cock, already full and hard, grew even larger that the end was near. He flexed his buttocks and tightened his thighs, and the moment arrived as he knew it would. What he hadn't expected was for Donnelly to reach down, grasp his erection, and unleash his irresistible milking technique to sudden, devastating effect. Suddenly Brandt, who had been content to be used by his horny partner, was on the brink of orgasm.

Donnelly gave one last, vigorous thrust, and then Brandt could feel his surging spasms as well as the tensing and flexing of the abs pressed against his back and the thighs pressed against his own. The sheet in front of him pooled with Donnelly's cum, and it splashed onto Brandt's thighs and all over his balls. He felt Donnelly's hand swab some of it up and then wrap back around his cock and resume its insistent stroking.

Brandt pressed back against Donnelly; he loved the strength and solidity of him, the way that he could leverage himself against and into him, a true partner in every sense. He arched his back and thrust into Donnelly's fist, feeling the quiver of orgasm begin to build deep inside. He leaned into it, his eyes shut so tightly that light began to sparkle around the edge of his vision. Reaching behind him, he pulled Donnelly even closer and held him there as he stepped off the cliff.

"Unnnh, fuck," Brandt moaned as his semen launched out of him and joined that produced by Donnelly a moment ago. He growled as Donnelly continued to work his hard-on, forcing every drop of cum from him until he twitched from overstimulation. He flipped over and crashed into Donnelly's lips, kissing him with all the force of the love inside him for the man who had come to be his entire life.

He looked Donnelly in the eye, dead serious. "I will always be here," he whispered.

Donnelly nodded, a smile of joy on his face. "We will always be together," he whispered back.

THE CCU family room was a less clinical space than the one outside trauma surgery. There were couches instead of stiff chairs with arms, plants in front of windows that looked out over a park, and a television in the corner making sotto voce offerings of car insurance. In this comfortable environment, the glowering of the Capellas was undertaken again in earnest. Their focus was, of course, Roman, as well as Nana Capella, who maintained her position as Roman's wingman in the arena of interfamilial battle.

The Capellas had just returned from seeing Justin for a precious few minutes. He had been settled into his room, but rounds were scheduled to begin soon, and he had quite a large team who needed to check and discuss his progress.

"How did he look?" Nana Capella asked when they resumed their seats.

"Like someone had tried to kill him," Capella spat in Roman's direction. "That's what happens when you associate with the wrong sort."

"Will we be able to see him soon?" Nana Capella said, undeterred by her son's angry demeanor.

"*We* will be able to see him again once rounds are finished," Mrs. Capella rejoined. "You," she continued, pointing at them both, "aren't going to see him at all."

Once again, Nana Capella simply patted Roman on the arm, counseling patience.

Around noon they were joined by another concerned soul: Donnelly.

"Mr. and Mrs. Capella, how is he?" Donnelly asked.

"He's sleeping," Mrs. Capella answered. "He looks so small and innocent." She blotted at her eyes.

"We've been able to go in a couple of times," Capella added. "They're changing his IV line right now, and then we can go back in for the rest of the afternoon."

Donnelly nodded and turned to Nana Capella. "You're still here?" he said, though he didn't sound surprised.

"Gabriel, it was so nice of you to come all the way down here again, especially when there is such important police work to be done."

He seemed about to protest, but she winked subtly at him, and he held his objection.

"But it really is very important that you get a good look around where the shooting happened, isn't it?"

Donnelly squinted at her, as if running sums in his head. "Yesss," he said, cautiously.

"I'm sure that once my son and daughter-in-law show you around the bakery, you can bring them right back."

"Oh," Donnelly said, nodding. "Yes, it should just take a moment or two." He turned to the Capellas. "Mr. and Mrs. Capella, I hate to impose upon you, but would it be possible for you to show me around the bakery, so that I can be sure we've gotten all of the evidence we can get?"

Capella frowned. "Didn't the crime scene people already do that?"

"Yes, but they didn't have the benefit of your guidance. There are likely things they missed, seeing as they'd never been there before. Sometimes the smallest clues can lead to evidence that we can use in discovering who assaulted Justin before the shooter arrived."

Capella looked at his wife. She shrugged tiredly.

"I'd be happy to drive you there and back," Donnelly said. "We could also stop at your house if you want to change clothes or pick up anything."

"We might as well," Mrs. Capella said. "We've been here for over twelve hours now."

"Excellent. Shall we?" Donnelly pointed the way, and he flashed Nana Capella a look of conspiratorial warning, as if to say she should make good use of the opportunity he had given her.

A few minutes after the departure of Donnelly and the Capellas, the CCU nurse came to the room and looked about. "Are you here for Justin Capella as well?" she asked Nana Capella.

"Why yes, we are," she replied, her voice suddenly sounding shaky and old.

"Would you like to see him?" the nurse asked.

"Very much." Nana Capella rose and took Roman's hand. "I'm his grandmother, and this is his brother, Roman."

"Walk this way," the nurse said, and she guided them down the corridor of glassed-in rooms until reaching the one at the end. She pointed for them to enter, and she followed behind. "He's still under sedation, but many doctors believe that in this state patients are aware of voices and touch, so we encourage family to sit close and engage with their loved one." She smiled at them, perhaps noticing the tears streaming down Roman's cheeks. "I'll leave you alone," she said, turning to go.

Nana Capella gave Roman a nudge. "This is your time, dear. Go ahead."

"Thank you," Roman said, his voice choked. He shuffled forward along the side of the bed until he reached a chair set at its head. He sat and leaned forward, whispering distance from Justin's unconscious form. He took Justin's hand and held it tight. "I'm so sorry, Juss," he whispered. "You are the last person in the whole world I would want to hurt." He rubbed Justin's hand gently. "I love you, Juss. I always have. When I lost you, I thought I could cover the hurt by never loving anyone again. But all that did was hurt me even more, and now it's hurt you. I will never hurt you again, Juss. Never." He leaned forward and kissed Justin's forehead.

Roman froze and looked at his hand, the one intertwined with Justin's. "He squeezed my hand. Nana, he squeezed my hand!"

"Of course he did, dear," Nana Capella replied, as if she'd expected this all along. "He loves you. Love is stronger than a bullet, every time."

Roman sat at the side of Justin's bed for the rest of the afternoon, whispering his devotion and telling stories of things that he and Justin would experience together. The nurse bustled in for end-of-shift rounds and found Nana Capella dozing in her chair while Roman slumped over the bed, his head on the pillow next to Justin's. They looked like they had just lain down for a nap. "Brothers," she said under her breath, smiling. She went to Roman and gently shook his shoulder. "Mr. Capella?" she said softly. "Mr. Capella."

Roman awoke and, finding himself next to Justin, looked up with a dreamy smile.

"A police officer called just a moment ago with a message he said was urgent. He says that he's bringing your parents back to the hospital, and he'll be here in a few minutes."

Roman straightened up. "Thank you," he said. "I'll go meet them in the family room." He looked over at Justin's sleeping grandmother. "Let's just let Grandma sleep, okay? She's been up so long."

The nurse nodded, and they left the room. The nurse returned to her station, and Roman to the family room. Once there, he looked out the window for a moment, cradling the hand that Justin had squeezed—he was sure of it. Sure of him.

"ROMAN, IT'S Officer Brandt."

"Hey, good to hear from you," Roman said into the phone.

"Where are you?"

"I'm just leaving the hospital."

"Did you get a chance to see Justin?"

"Yes, thanks to Donnelly and Justin's grandma. I got to spend a couple of hours with him—he squeezed my hand. The nurse said we couldn't expect anything like that, but he squeezed my hand."

"That's great, Roman. Gabriel's just taking the Capellas back to the hospital now. He's going to bring you back downtown with him, if that's okay with you."

"Um, sure?" Brandt could hear the exhaustion in Roman's voice. "What for?"

"The coroner needs you to make a positive ID on Marcus Verona." There was a long pause. "Roman, you there?"

"Yes, I'm here. I just… I didn't think I'd ever have to see that guy again."

"Well, he's still dead, if that helps."

Brandt's attempt at gallows humor seemed to help Roman's mood. "Okay. I'm out in front of the hospital now—can Gabriel come and pick me up here?"

Brandt tapped and swiped at his phone for a moment, texting Donnelly. The reply came almost immediately. "He'll meet you there in a couple of minutes."

About a half hour later, Donnelly and Roman walked into the coroner's office, where Brandt was waiting for them. They were conducted into the morgue by a technician, who slid open a drawer and revealed the bluish face and shoulders of a man whom death had found in midsnarl, his lips still contorted in rage.

Brandt and Donnelly peered into the face of the man they had killed and nodded to the technician. Then Roman stepped up, keeping his face averted. He took a deep breath before lifting his gaze to the stainless steel tray. His face was impassive, Brandt thought, revealing none of the emotions that the officer would have expected from someone confronting the corpse of the man who had brutally raped him and then attempted to kill him—twice.

"That's him," he whispered.

"I need a name, for confirmation," the technician said softly.

"Marcus Verona," Roman answered. He shook his head slowly, then turned away.

"All right, let's go," Donnelly said, guiding Roman out of the room by the shoulder.

Back in the car, Donnelly rode with Roman in the back seat. "We have just one more thing we'd like you to do, Roman. It would really help us out."

"What's that?" Roman's voice clearly showed his exhaustion.

"We need you to come to our office and look at a couple of mug shots."

Roman looked at him with a frown. "But I just saw him. I know it was him. What more do you need?"

Donnelly flashed Brandt a look, then answered Roman. "There's some paperwork that doesn't quite line up, and we think you can help us with it."

"Okay. I would do anything for you guys. You saved my life—and Justin's."

At their office, Donnelly seated Roman in the conference room while Brandt brought in his laptop. His fingers raced across the keyboard, and suddenly the face of Marcus Verona peered back at them from the large monitor on the wall.

"This is a photo that was taken a couple of years ago," Donnelly said, pointing at the screen. "Can you identify it?"

"Well, this looks like it was taken before he got all 'roid ragey, but that's Marcus all right." He looked at the confused faces of the officers. "Marcus was a pretty hard-core bodybuilder—I think it's part of what made him so violent."

"How about this one?" Brandt brought a new face up on the screen. "Do you know him?"

"Yes." Roman said. His startled tone indicated this was another face he had not expected to see again.

"Do you know his name?"

Roman shook his head. "I only saw him at Marcus's place in the Heights. He was there every time—he always answered the door, except for that last time. We were never introduced, but then again Marcus and I were barely on a first-name basis." He shivered. "That's the guy Marcus sent to beat up Justin before I got to the bakery. Did you find him?"

"He was picked up earlier today by Metro police during a traffic stop," Brandt explained. "They're holding him on an out-of-state warrant."

"Let me guess—he and Marcus have roughed up people before," Roman said.

"Well," Donnelly chimed in, "yes and no."

"What does that mean?" Roman asked.

"He means that this man has no known association with Marcus Verona," Brandt answered, "because, as far as we can tell, Marcus Verona never existed."

Roman just stared, vacant-eyed, at Brandt. Then he turned to Donnelly and did the same. "He doesn't exist? Are you saying I imagined him? Because my ass remembers him."

"We didn't find any identification on the body when we checked him over at the bakery. The medical examiner searched more thoroughly, and she didn't find anything either. All he had in his wallet was a wad of cash and this," Brandt said, tossing an evidence bag across the table to Roman. "Half of a gym membership card. The name and photo were torn off, but we could make out the name of the gym."

Donnelly picked up the story. "There were three gyms in the chain—regional outfit in a suburb of New York City. I e-mailed a photo of Verona to each of them. A little ghoulish, I know, but I put a warm Instagram filter on him, and he still looked mostly alive."

Brandt stifled a laugh, prompting a scowl from Donnelly. "Sorry, please continue," Brandt said, overcompensating grandly for his outburst.

Donnelly sniffed haughtily. "As I was saying, I sent his picture to all three gyms, and the manager of one of them replied right away. He identified Verona as one Mark Tibble, whom he seemed to be gladly rid of as a customer of his gym. There were, apparently, some anger management issues in the weight room."

"But that's not the most interesting thing we learned about Mr. Tibble," Brandt prompted.

"I was getting to that," Donnelly cried. "You'll have to excuse my partner, who is completely useless at storytelling. Anyway, the gym manager made reference to a second identity used by Mr. Tibble. He said in certain circles he went by the name of 'Mercury.' A quick search of the newspaper database for the area revealed that this Mercury had caused a bit of a stir as an escort with a certain specialized skill set."

"I believe I'm familiar with his skill set," Roman commented ruefully.

"Part of it," Brandt said. "Bondage was his core competency, it seems, but he at some point began to add something more: blackmail.

His clients were mostly wealthy married men who liked to be roughed up a bit."

"So he branched out into tapping their wallets as well?" Roman asked.

"Nicely put," Donnelly replied. "Anyway, that's what we think. We're having his associate transferred here from Metro for questioning. We'll see if he can flesh out the story for us."

"Would you be willing to observe the questioning?" Brandt asked. "We could have the video piped in from downstairs."

"It might jar your memory about some detail Tibble might have mentioned, some information he might have let slip," Donnelly explained. "We're trying to be sure that he didn't have a larger network in the area that could be a threat even with him out of the picture."

Roman seemed to ponder this for a moment, then nodded. "Okay. I'll do it."

About an hour later, during which time Roman dozed in a chair while Brandt typed up notes on his laptop, the monitor in the conference room came to life.

"I should get down there in case Gabriel needs me," Brandt said, rising. "You stay here, and if anything seems significant to you, write it down and note the time in the lower-right corner—that will help us get to the exact point in the questioning."

"Got it," Roman said.

Brandt took the two flights of stairs at a jog and met Donnelly outside the room where their suspect was waiting to be questioned. "Ready?" he asked.

"I was born ready," Donnelly replied, as he always did.

And as he always did, Brandt felt a surge of heat in his chest seeing his partner's confident swagger. What endeared Gabriel to him was his sweetness, his thoughtfulness, his ability to see the good in other people. But seeing him aggressively question a suspect, trying to protect the innocent? That made Brandt's heart pound.

"Go get him, tiger," he said, with a sock on the shoulder that was both police-brother routine and boyfriend intimate.

Donnelly nodded, then opened the door and strode in. "Good evening, Mr. Perry," Donnelly said, sitting at the table across from his subject. "I understand you have been read your rights and that you have waived your right to be represented by counsel. Is that correct?"

"Yes," Perry replied dully.

Whatever Metro had done to soften him up really seemed to have worked, Brandt thought as he watched on the monitor in the room next door.

"How do you know Mark Tibble?"

"He's a friend," Perry replied. "Or, he was until someone killed him." He fixed Donnelly with a hateful stare.

"Yes, that is a shame. Can you tell me when Mr. Tibble relocated to our fair city?"

"We moved here two years ago."

"We? Were you and Mr. Tibble in a relationship?" Donnelly asked, voice devoid of judgment.

"We had a *business* relationship," Perry replied, acidly.

"Involving extortion, I believe?" Donnelly said brightly, as if inquiring whether Perry and Tibble had shared a paper route.

Perry sighed. "Mercury had some wealthy friends. These friends found him very attractive. They offered him gifts as a voluntary reward for his companionship. Sometimes relationships end badly. People accuse other people of all kinds of things when a relationship is over."

"He's the first one I've ever come across who decided to poison an entire wedding because of a bad breakup."

"That isn't why he did it," Perry said.

Donnelly leaned across the table. "Then why don't you tell me why he did it, and how, and who else was involved, and we'll see about not charging you as an accessory to manslaughter."

"The fuck? Manslaughter?"

"Peter Laurence, one of the grooms at the wedding, is dead."

Perry looked like someone had kicked him in the gut. "Shit."

"Indeed," Donnelly replied. He sat and waited for more to come. In this he was not disappointed.

"Okay." Perry heaved a deep breath, and a dam inside him seemed to break. "I met Tibble about five years ago, working out at the same gym. We started by spotting each other, shooting the shit. Then one day he comes to me and says that some guy offered him like five hundred dollars to go to his house and like, pose and shit. He's like 'Should I do it?' and I'm like 'Rich fag wants to watch you pose for five bills, hell yeah you should do it.' So he says he'll do it, and then he gets kinda scared and asks me to come with him and wait in the car case the guy wants to go Dahmer on him. So I go, and I sit in the car all fuckin' night. He comes out of the guy's house like four in the morning, and he's got a wad of money—just a fuckin' wad. So we drive to a diner to get something to eat, and he tells me the guy wanted him to pose naked. And I'm like 'Well, no shit, what did you think he wanted?' But then the guy got all handsy with him, and he had to rough the guy up a little bit. Turns out the guy liked that, so he did it some more, and pretty soon he's got the guy tied up and he's smackin' him around, and then the guy goes 'I'll give you a thousand dollars if you fuck me right now and make it hurt.' Well Tibble goes 'It always hurts,' because he was hung like a fuckin' thoroughbred and no shit."

Perry paused to take a sip of the water that the officer who seated him had set on the table for him. He wiped his mouth and continued his story.

"So he just rails this guy for like a half hour. I ask him, 'How did you even get a fuckin' boner so you could shove your dick up some guy's shitter?' and he's all 'I just rubbed the money on it'—that's how Tibble was. He was as straight as they come, but he could fuck anyone or anything if there was money in it for him. Anyway, that guy was Tibble's first client. Turns out he had some friends who liked it rough too, and they started asking him to hook them up with Tibble. So I tell him, I'm like 'Man, you gotta make this your business, you know?' and pretty soon he puts up a little website with some pictures that this fag at the gym took, and he starts callin' himself Mercury, because he would always meet his customers at their place, not his. You know, like Mercury the messenger guy in Greekology?"

Donnelly nodded. "Roman," he said.

Perry startled at the mention of Roman's name. "What did you say?" His voice was low and tense.

"Roman mythology. Mercury was the messenger of the gods in Roman mythology. The Greeks knew him as Hermes."

"Oh, yeah, right," Perry replied with what Brandt thought was an ill-conceived attempt to cover up his panic at the mention of Roman's name. "Anyway, Merc built a clientele of rich, closeted fags who gave him money for tying them up, knocking them around a bit, and then fucking them until money came out of every hole they had."

"What a colorful image, Mr. Perry."

Perry ignored the interruption. "Once in a while, one of the old wrinkly farts would stop paying, and Merc would threaten to expose him—not directly, but by saying that someone had somehow gotten pictures of an incriminating nature. That someone was me. Anyway, that got the tap flowing again. So everything was copacetic until the law changed."

"Mr. Perry, extortion has always been against the law," Donnelly stated.

"Not that law. The gay marriage law. That fucked things up but good."

"I don't understand."

"Then you don't know how fags think, do you?"

Brandt gasped, but in the interrogation room, Donnelly's expression didn't change. Brandt leaned closer to the monitor, wondering how his partner was going to handle this.

"Why don't you enlighten me, Mr. Perry?"

"Blackmail works when some information that one party—say, me—knows about another party—say, you—would cost that second party more if it went public than the price I'm asking to keep it quiet. Merc's clients would pay a metric shit-ton of money to keep their wives and business associates from finding out they like to spend their weekends getting tied up and dancing like a puppet on the end of Merc's foot long. But once gays start getting married, the whole dynamic is off. You know, the first few guys down the aisle get their picture in the paper, and everyone goes crazy. But once people get used to the idea, they start to accept fags in other ways too. And pretty soon Merc's clients started to get the idea that maybe their lives wouldn't end if their secret got out. Sure, maybe some rich wife gets pissed and throws one of them out of the mansion, but it's not like he's going to get fired and run out of town on a rail. It was only a matter of time before someone decided he could go to the police crying blackmail, and we had to get the hell out of there. We came here because it seemed like the last place in the country that would allow gay marriage. And we wanted to keep it that way, so once the court made it legal, we decided to… discourage people from doing it."

"You didn't seriously think that making people sick at a wedding would make the state repeal marriage equality, did you?"

Perry laughed derisively. "We weren't fucking stupid. All we wanted to do was bring back a little of the stigma. Our clients paid because they feared what would happen to them if they went against what's normal. It doesn't take much to keep that fear simmering in the backs of people's minds."

"That is a startlingly cynical business model, Mr. Perry."

"Thank you," Perry replied.

"Whose idea was the poison?"

"It wasn't poison. It was that shit they give kids who swallow drain cleaner or whatever. It wouldn't kill anyone."

"If a person gets enough of it, it can be deadly."

"Well, we didn't think that would happen."

Donnelly nodded skeptically. "And how did Roman Montgomery get involved?"

Perry erupted with a snarling laugh that did nothing to enhance his credibility to Brandt. "I don't know anything about what happened to him."

"Don't worry, Mr. Perry. Young Mr. Montgomery is fine. I saw him not a half hour ago."

Perry froze, as if trying to sort out this new information. Brandt leaned closer to the monitor, watching his face to see if he would reveal that he knew what was supposed to have happened to Roman. But he blinked twice, and some con-man circuit breaker flipped in his head and he was back on his game.

"Oh, that little twink," Perry said with a dismissive chuckle. "We met him at a club a while ago, and he seemed to take a shine to Merc. Some boys like it rough, you know. Once we found out who he was, all we had to do was string him along a little—a slap and tickle couple of times a week—and he would do anything Merc asked of him. He was a mule, just as useful and just as stupid."

"Where did you get the poison?"

"That was the easy part. Merc met a pharmacist who didn't want anyone to find out that he liked electricity applied to certain parts of his body while hanging upside down in a straitjacket. He got us the stuff—Merc said he didn't know where he got it."

"Do you know the name of this pharmacist?" Donnelly asked.

"Hell no. Merc kept all of that in his head—he never wrote anything down, never told me the details. All I did was take the pictures and make the threats, and he did the rest."

"Was there anyone else in on this little plot?"

"Blackmail is hard work, Officer," Perry reprimanded Donnelly. "Why would we want more people to share the take? It was just Merc and me."

Donnelly looked down at his notes for a moment, then moved casually into the next line of questioning. "So, once you made everyone at that wedding puke, job well done, and you were just going back to shaking down closeted money?"

Perry looked at a loss for the first time. He sighed and looked at the ceiling as if not sure which version of the truth to tell. "I was done. Too many people were asking too many questions after that mess. I wanted to clean up and clear out, but Merc was on about doing more—'Taking it to the next level,' he kept saying. Honestly he was starting to go a bit off the rails. Those gel cap things he worked out for the flowers? That was the real reason for what he did at the wedding. He was testing the best way to deliver...." Perry fell silent, as if he'd said too much.

"You should get it all out now, Mr. Perry. This is your best shot at a deal, and anything we find out about after this interview ends accrues to you, not the dead Mr. Tibble."

Perry took a deep breath, let it out slowly. "This was all him. He kept me out of it, which was fine with me. He sat there doing research and stuff all fuckin' day. One time he was out working over one of his clients, and I took a look at his laptop. He was doing searches on stuff like ricin and sarin. I freaked the fuck out. I told him when he got back he was goin' too far, and I never signed up for killin' people. Never said another word about it. But I think he kept workin' up plans. I was about ready to get the hell out, even though the money was still good, when he said we needed to burn and run, stay under for a while and let this all blow over."

"So you expect me to believe that you had suddenly found your moral compass and were planning to abandon your still-lucrative business partnership with Mr. Tibble?"

"Look… I'm not one to speak ill of the dead, but Merc was getting along. We'd been running this scam for more than five years, and he was starting to show some wear. He kept spending our money on things like steroids and botox and acid peels and whatever, but the truth is his days as a spanky whore were numbered. A guy who wants to be tied up and fucked until he passes out can walk into a club any night of the week and find a dozen leather daddies who will be pleased to do the job. But Merc looked like he was captain of the water polo team. The All-American boy with a leather crop and a dick as big as your arm—there's something you don't find every day. But Merc was nearing thirty, so the business model was going to have to change. Maybe it's a good thing it ended this way. Before he was too far gone."

Donnelly sat back in his chair, as if weighed down by the sheer extent of the lunacy he had just heard. "Mr. Perry, what you've described goes far beyond the garden-variety blackmailing-dom scenario. What you're describing rises to the level of a terrorist threat. You'll excuse me if I characterize this in my report as the insane grasping of a psychopath."

Perry laughed, then kept laughing until he sounded a bit unhinged. Finally, he recovered his composure. "Yeah, that was him. Insane. But most of the shit he tried paid off eventually. I just learned over time to go along with him, and we'd land on our feet."

"I will simply point out, Mr. Perry, that where he landed you was in police custody."

Perry chuckled. "This one didn't work out so well. But it was a good run, Officer. A good run."

"Well," Donnelly said, rising from his chair, "I think I have everything I need. Thank you for your cooperation, Mr. Perry. I will let the DA know how much you helped us get this sorted out."

"Is the kid okay? The baker?" Perry asked, as if he'd just remembered that he'd roughed up Justin and left him in a pool of blood.

"We hope so. He's in critical condition, and if he dies that will add to your tab significantly. I suggest you start hoping for his full and swift recovery." With that, Donnelly left the interrogation room.

Brandt met him in the hallway. "Nice work, Officer."

Donnelly bowed his acknowledgment of the accolade as they walked toward the stairs. "We should be sure that forensics gets Tibble's laptop out of his car and checks it for search history, and whatever else they can find related to poisons."

"You think Perry was telling the truth about that? Maybe he was pumping it up to make the ipecac seem like no big deal."

Donnelly nodded, as if this had occurred to him as well. "That may be. But at least we got to him before he could wipe the laptop, so if there's evidence there, we'll find it."

Brandt and Donnelly climbed the stairs to the conference room, where they found Roman sitting with his head down on the table. He looked up when they entered the room.

"Well, that was horrifying," he said by way of greeting.

"Sorry," Donnelly replied. "That must have been really hard to listen to."

"That guy could give a snake lessons on being cold-blooded." Roman shivered. "I was creeped out every time I saw him, and now I know why. But one of the things he said did make me remember something that might be useful," he offered.

"Anything could be useful," Donnelly replied encouragingly.

"That part about the pharmacist"—he consulted his notepaper— "at 18:06. The guy who got him the ipecac? I think that whole thing happened before I met Marcus, but one night I heard them talking about him—at least, I think it was him. It was kind of hard to tell because I was upstairs and their voices were muffled."

"Did they mention a name?" Brandt prompted.

"I didn't think so, not at the time. But now I'm not so sure. They kept calling the guy a seeker—like a drug seeker, which seemed appropriate for a former pharmacist who's maybe a former pharmacist because he was stealing the drugs. But they never said 'drug-seeker,' they just always called him 'seeker.' Like maybe that was his last name, or part of his name." Roman shrugged but then froze when he saw the troopers' reaction to the name. "What?" he asked.

Brandt and Donnelly exchanged a look.

"We may have a theory as to whom they might have meant," Brandt said. "Thank you for that information; it could prove very useful indeed."

"I'll take you home," Donnelly offered. "You look completely wiped out."

"I kind of am," Roman said. "I don't even know what day it is anymore."

"It's still Tuesday," Donnelly answered, looking at his watch. "At least for the next seventeen minutes."

"Can hardly wait to find out what tomorrow will bring," Roman said with a sad shake of his head. Then his face turned more thoughtful. "But you know what really gets me?"

"What?" the troopers replied in unison.

"I thought I was the shit," he said. "Thought I had it all figured out. I was having a big 'Fifty Shades of Gay' adventure. Now I find out I've been played. Completely played. He chose me because of the company my family runs. He told me exactly what I wanted to hear, and I let him do whatever he wanted to me. He never wanted me for me."

"He made a living deceiving and threatening men much older and more experienced than you, Roman," Brandt said compassionately. "You can't beat yourself up for being taken in."

"In fact," Donnelly added, "once we write this up for the DA, I think we can convince him that prosecuting you for putting the ipecac in the cake doesn't make sense. You've suffered enough. You were as much the victim of his manipulation as everyone else, and you helped us uncover a potentially much more devastating plot."

Roman blinked back tears. "You would do that for me?" he asked in a small voice.

"Of course," Brandt said warmly. "Now, let's get you home so you can rest. Justin could be awake tomorrow, and you'll want to see him."

"Not that his parents will let me anywhere near him."

"We'll just have to come up with something to get them out of the way again," Donnelly replied with a laugh.

Chapter Thirteen
Fathers and Sons

ROMAN LAY awake in his bed, listening to the clock in the living room tick away the minutes. Every quarter-hour brought chimes, which he had now heard six times. Seven long bongs of the main chime told him the time, and he sat up in bed, giving up on sleeping any more this morning.

He stumbled to his bathroom, turned on the shower, and regarded himself in the mirror. He looked exactly as bad as he felt. Like he had been beaten and abused. Like he had spent a night in the hospital. Like he had watched his best friend—the one he had lost as a boy and almost lost again as a man—take a bullet for him. No one should have to go through what he had been through, and yet here was another day to live through.

For Justin. For him he could keep going.

He cranked on the shower and peed in the toilet while clouds of steam developed, filling the room. In the shower he tried to scrub the entire experience off of him: the blood, the disinfectant, the shame. He wanted to scrub until he got down to the hope, the hope he used to have when he was young. He'd had it until they took it all away and left him bitter beyond his years.

He dried and dressed and headed downstairs to the kitchen. Normally they would all be at the shop by now, but today was another in a string of not-normal days. His father was already there, pulling the long shots of espresso that normally powered him through the predawn part of the workday. He was focused on this task and didn't turn around when Roman entered the kitchen.

"Morning, Dad," he said.

Monty started and turned around with his steaming mug of strong brew. "Morning, champ," Monty said, as he almost always did—at least before the mess that the last couple of weeks had become. "Coffee?"

"Love some, thanks," Roman replied, his voice carefully casual.

Monty pulled a second espresso and then dropped a cube of sugar into the cup before handing it over to Roman. "Come sit for a minute?" he asked, tipping his head toward the breakfast table by the windows that overlooked the garden. A riot of flowers was visible through the glass. Monty sat on the banquette and motioned for Roman to join him.

Roman sat, somewhat gingerly, and sipped his coffee. He smiled at his dad, though he was reluctant to begin their conversation.

"Yesterday, at the hospital," Monty began, speaking with deliberation, as if he'd rehearsed this speech, "Cap said some awful things to you."

Roman nodded but then shrugged it off. "It wasn't the worst thing I've ever been called," he said.

"But they were hurtful and mean and...." Monty trailed off as if searching for the right words. He took a breath and started again. "They were words I realized I've thought myself. About you... about my own son. And I'm not proud of that."

Roman winced at his father's contrition. "That's okay, Dad, a lot of people—"

"No," Monty interrupted. "It's not okay. It's not okay at all. Hearing those words come out of his mouth, well, the hate in them was suddenly so clear. I should never have spoken them, even just to myself. The lawsuit, and the wedding, and everything that's happened... I kept telling myself it was about values and tradition and religious freedom. But it was only ever about one thing. My fear. My dread that you, my only son, the most important person in the world to me, were—" He leaned close to Roman, and whispered. "—gay."

Roman smiled, amused by his father's heroic attempt to manage that dreaded word.

Monty wouldn't have noticed Roman's change of expression, however, as he had averted his eyes in the wake of summoning the courage to say that momentous word. He sipped a fortification of coffee and continued. "I know we haven't been as close in the last few years as we had been before, and I wanted to believe that it was because you were at college and it was natural that we'd have some distance. But yesterday was the first time I'd been on the receiving end of that prejudice. I felt how much Cap's words hurt you. I never want to hurt you, Roman. I want to be a part of your life, and I know that can't happen if you think I disapprove of who you love. And I hope you can forgive me for how I must have made you feel over the years when you felt my disapproval. I'm truly sorry, Son."

Roman wiped his eyes, startled by his father's impassioned apology. "Thank you," he choked out before his voice failed him.

Monty patted his son's knee, tears creeping into his eyes. "Now, I want to start our new relationship with a clean slate," he said. "We've never talked about what happened between you and Justin in third grade, and that's wrong. I couldn't let myself even admit the possibility that you might be gay, and so I made sure the entire family buried that whole incident. But given what's happened in the past few days, I've come to see that I pretty seriously overreacted back then and may have actually completely ruined your entire childhood with that one mistake."

"No, Dad, don't," Roman said immediately. "Don't think that. You did what you thought you needed to. And it wasn't all bad." He chuckled impishly. "You have to admit that if your intention was to be sure I stayed away from boys, sending me to all-male schools was probably not the best way to go about it."

Monty's eyes went wide. "Oh," he said, clearly stunned. "Do you mean that you... and the other students... oh my God...." He swallowed hard, then nodded as if settling an internal debate. "Okay, now that you say it out loud, I see what happened there. I kinda threw you into the briar patch, didn't I?"

"That you did, Dad," Roman replied with a chuckle. "There were some sweet berries in that patch, though."

Monty jerked back with a wince.

"Too soon?" Roman asked mischievously.

Monty nodded and looked away as if he'd had a glimpse of something he'd rather not have seen. He shook his head to clear it and then smiled at Roman. "We may need to go slow on the details, okay? I'm still kind of new at this."

"Deal. Now, there is something I really need your advice on."

Monty looked a little fearful at the prospect but nodded. "I'll do my best."

"Mr. Capella doesn't want me to see Justin. It's like my third grade field trip happened yesterday for him. He just wants me to stay out of his son's sleeping bag."

"How does Justin feel?" Monty asked.

"Funny thing is that you and I and Mr. Capella have been wrapped around the axle of that field trip incident for years, and Justin hardly remembered it at all. I had to tell him the whole story, and he acted like he was hearing it for the first time."

"And how did he react to it?"

Roman blushed. "He kissed me."

Monty nodded sagely, then chuckled nervously. "I can't believe we're talking about this, about you kissing Justin. It's all so strange to me," he said, but then held up his hands as if to apologize for his reaction. "My issue, not yours. It'll just take me some time."

"I appreciate the effort you're making. I really do."

"Now, about Justin. Seems like he feels the same way you do, because of the… you know… kissing."

"We did more than kiss, Dad."

Monty took a deep breath and blew it slowly out through puffed cheeks.

"Sorry. Too soon. I'll try to stop doing that."

"Thanks." Monty took two or three more deep breaths. "Okay, so. You can do this two ways, seems to me. First would be to have a heart-to-heart with Cap, tell him what's going on between you two." He held up a hand. "Not everything that's going on, because that fat bastard would have a heart attack—just so he could clutch his chest and fall forward, crushing the life out of you as he drew his last breath. That man and grudges, I tell you what." Monty shook his head. "Second plan would be to sneak in when he's not looking, but that's only going to work so long before you get caught and he gets you thrown out for good."

"So I'm basically screwed," Roman said dismally.

Monty looked at him sympathetically. "You love him?"

"I do. Always have. I thought I'd gotten over him, moved on, but seeing him again the last couple of months… he's the one, Dad. He's the one."

"And he feels the same way?"

"I think he does. I have to believe he does. Yesterday, when Nana Capella got me in to see him, he squeezed my hand—I'm sure of it."

"Then we will find a way." Monty held out his cup and touched it to Roman's. "Promise."

BRANDT AND Donnelly drove in the early afternoon to a place they never thought they would visit again: the bungalow that housed Organic Unions. They stood on the porch and knocked.

"Ugh," said Donnelly, nose wrinkled. "I forgot about the wall of patchouli."

"And snake oil," Brandt groused sourly.

Donnelly chuckled, and Brandt joined in when the contagious laughter got to him.

"Enter in joy" came the lilting, spaced-out voice.

"He won't be joyful once we finish with him," Brandt muttered.

Donnelly shushed him and opened the door.

"Ah, the goddess has brought you back," Seeker intoned from his meditation room. "Welcome. Please, come sit."

Brandt and Donnelly seated themselves in the same places they had occupied on their first visit two months ago.

"Now, how may I support your enlightenment today?"

"Well," Brandt said, smiling placidly, "we are here in a more official capacity than last time."

"Mm-hmm." Seeker nodded, but Brandt noticed a slight twitch in his eyebrow, as if his meditative flow had been disturbed.

"We'd like to find out about any association you might have had with a gentleman we know."

Seeker fidgeted, then took several cleansing breaths. "And what would this gentleman's name be?"

"Mercury," replied Brandt.

The name hit Seeker like a bomb blast. He gasped and practically fell over, knocking his incense burner to the ground. He leapt to his feet and stomped out the cinders before they could set his tatami mat on fire. Panting, he turned to face the officers.

"Never heard of him, I'm afraid," he said, a smile pasted awkwardly on his face.

"Really," said Donnelly. "That's too bad. Especially since he's dead now."

Seeker froze. "Dead?"

"Dead. And from what we know, people who did know him would have had little cause to be upset by his untimely demise. Perhaps you would be in that camp?"

"You're not suggesting that I had anything to do with his death, are you? I hadn't seen him in over six months."

"Of course not," Brandt chimed in. "We killed him."

"But thanks for admitting you did know him," Donnelly said with a smile.

Seeker plopped down on the floor and stared at the officers, flabbergasted.

"You might as well tell us what happened, Seeker," Donnelly said. "And don't forget the part about the ipecac, okay?"

This was the final blow. Seeker could hardly catch his breath.

"Take a deep, cleansing breath, find your center, and spill your guts," Brandt counseled, a bit gruffly.

Seeker took a moment to compose himself and then began. "I met him about a year ago. I was working as a pharmacist out in the suburbs, giving rich white women their diet and depression pills and their daughters Plan B. On the weekend I'd come into the city and hit the clubs.

"I like to think that Mercury was an old soul," Seeker said, looking into the distance above the officers' heads. "He seemed to know instinctively what people wanted, and then he'd tie them up and give it to them. Hard. Problem was, once he had given it to you, you'd find out that there were pictures of you taking it, and then you had to pay. If those pictures got around, I would have been drummed out of the pharmacy. Discretion is paramount when you are selling boner pills to every woman's husband, boyfriend, and gardener, all of whom will use them in her company. So one hint that I liked anything… unconventional… would have resulted in my having to find a less remunerative occupation.

"But he didn't want money from me; what he wanted was for me to find old stockpiles of ipecac juice. Turns out most of it had been transferred to homeopathic remedy distributors, and I was able to use my connections there to gather up what he needed. He made it clear that if I told anyone what I had given him, he would send the pictures to my boss. So I kept quiet. And I got out of that job as soon as I could so he wouldn't have that over me anymore. Of course, he still had the photos of me getting my balls shocked, but in my current line of business, no one really cares about that. In fact, some might think of it as appropriately therapeutic."

"Wow. That's some story, Seeker," Donnelly replied. "And it answers most of our questions, right, Ethan?"

"It's not illegal to possess ipecac juice, is it?" Seeker asked, wincing.

"No, but are you aware that the ipecac was used to poison a wedding cake last weekend?" Donnelly asked. "Made a lot of people ill."

"I saw that on the news, and I hoped Mercury wasn't behind it. Honestly, Officers, I had no idea what he wanted to use it for."

Donnelly fixed him with a quizzical look. "But you warned us last time we were here—you said we shouldn't eat the cake."

Seeker smiled. "Oh, that. Funny thing about that. I really got that message from looking at your auras. It was like I was reading it off a piece of paper, it was that clear." He chuckled softly. "I guess not having an electrode up my ass on a regular basis has opened my mind to another plane."

"Yeah, I'll bet that's it," Brandt deadpanned. "Well, thank you, Seeker. You've been very helpful."

"Have you decided on which enema ritual you would like for your wedding day?"

"As a matter of fact we have," Brandt replied. "We're going to go with the ritual where you never have a wedding enema ever and pretend that such a thing never even existed."

Seeker nodded sagely. "I see you still have a small pocket of doubt blocking your acceptance."

"You could call it that. Thank you for your time." Brandt was happy to close the door on the patchouli bungalow for good.

DARKNESS.

Then, out of the darkness, a sound.

A familiar sound. His name? Was that what his name sounded like? It had been so long.

"Mom?" It's what he tried to say. But instead, he croaked. His throat was sore—so sore.

Did he really make a noise at all?

"Justin? Justin, I'm right here."

The voice was clearer now, and light started to edge into the darkness.

"Mom?" He could hear the word this time, not just the croaking.

"Oh, Justin! Oh my God, Justin."

Yep, that was Mom.

It occurred to him that he could see better if he opened his eyes. He wasn't sure he could—they felt glued shut. But he pulled hard, and they fluttered open.

Too bright. He clamped them shut again.

"Robert! Robert! He's waking up!"

Mom, always making a big deal out of everything. Like Dad had never seen him open his eyes before.

He tried to lift his hands to his brow to shade his eyes, but only one would work; the left arm didn't respond to his command. Hmm. The right one came up, though, and he tried to open his eyes a little in its shade.

The room seemed to be an undifferentiated landscape of white, which seemed a cruel choice when one is opening one's eyes for the first time in several days. As the field of his vision came into focus, the only things that were not white were the shadowy blobs on either side of his bed. These gradually resolved into his parents.

"Justin, dear, you are in the hospital," his mom enunciated with pained precision.

"I know," he replied. He hoped she could understand him; repeating himself would be too painful.

With his right hand, he felt his left shoulder and down his chest; there was a complex network of bandages where his chest should be.

Oh.

He remembered how that happened.

He remembered that night.

"Roman?" he asked. He looked at his mom-blob and tried to tell her with his expression all of the questions he was asking in that word. Was Roman alive? Did Roman still love him? Was Roman just a dream he'd had once upon a time?

The dad-blob expectorated a disgusted sigh and faded back out of Justin's range of vision. He looked harder at his mom. She must understand—she had to. His life depended on it.

"You get some rest," she said with firm gentleness. "You're talking nonsense."

"Is he here?"

"Yes, rest will do you a world of good. Just rest, sweetie."

Justin, unable to be understood, gave in to the exhaustion that he had managed only by force of will to beat back. The darkness crested over him again, and he welcomed it.

He wasn't sure how much time had passed when he came to himself again. It was easier this time, as it seemed to be darker in the room. His vision was clearer this time, and the soreness in his throat had abated. He lifted his head and looked about the room. His parents were sitting in the chairs at the foot of the bed.

"Mom? Dad?"

They jumped at his voice and scurried to take up their stations on either side of the bed.

"Justin, it's so good to see you awake again," his mom said. "Last time they had just taken out your breathing tube, and they said talking would be hard for you. But you sound much better this time."

"How're you doing, Son?" his dad asked.

"My shoulder hurts," Justin said, not wanting to complain, just stating a fact.

"They had to dig a bullet out of it, Son. There were pieces all over—it was a mess. But they say they got it all, and you're going to be fine."

"Oh you gave us such a scare," his mom said, clutching his right hand. "But you're going to be fine, Justin, thank God."

"Where's Roman?"

"Oh, he's—"

"He's not welcome here," his dad interrupted. "Don't worry, you'll never see that piece of filth again."

"Dad, I need to see him. You have to let him in to see me."

"I don't have to do any such thing."

"Mom, I need to see Roman. Please."

"You listen to your father, Justin. He knows what's best. Now we'll not say that name again."

Justin looked at his mother, then at his father. Their faces were set in a frown and an angry frown, respectively. He took a deep breath and set his own jaw as his parents had taught him to when faced with a challenge.

"Mom," he said, turning back to her. "Is there a call button for the nurse?"

"Yes, of course, dear," she said, clearly pleased to be of use to her son. She took the button from where it was clipped, just above his pillow, and handed it to him.

"Thanks." He pressed the button.

"Is there something you need?" she asked as she clipped the button back in place.

"I just need to see the nurse."

A moment later the nurse came into the room. "Do you need something?" Then she saw that Justin was awake and strode to his side, nudging his father out of the way. Both parents retreated to the far end of the room.

The nurse checked his lines and monitors, then looked in his eyes. "How do you feel?"

"I'm feeling pretty good," he replied. "I just wanted to check on something."

She nodded encouragingly. He tipped his head to beckon her closer so he could whisper to her.

"As an adult, I can choose who visits me in here, right?"

"That's right."

"Great. Here's what I need your help with. I don't want to see these people"—he pointed to his parents—"until they let my boyfriend in to see me."

The nurse's eyes widened a bit, but she settled her face back into a medical professional's mild expression of engaged objectivity. "I see. And these people object to his being here?"

He nodded.

"I understand. Leave it to me." She turned and, smiling pleasantly at the Capellas, made her exit.

"What was that about?" his mom asked him as soon as the nurse left.

"Just wanted to ask about kind of a sensitive issue," he replied.

"Ah," his mother replied, clearly imagining that he meant something having to do with a bedpan.

A few minutes later, a man in khakis, a plaid shirt, and a lab coat came into the room. "Mr. and Mrs. Capella?"

"Yes," Capella replied.

"I'm a social worker here at the hospital. The nurse asked me to come talk with you about visitation policy."

Capella shot a glance at his son. Justin knew full well what that look meant. And for the first time in his life, he didn't care.

"I understand Justin has asked for his boyfriend to be allowed to visit him."

"That's impossible," Capella spat. "He doesn't have a 'boyfriend.' The human filth he's referring to is the reason he's in here. He's why my son was shot."

The social worker turned to Justin. "Justin, is this true?"

Justin shook his head. "I got shot because I was protecting Roman. After he got knocked down for protecting me." He knew that this—entirely accurate—description of the fight with Marcus would push every PC button the social worker had.

"And you wish to have Roman visit you here?"

"More than anything."

The social worker turned to the Capellas. "Hospital policy is clear. We cannot keep anyone from visiting if the patient wishes to see them, and if the doctors feel his condition allows visitors." He checked his clipboard. "Justin's doctors have put no restriction on the number of visitors he can have, as long as there are no more than two in the room at any one time."

"We're the two, and we're not leaving," Capella snarled.

"I don't want them here, not until I see Roman," Justin said with an emotional detachment that surprised even him.

"Very well. Mr. and Mrs. Capella, will you come with me, please?"

"The hell I will," Capella blustered, his voice rising to a shout.

"Mr. Capella, I can bring security in, but then hospital policy would require that you be banned from visitation for a full week. Wouldn't it make more sense to just agree to your son's request?"

Capella stepped right up to the social worker, toe-to-toe, and looked him fiercely in the eye. "I will leave, and I will go directly to my lawyer's office. This will not stand, sir. It will not stand." Capella motioned brusquely for his wife to follow him, and they stormed out of the room.

The social worker turned to Justin. "They'll calm down once their attorney tells them they don't have a case. Now, does your boyfriend know you're here?"

"I don't know, actually. I would hope he'd have tried to visit me, at least."

The social worker stepped out into the nurses' station and motioned for Justin's nurse to come in. "Has Justin had any other visitors than his parents?"

She swiped for a few seconds on her tablet, then nodded. "The log says that yesterday he was visited by his parents, his grandmother, and his brother."

"I don't have a brother," Justin said, confused.

"That's how he was signed into the log." She tapped and read. "At 12:20 p.m., Carlotta Capella, grandmother, and Roman Capella, brother." She looked up. "Oh."

Justin burst into gleeful laughter. "He was here! I knew he'd find a way. I just knew it."

"Well, we'll see if we can get him back in here," the social worker said. "Do you have a phone number for him?"

"I don't know where my phone went."

"I'm sure we have it in your personal effects locker," the nurse said. "We'll get it charged up and you can call him yourself after dinner. The doctor wants you to try some liquids tonight. Why don't you try to get a little rest before then; having your parents thrown out has to have taken a bit of a toll." She smiled warmly and walked with the social worker out of the room, shutting the door behind her.

He was here is all Justin could think. *He was here.*

"MONTY? THERE'S someone here to see you." Diana, the long-time office manager, stood in the doorway of Monty's office in the back of the shop.

"Can someone else handle it? I really don't have it in me to deal with people today."

"He says he needs to talk to you." She took a step into the room and whispered conspiratorially. "It's Mr. Capella—and he seems angry."

Monty sighed. "Never known him to be any other way."

"How about I show him into the corsagerie? No one's using it today."

The florist nodded. "Thanks, Diana. I'll be there in a minute." He drank the rest of the coffee in his battered "Kiss Me I'm Irish" mug and walked slowly down the hall to the small workroom they used for making wedding boutonnières and corsages during prom season. Just outside the entrance to the room, he stopped and worked up the most personable smile of which he was capable at the moment. He took a deep breath and walked in.

"Cap, good to see you," he said in a voice that almost sounded chipper.

"Cut the crap, Monty. You know as well as I do we never wanted to have this conversation."

Monty drew up a stool and sat. "What conversation would that be?" His eyebrows were raised in disingenuous expectation.

Capella heaved himself onto a stool as well. "I thought this was all settled when you pulled him out of school. You did the right thing back then, but now he's back like a bad penny, and he's got his hooks into my boy."

"Now hold on a minute—"

Capella thrust his hand into the air and shook his head. "No, stop. I'm not blaming you. You did what you could. But now you have to do something more... permanent."

Monty looked at Capella with his mouth hanging open. "What the hell is that supposed to mean?" he demanded.

"Look, I know this is hard to hear about your own flesh and blood, but you need to send him away. Get him far from here. Open a branch in fucking Belgium or something. Just keep him away from my son."

Monty sucked in his cheeks and looked Capella up and down for a long moment. Then a light seemed to break on his face, and he smiled, a little wistfully. "Cap, we been friends for how many years now?"

Capella scowled at this sudden departure from his topic, but he seemed willing to go along for now. "Gotta be fifty years if it's a day. And our dads were friends long before that."

"What happened between us?"

Capella looked intently at the worktable before him. "You know what happened. Your kid tried to rape mine. In third fuckin' grade, Monty. Third grade!"

"If I had that day to live over again...," Monty said sadly.

"It wasn't your fault. And you did the only thing you could do."

Monty shook his head. "No. I did completely the wrong thing. I threw my son under the bus because I was embarrassed. I was ashamed of him." He paused, heaved a sad sigh, and wiped his eyes with a rough hand. "If he had tried to kiss a girl, I would have talked with him about it, told him that it wasn't appropriate in that setting, but it would be someday. I might even have been a little proud of him. But since he kissed a boy, I threw him out of my house. I did what everyone said I should do, instead of just... loving him for who he is."

"What kind of bullshit is that?" Capella demanded angrily.

"I lost my son. I lost the chance to spend his childhood with him. I made him feel he was wrong, and broken, and defective, and perverted. I pushed him away, and...." Monty took a deep breath and exhaled decisively. "And I won't do it again." He fixed Capella with a determined stare. "My son is gay, and I love him. And if he and Justin have fallen in love, then I am happy for them. And if they someday get married, I will arrange the flowers myself, and I will dance at their wedding, and I will toast to their happiness because I love him. I love my son, and I will not listen to you call him a pervert and tell me to send him away. Because that won't change anything. It won't change him. And it won't change your son either, Cap. If Justin feels the way Roman says he does, then the sooner you accept that the better off you're going to be. Don't make the mistake I did."

Capella sat with his mouth hanging open. "I can't believe what I'm hearing."

"I wouldn't have believed it either, if someone had told me this a coupla months ago. But after all the crap we've been through—the lawsuit and the boycott and all those poor people painting the walls of the Grand Central Hotel with your cake—the one thing I've learned is that love wins. I don't mean that in the 'love will conquer all' sense; I mean that, in the end, love is hard wired. It's what makes us human. You can fight it, and you will lose. So you need to take that suspicion and that anger and everything else you're feeling about this whole mess and just focus on this: how can you make the people in your life happy? You can love them, and you can be happy that they have found people to love. Forget about all the rest of it. Forget about judging them for who they love. Just be happy for them, because a life with love in it is worth living."

"Oh my God, you've gone full hippie."

The florist shook his head pityingly. "Far from it. I'm just being realistic. Getting all worked up about my son kissing a boy lost me a lot of years I could have spent with him. And I guarantee you will lose Justin if you push him on this." His voice softened, and he put a hand on Capella's arm. "He jumped in front of a bullet for Roman. Remember that. Be *proud* of that. You raised a son who was willing to give his life for the one he loves. Isn't that selflessness and love exactly what Father Mooney tells us every Sunday should be our highest aspiration? Your son is a good man, Cap. And so is mine. And if they find happiness together, then the world will be a little better."

Capella slumped against the table. "I just can't...," he mumbled but then lost the thread.

"Then don't. Don't stand in their way. Just step back and let them figure it out for themselves. They know you're not suddenly going to climb on a float and dance around under a rainbow. But you can give them the space to figure out what they want. And the best part is that you can still have your son in your life. Don't push him away. Don't do what I did."

"I gotta go," Capella muttered, rising to his feet. He took a long look at Monty, shook his head slowly, and walked from the room.

"Good luck, my old friend," Monty said under his breath as he watched Capella trudge joylessly down the corridor.

JUSTIN OPENED his eyes when he heard a voice call his name. It got easier every time he woke up: the room came into focus sooner, and he didn't feel as though he was cheating Death himself by regaining consciousness.

He was here.

"You made it," he said.

"You made it," Roman replied.

Justin hadn't thought it possible to smile and cry at the same time, but here he was doing just that.

"I came as soon as I got your text," Roman said, grasping Justin's hand. "I didn't think they would let me in."

"You're the only one I wanted to be here," Justin replied.

Roman handed him a tissue. "You saved my life."

"You were going to dent my good copper pan banging it on that guy's head, so I had to do something," Justin said with a grin.

"I am so sorry. For everything."

Justin shook his head. "No. Don't be sorry. Don't be sorry about anything that brought us back together."

"You still want to be with me?"

"I'd prefer that it not be in the hospital, but yes, I still want to be with you. I've kind of been in love with you for a long time."

Roman blushed. "I wish I were as smart as you are. It took me forever to see it. They were so good at making me think that loving you would land us both in Hell that I blocked it out completely." He reached up and brushed Justin's hair out of his face. "You were so brave. I owe you my life," he whispered.

"I wasn't going to let anyone take you away from me again," Justin said, and he brought Roman's hand to his lips for a kiss.

Chapter Fourteen
Anything for Love

Nana Capella was standing at the front door waving gaily as Roman pulled into the driveway, bringing Justin home from the hospital.

"Ready?" Roman asked as he switched off the car.

"As I'll ever be," Justin replied with a sigh. "I hope that two weeks of the silent treatment is enough for them, and we can just get over it."

"It was kind of rough of them to stay away the entire time you were in the hospital."

Justin shrugged. "That's pretty much Dad's MO. When he decides he's against something, he can hold out until everyone else has just given up."

They walked through the garden to the front door, where Nana Capella threw her arms wide and welcomed her grandson home. "Oh, sweetie! Look at you, up and about and looking so strong." She embraced him, hugging with a vigor that surprised him. "And Roman, taking such good care of our boy. Come here, dear." She enveloped him in a fierce hug as well. "Come in, come in."

She stepped back in to the house to allow them room to enter.

Justin looked around. "Seems pretty quiet," he said softly. "Mom and Dad at work?"

"Let's sit and have a nice cup of tea," Nana Capella replied, bustling to the kitchen to put the pot on.

Justin and Roman sat in the living room. The short walk from the car had winded Justin a bit, and he welcomed the chance to catch his breath.

Soon, Nana Capella returned from the kitchen with tea and cookies. "I made some of your favorites, dear," she said to Justin, holding out a plate of chocolate-dipped shortbreads.

Justin took a cookie and handed one to Roman.

"Oh man, I forgot about these," Roman said after biting into it. "Nana Capella, you make the best cookies."

"You always were the sweetest child, Roman," Nana Capella said with a smile.

Justin sipped his tea and then set his cup down. "Nana, where are Mom and Dad?"

Nana Capella shifted uncomfortably in her chair; she straightened her skirt and took a deep breath. "They're not here, dear."

"I kind of figured that," Justin replied with a smile. "I wasn't expecting a brass band, but I kind of thought they'd be here."

"Justin, your father is a traditional man," Nana Capella began, starting into a script she had clearly prepared for the occasion.

"You don't need to make excuses for him, Nana. I know what Dad is like."

She nodded and seemed to decide to take a different tack. "They're gone."

Justin waited, sure there was more to that statement. But nothing seemed to be forthcoming. "Gone… where?"

"They moved, honey. They're gone for good."

Justin was stunned. "They moved?"

Nana Capella nodded. "After that confrontation with you in the hospital, their lawyer told them there was no way for them to stop Roman from seeing you. Your father went to see Mr. Montgomery, to try to get him to send Roman away again. Well, you can imagine how that conversation went. Then he went to the police, but since those nice officers had convinced them to drop the charges against Roman for that nastiness at the wedding, they refused to do anything. So he came home and told your mother that they were leaving. Leaving the city he grew up in, leaving the business his father had inherited from his own father—just up and moving."

"Where did they go?"

Nana Capella shook her head. "They wouldn't tell me, dear. Somewhere warm, I think, because of your mother's arthritis. But they didn't want anyone to be able to contact them, so they just went."

"What about the business?" Justin asked, his voice rising as he took in the insanity of this turn of events.

"He left it to you. He said that times had changed, and he couldn't change with them. He said that you could run it as you see fit."

"Wow," Justin said, shaking his head. "And the house?"

"It was already in a family trust, so we didn't even have to do any paperwork." She looked at him, an anxiety creeping into her expression. "Is it okay if I keep living here?" she asked.

"Of course, Nana—don't be silly. I want you here forever." He turned to Roman, shaking his head in bewilderment.

"How are you doing with all of this?" Roman asked.

"It's just… shocking. I can't believe he would uproot his entire life and move away from everything he built here just because he couldn't handle me being gay."

"Maybe he did the only thing his conscience would allow him to do, under the circumstances," Roman replied. "He couldn't accept me and you being together, but he didn't want to throw you out of the business. He must have known that your designs and vision were the future of the company. So he left it to you." Roman paused for a moment. "If you think about it, it's a pretty selfless thing he did, in his own homophobic way."

Justin marveled at the maturity Roman exhibited and all of the ways he had grown in the short time they'd been together.

"That's a lovely way to think about it, Roman." Nana Capella looked at Justin with a sparkle in her eye. "Never let this one go, you hear me?"

"I don't plan on it," he said. He turned serious again. "I don't know how I'm going to run the entire business, especially while I get back up to full strength."

"You've got good people working for you, dear. Some of them have been there their entire lives. Not one of them quit when your father left. Of course, they might simply have welcomed a quieter, less angry workplace."

"So it's been running okay without me?"

"In a lot of ways, yes," Nana Capella said diplomatically. "And it's been a lot of fun for me to be back in the bakery after all these years. But…."

"But what, Nana?"

"For two weeks we've been producing designs you had already sketched out. The customers have been ecstatic with those, as usual, but we haven't signed a single new contract, despite all of the people who have been calling to make appointments. They all want you, dear. There's no one else who can design like you can."

Justin blushed to be praised so highly by his grandmother. "It will be nice to get back into the shop. I guess I'll stick with working the front of the house from now on."

"Funny," Roman said. "That's exactly what my dad told me last week. He's been talking more about retiring, and he's been letting me handle the designs and meet with customers. I guess we're more useful being the pretty faces at the front counter."

"I just wish it was the same counter—we'll never see each other!" Justin cried.

Roman's eyes widened. "You know...."

"Oh my God, that's a perfect idea."

"I know, right?"

"Would your dad go for it?"

"Oh hell yeah. I'm sure of it."

"Well, aren't you two the perfect old married couple," Nana Capella hooted. "Talking in half sentences and getting each other all worked up. So tell me, what are you plotting now?"

"What would you think about a new one-stop shop for wedding cakes and flowers?" Roman replied. "Capella & Montgomery?"

"We could consolidate in our front shop, since it's a little bigger," Justin said.

"And it has more windows facing the street, for better visibility," Roman added, with an ill-concealed giggle. Justin whacked him in the chest with his good hand.

"We keep both facilities running for production, but consolidate for marketing and meeting with clients." Justin beamed at his grandmother. "What do you think?"

Nana Capella clapped her hands and bounced up and down in her chair. "I think it would be the happiest place in the entire city, and I would be thrilled to help out however I can."

"Looks like we have some work to do," Justin said. "I should probably get some rest, though. It's been kind of a big day, and there are bigger days ahead." He rose and began walking slowly toward his bedroom. Then he stopped and turned around. "Come tuck me in?"

Both Roman and Nana Capella rose and then looked at each other and laughed.

"I had my turn when he was a little boy," Nana Capella said, sitting back down. "I deliver him into your capable hands."

"I'll take good care of him, I promise," Roman answered with a bow.

"Remember, he needs his rest," called Nana Capella after the boys as they walked down the hall hand in hand.

"LOOKS FUCKING amazing," Roman said, looking at the new storefront from the sidewalk. The quaint, lacy tea-room decor and leaded windows had been replaced with a sleek and modern façade, marble and steel taking the place of brick and wrought iron. Above the gleaming windows, spanning the entire width of the storefront, was the new "Capella & Montgomery" sign.

"It finally feels like ours," Justin added. He kissed Roman on the cheek and beamed at him.

It was Labor Day weekend, the official end of the summer wedding season, and the scions of the cake and floral dynasties were finally out from under the crushing load of orders that had dominated their every waking moment for the past two months.

"Now," Justin said, turning to Roman, "what's this big surprise?"

"If I told you...," Roman said, pulling open the door to the shop. "Now go tell everyone we're leaving, and won't be back until Tuesday."

Justin looked into the back of the shop. "Everyone's gone already, and tomorrow's Labor Day, so they know we're closed. Looks like you'll just have to tell me the surprise now."

"Ha-ha. Lock up, and I'll pull the car around."

"You have to tell me where we're going," Justin pleaded.

Roman laughed maniacally and dashed out the door.

Justin shook his head at his crazy, impulsive boyfriend and went to the back of the shop to lock up. The final lights to be turned out were the ones in the room with the big butcher-block table, where his life had changed. A couple of times. It was here that he had first kissed Roman—or anyone, for that matter. And it was here that Roman had betrayed him, and then defended him, and ultimately redeemed himself. Though the bakery had been renovated, this room would stay the same for as long as Capella & Montgomery was in business.

He turned out the light and walked through the front of the shop to the sidewalk. Just as he shut and locked the door, Roman drove up to the curb. He honked gratuitously and pushed the passenger door open for Justin to climb in.

As they pulled away from the curb, Justin looked for the GPS unit so that he could discover their destination.

"I put it over here," Roman said, reading his thoughts. "There's no way you're going to find out where we're going until we get there, mister."

"No fair," protested Justin, but inside he was perfectly happy to surrender to the whims of the man he knew would never hurt him—he knew this better than most because he had seen what Roman was capable of when the person he loved was in danger. Justin settled in for the ride, resolving not to let himself even think about where the car was headed.

He drifted off as the car left the city; the week had been a busy one, with a half-dozen weddings scheduled for Saturday. His entire crew had been in frenetic motion all week, and especially on the weekend. He had spent the earlier part of the day cleaning up and ordering supplies for the next month and then reconciling payroll with the accountant. His exhaustion defeated his excitement at the prospect of a surprise adventure with Roman, and he slept until he sensed the car slowing. When he opened his eyes they were in the brightly lit streets of Springfield.

"You drove us all the way to Springfield?"

"For you, love, I would drive to the ends of the Earth."

Justin made a gagging sound and clutched at his throat. "You are just completely full of shit these days—pink sparkly shit." But he was inwardly delighted at every silly romantic gesture Roman made, and he made a lot of them lately.

The GPS guided them through the streets of the city Justin had been to only a handful of times.

"Where are we going?" he asked as they ventured deeper into what seemed to be a neighborhood full of brick houses and not much else.

"Still a surprise," Roman said as he carefully followed the instructions of the GPS mounted to his side of the windshield. Ahead of them, at the end of the street, loomed a large, dark, brick building. It was surrounded by a chain link fence, clearly having been abandoned long ago. Roman pulled up at the side of the block-long building.

"Roman, it looks like it's completely closed off."

"I was looking for something private," Roman replied playfully. He got out of the car and walked over to the gate that was locked up tight with a heavy chain and a padlock that must have weighed three pounds.

Justin watched from the passenger seat, trying to decide whether he would give chase if Roman leapt over the fence. But Roman walked up to the gate and grabbed hold of the padlock. Impossibly, he slipped a key into it and—it opened. He unwound the chain, and the gate swung wide. He turned back to the car and beamed at Justin. Then he walked back to the driver's side of the car and drove carefully through the gate, coming to a stop next to the looming, two-story block of a building. He shut off the car, got out, and then closed and locked up the gate again. Finally, he opened the passenger side of the car and gestured gallantly for Justin to alight.

"This is the surprise?" Justin asked as he stepped out of the car. "A tour of an abandoned building? You planning on shooting some kind of horror movie tonight?"

Roman took both of Justin's hands in his. "Trust me?"

Justin looked him in the eye. "Anywhere you go, I will go with you," he said, far more solemnly than he had intended to. But he felt, in that moment, that he was making a vow to Roman, which he meant as seriously as any he had ever made.

"Then come with me. I have something special to show you."

They walked up to the door of the building, and Roman opened it.

Justin peered inside. What he found was a school gymnasium, transformed. Hundreds of tiny tea lights flickered all around the room, bathing the interior in a soft glow. He stepped through the doorway and realized that this was the very same gymnasium in which they had spent an ill-starred night all those years ago, in third grade.

"Oh my God, Roman," Justin whispered. "Is this really…?"

"Yes, it is," Roman answered, looking about the looming space. "It really is."

"How did you do this?"

"Turns out someone bought the school from the city last year. They're planning on turning it into a brewery/restaurant complex. I got in touch with them, and found out that they're going to begin renovations at the end of the month. I asked if we could use the gym tonight. They seemed kind of reluctant until I explained why—then they were really happy to let us have it. Brotherhood of the gay hospitality industry, right?"

Justin laughed. "This is amazing. It seems so much smaller than when we were here last."

"Candlelight will do that. Come here," Roman said, leading Justin to the center of the room, where there was a larger grouping of tea lights flickering warmly.

"Sleeping bags? And is that—seriously?" Justin leaned down and picked up a bag of circus peanut candy. "I can't believe you remembered."

"That you threw circus peanuts at my head until everyone else had fallen asleep? There's nothing about that night I don't remember."

Justin plopped down on a sleeping bag and looked around the room in wonder. "This is unreal."

"It gets better. We don't have to live by circus peanuts alone—I got that amazing new caterer in town to pack us a picnic dinner you will absolutely love. I'll grab it from the car."

Justin was lying on the sleeping bag, looking at the ceiling, when Roman returned from the car. "I remember now," he said quietly, trying not to disturb the ghosts of his youth. "Come lie here with me." He patted the sleeping bag next to him for Roman to lie down.

Roman stretched out next to him and looked up at the ceiling as well. Justin laced his fingers into Roman's, and they lay there for a long moment staring up into the darkness high above them.

"I listened to you breathing," Justin said, the echo of long-distant memory in his voice. "I tried to breathe along with you. I thought if I could make myself more like you, you would see how much I...."

"You felt that way, about me? Even then?" Roman asked in a low murmur.

"I did. I feel it all again, being here."

"Why didn't you say anything?"

"There weren't words for it, back then. How would I have told you what I couldn't even say to myself? The words that might have described what I felt were all swear words when we were in school. I couldn't say anything that might have conveyed what I was going through without getting sent to the principal's office. That's how they kept us from feeling those things: they kept us from even having the words to describe what we felt." He turned to look at Roman. "You found the only way. You didn't bother with words. You just did it. You kissed me to tell me everything we couldn't say. That was an amazingly brave thing you did, Roman. I didn't know it then, but I know it now. You risked everything to let me know."

"Paid a pretty big price for it, too," Roman replied. "I thought you hated me all those years after I got sent away."

"We lost so much time. But you came back, and that's all I care about. I can't believe you did this for me. It's like you're giving me back my childhood. I'm not alone anymore."

Roman turned onto his side and put his hand on Justin's cheek. "As long as you will have me, wherever life takes us, I will be by your side." He kissed Justin gently, sweetly, defying the echoing darkness of the school gymnasium.

Justin returned his kiss, deepened it, pulled him closer. He kissed his once-and-forever love until he remembered how to breathe. Lying back, he looked up at Roman, amazed at what this man—his man, now—could accomplish. "Hey Roman, want to get in my sleeping bag?"

"I've waited years for you to ask me that," Roman replied. "But I don't think we'll fit with all of these clothes on." He started unbuttoning Justin's shirt, kissing the soft skin revealed with each button that yielded to his sure fingers.

As Justin's chest was laid bare, he reached up and pulled Roman's shirt off over his head. The muscles of Roman's torso stood out in flickering relief, making Justin's head a little light. "You're… beautiful," he whispered, running his fingers down Roman's chest and the ridges of his abs.

"It never occurred to me before that our jobs—cakes and flowers—are two of the most feminine jobs, and yet hefting bundles of greens and squeezing pastry bags have given us these," Roman said, sweeping his fingers along the full roundness of Justin's pectoral muscles.

"Real men make cakes, buddy," Justin said in a reverberant voice. "And, you know, pretty bouquets."

Roman's response was to launch an all-out tickling attack on Justin's bare ribcage. The gym was filled with delighted squealing at Roman's onslaught and Justin's lightning counterattack. Finally, panting with exertion, they returned to their first task of making each other naked. Roman slid Justin's pants off, flinging them across the room, and Justin returned the favor. They slid into the sleeping bag with their underwear on, a nod to the authenticity of the experience.

"This is how we were that night," Justin whispered. His hand found Roman's crotch. "And you feel just as hard as you did then—though probably three times the size." He gave Roman's hard manhood a lingering caress.

Roman conducted an exploration of his own under the cover of the sleeping bag. "I think it's contagious," he murmured. "You seem to be similarly affected." He slipped his hand into the waistband of Justin's boxer briefs. "I think I need to take a closer look."

With sure hands he eased Justin's underwear down and off his legs, which was an operation of some complexity, given the logistics of the sleeping bag. But he reached his goal with determination and was soon handling the bare skin that Justin had only ever shared with him.

"I think we're ready to get past third grade, don't you?" Roman asked, his voice full of insinuation. He slipped his own underwear off.

"I thought you'd never ask," Justin replied breathlessly.

"Are you sure the doctor thinks you're up for it?"

"He said that I could resume normal sexual activity. I didn't tell him that normal for me is jerking it to Str8FratDudes.com and then crying myself to sleep."

"I'm your new normal, mister," Roman said, his voice full of bravado.

"I highly doubt that anything you do could be considered normal, but that's why I love you," Justin replied with a laugh. "I will simply point out that I've been completely naked for a full minute and you have yet to assail my virtue. That had better not be the new normal."

"Hold on tight," Roman said, climbing atop Justin, straddling him with his strong legs. He kissed Justin from his forehead all the way down to his bellybutton, making stops along the way for his lips and nipples and those amazing V-cuts that formed the base of his torso.

Justin writhed with anticipation, and he clutched the sleeping bag as Roman wrapped his hand around Justin's rock-hard cock. He ran his tongue up its length, from the soft gathered skin at its base all the way to its flared head, causing Justin to moan with want. With one fluid motion, Roman reared up and slurped nearly the entirety of Justin's penis into his mouth. Justin babbled incoherently, dizzied as the room whirled around his pole. And then, just as suddenly as he had engulfed it, Roman let it slide out of his mouth.

"Remember when your dad said I slipped into your sleeping bag and tried to rape you?"

"Uh-huh," Justin grunted in reply, hoping that this was the last time Roman would mention his father while holding his dick.

"Well, I think it's time for that one to come true." Roman reached over to his own sleeping bag and pulled out a small bag. "I have come prepared this time," he said with a laugh. "And you should be prepared to come." He held up a condom and a small bottle of lube.

"Uh, Roman? I'm not sure I'm ready for you to—"

"I think you are," Roman interrupted, squeezing Justin's steely erection.

"But I don't know how to—"

"Shh. That's the upside of having a slut boyfriend. Let me take care of everything. You just lie back and try not to pass out from dehydration. Because you are going to come like you never have before." Roman flipped the top of the lube bottle open and squirted a dab of the slick gel on the head of Justin's cock. Then he put a healthy dollop onto the tips of his fingers and ran his hand down between his legs. He set the bottle down and ripped open the condom packet. Unrolling the condom over Justin's cock was the work of but a second, as it was already slicked with lube. Roman drizzled more lubricant on Justin's sheathed cock.

Justin watched this ritual with terrified fascination. "This is like watching you arrange flowers," he said reverently. "You are so... confident."

"Justin, honey, sex is not a test. It's something humans do because it feels better than anything else we can do with our bodies. And if you share it with someone special, it's the best feeling in the world." Having finished his prep, he settled his buttocks just above Justin's navel. "Now, just relax." He reached around behind himself and took hold of Justin's slippery prick. He lifted it slightly and then backed onto it, rubbing it up and down the crease between his buttocks. "Feel that?" he asked as he played Justin's cockhead around his anus.

Justin groaned. "It's so hot."

"Oh, just you wait," Roman said with a deep chuckle. He positioned Justin's cock, and moved back and down just enough to slide the tip of it in.

"Oh my God," Justin groaned. "It's so tight! And hot. And amazing...."

"And that's just the beginning," Roman said, rocking himself back and forth in tiny increments, bringing more of Justin inside him with each movement. Soon he was sliding most of his lover's manhood into his body.

Justin couldn't believe he was actually doing this. All his life he dreaded the very idea of having sex because it meant figuring out how to do it with a woman; then, as he became more secure in his sexuality, he couldn't imagine being confident enough to do it, nor flexible enough to allow it to be done to him. But Roman had made it possible, just by being who he was. And now Justin was nearly completely buried inside the most private place of the man he loved most in the world. Caught up in the moment, he tipped his pelvis forward—a little surge of sexual energy, an instinct coming to life.

"Oh, fuck!" cried Roman, pitching himself forward onto Justin's chest.

"Did I do it wrong?" Justin asked in a panic.

"Oh God no," moaned Roman. "You did... something amazing. Your cock was right against my prostate, and then you pushed, and I swear to God I just about came right then."

"You can come just from me... doing this?"

"Oh hell yeah. Your cock is just perfect—perfect size, perfect angle, and when you thrust like you just did—fucking perfect."

"Like this?" Justin asked, and he again timed his thrust for the moment when he felt almost completely consumed by Roman's ass.

"Fuck! Yes, that's it. It's like we were made to fit together."

Justin obliged by continuing to thrust, sending Roman into spasms of joyful bouncing toward orgasm.

Then, Roman froze. He made a growling, rumbling noise from deep in his chest, and he looked down, wide-eyed, at his own hard cock as it began to bob rhythmically.

Justin felt Roman's ass clamp down hard on his cock, milking it along its entire length. He gave a few last, twitchy thrusts, and he could feel a lump that he hadn't felt before. Roman jumped and moaned when his cockhead grazed it, so he aimed right for it and jerked his hips upward at it.

Roman cried out, and his cock began erupting without his touching it. A surge of hot white gushed from its head, lacing Justin's sweat-glazed torso with its slippery heat. It was followed by blast after blast of heavy spunk, each landing higher and higher up Justin's writhing body until the last landed on his chin and cheek. It was at that moment, when he felt Roman's semen land, hot and wet, on his face that the seizure started. His hips launched into crazy motion as the orgasm tore through him. He clamped his hands onto Roman's thighs, fingers digging into the muscle just below the surface of smooth skin. He bucked and cried out, and felt his cock take on a life of its own. He had never experienced anything like this, and it swept him almost out of the realm of sanity. His body, somehow, knew what to do, and he just let it beat out its primal rhythms and fill Roman with his own gift of seed.

Finally, he, and Roman, and the entire room, stopped moving. Justin breathed hard into the stillness, trying to recover without letting the moment end. He looked up at Roman and felt the warmth of a smile work its way across his face. Roman beamed down at him and then leaned down for a kiss, all without relinquishing his cock. It stayed snug in its new home, buried deep inside.

"That was fucking amazing," Justin whispered when their kiss finally ended.

"That was amazing fucking," Roman countered, smiling broadly. "You are a natural at this. I've never had anyone hit all the buttons at once. You are incredible."

"I had a gifted teacher," Justin said with a grin of pure joy.

They collapsed together and, in the stillness of the gymnasium, in the middle of the night, they were complete for the first time in their lives.

"SO THIS is a thing now, people cooking outdoors?" Bryce asked, surveying the backyard of Brandt and Donnelly's house. A smoking grill in the corner of the yard filled the neighborhood with the aroma of seared beef.

Brandt and Donnelly were making the rounds, handing out beer. "It's traditional on Labor Day to grill huge quantities of meat," Donnelly explained, "and then stand around in the yard, drink beer out of bottles, and talk about how the working man gets screwed on the other 364 days of the year."

"As much as I like that last part, the rest of it looks like something from one of those magazines in my dentist's office that showcase primitive cultures. You know, *National Geographic*—or *Midwest Living*."

"Welcome, my dear sir, to our primitive culture," Donnelly replied, bowing grandly and then handing Bryce a beer. "I thought you might prefer a long-neck to start with." He winked as Bryce took the tall bottle from him.

"Thank you, Gabriel." Bryce regarded the bottle warily. "It does remind me of someone I met last weekend," he said thoughtfully. He placed his lips delicately around the top and took a sip. "Ah, it's bubbly like champagne, but tastes of oatmeal with—" He smacked his lips thoughtfully. "—fresh grass clippings on top. What an exotic treat you have provided me, darling." Bryce smiled brightly.

"Always happy to broaden your horizons," Brandt said with a laugh as he and Donnelly returned to the grill to tend the meat.

"So you *are* capable of inviting people to your home for a meal," Donnelly's sister Chris called as she and Billy Walters made their way to the corner of the yard, where the grill and several drink coolers were located.

"Oh shush," Donnelly replied, wielding his spatula on the grill. "We've had you over before."

"For the Super Bowl. When our cable was out. And we brought the food."

"And yet I see you have neglected to bring a hostess gift this time," Donnelly groused with a playful glance at Brandt.

Chris pulled a six-pack of Donnelly's favorite local microbrew from behind her back. "This is how it's done, bitches," she cried with a laugh.

Donnelly leaned over and kissed his sister on the cheek. "That's my girl," he said warmly.

"Walters, I got one here with your name on it," Brandt said, stacking the fourth hamburger patty onto a bun. He stuck a bun on the top and held the plate out to his colleague.

Walters sized up the burger with a squint. "It'll do for a start," he said with a shrug.

Chris rolled her eyes. "Thanks, Ethan. Now I'm going to have to make him jog home while I rev the car behind him so he can work that thing off."

"All part of the service we provide," Brandt replied with a smile.

Chris took one of Donnelly's grilled chicken breasts and followed Walters to a table.

"You know, this is the first time we've had Labor Day off since joining the force," Brandt said to Donnelly. "I guess special assignments have their benefits."

"Yeah, it's almost worth getting barfed on by society's elite, shooting a guy, and then doing nothing but paperwork and 'post-fatality review' sessions for the next two months."

"I'm really glad that's all behind us now," Brandt said with a sigh. "The details of Tibble's ricin plot made for fascinating reading in the terrorism task force report. You have to admit, we managed to keep some pretty serious stuff from going down."

"As bad as it's been, it's nothing compared to what Greg Sampson's been through," Donnelly replied. "Did he say he was coming today?"

Brandt shrugged. "He said he'd try. I don't think he's been out much socially since the wedding."

"Can't blame him," Donnelly said, turning back to the grill. "I don't know how you come back from something like that."

"Hey, look who did make it," Brandt said, pointing to the most recent arrivals walking through the side gate of Brandt and Donnelly's bungalow.

Justin and Roman came around the side of the house carrying a large cake and a huge spray of flowers, and Brandt jogged over to help them find a place to put them.

"Hey, guys! Great to see you. Glad you could make it," Brandt said, taking the cake from Justin and carrying it to a table where it completely outclassed everything else that anyone had brought. "Beautiful cake."

"Thanks," Roman said. "It was my first attempt. But I had a good teacher." He kissed Justin, who blushed at the public display of affection, even in this safest of environments.

"Nice work," Brandt replied. "And did Justin try his hand at flowers?"

"I did," said Justin modestly. "For as many things as Roman has taught me in the last couple of months, I think this one might take the longest for me to get the hang of."

"He's a pretty quick study on the other stuff," Roman said with a leer and a nudge at Justin's ribs.

"You guys look so good together," Brandt said with a laugh. "It's just great to see you settling in after all you've been through. And you brought Nana!" Brandt held out his arm for Justin's grandmother, whose small stature had resulted in her being completely obscured by the two young men.

"Why, how gallant," she said with a spry laugh. "Lovely to see you again, Ethan."

"What can I get you to drink?" he asked the newcomers. "Beer? Wine?"

"Beer would be great," Justin said, grabbing one out of the large iron washtub full of ice and bottles. He handed one to Roman as well.

"I think an old woman with a bottle of beer looks ridiculous," Nana Capella said. "Perhaps a bourbon?"

"One bourbon for Nana, coming up!" Brandt called as he settled the old woman at a table. Apparently Justin and Roman found this quite humorous, though Brandt wasn't sure why.

"Welcome!" Donnelly called as Justin and Roman approached, smiling and sipping their beer. He set his spatula down and embraced both Justin and Roman. "So good to see you. Ethan and I drove past the shop last week; it was looking really good. How's business been?"

"Oh my God, I don't know if we can keep up with the orders," Justin said with a helpless gesture. "Seem like every gay wedding in the state wants us all of a sudden."

"Plus we do have to serve some straight couples once in a while," Roman added. "Just to keep up appearances." He and Justin laughed at their good fortune.

"Heard from your parents, Justin?" Brandt asked, his voice quiet.

Justin shook his head. "Mom sent a postcard that I think Dad probably didn't know about. No return address, but it was postmarked Santa Fe. Still, it is nice to know they're out there somewhere."

"They'll come around," Donnelly said. "They just need some time. Lots of years of prejudice need to be worn away, and that can take a while."

"Gabriel knows a thing or two about parental prejudice," Brandt said, stroking his partner's strong arm.

Donnelly shrugged. "Some parents take longer than others. But I still think most will come around eventually."

"At least I have Roman—and his family is great. Plus Nana, who's turned out to be this amazingly awesome person."

Donnelly laughed. "I think Nana Capella will bury us all."

"Not if she dies of starvation before someone brings her a hamburger sandwich!" she called from the table where the boys had seated her on their way in.

"Man, is she sharp," Brandt said, serving up a burger for Nana Capella.

"Yeah, we kind of have to work on being quiet when we're... together," Justin said under his breath.

"Yes, it's a good thing your old grandmother likes to watch *Queer as Folk* reruns in bed at such high volume," Nana Capella shouted in an aggrieved voice, then smiled wickedly.

"I'm just going to go die of embarrassment now," Justin whispered, blushing furiously.

"I think she's awesome," Roman said, putting his arm around his mortified boyfriend. "She was really cool with me moving in and everything."

Brandt, having handed Nana Capella her bourbon, raised his bottle. "To Capella and Montgomery, a true partnership," he called. Everyone drank a joyful toast, including Nana Capella, who put away her bourbon in a single gulp and looked about for a refill.

After dinner many of the guests had drifted into the house to watch the opening game of the university's football season. Brandt and Donnelly gathered with the nonsporting guests around the fire pit, and a bottle of Jaegermeister made a slow, spicy circuit of the assembled friends. Until it got to Bryce, that is, who regarded the square green bottle with horror and passed it along with his fingertips.

"Now darlings, about your wedding plans," Bryce twittered to Brandt and Donnelly. "We have so much to discuss!"

"Wait," Brandt said, eyes narrowed. "I thought we had that all taken care of."

"Oh no, dear, no," Bryce cried. "You have someone to plan the ceremony and the party, but what about the honeymoon? We have decisions to make. What if you go somewhere warm and tropical? You're going to need swimsuits—tiny, tight little swimsuits. But what about a whirlwind tour of Europe? Do you have enough skinny jeans? So much, darlings, so much to see to!"

"Bryce," Donnelly said gently, "we haven't even started thinking about a honeymoon."

"And that's why you have me. I'll draw up some options, and we'll brunch soon. Somewhere tasteful, perhaps?" Bryce raised his carefully groomed eyebrows slightly in good-natured judgment.

"We'd be happy for you pick the place. Just another decision you can take off our shoulders," Brandt said, grateful that the Jaeger had made it to him so that he could take a nice long swig.

Bryce took a long, loving glance at the strong shoulders of the troopers and smiled.

The party was still going strong when a late arrival caused all heads around the fire to swivel. In the gathering dusk, a tall silhouette walked toward the group.

Donnelly tapped Brandt on the shoulder. "Greg made it."

No longer a news anchor, Greg Sampson still cut a dashing figure as he strode across the yard, bearing a bottle of wine that certainly cost more than all of those assembled by Brandt and Donnelly in preparation for their party.

"Greg," called Donnelly, striding to meet him halfway across the backyard. "Great to see you, man." He pulled Greg into an embrace that he returned warmly.

"Cute spot you two have here," Sampson said, handing Donnelly the wine bottle and giving Brandt a back-slapping hug as well. "Thanks for the invite."

"Our pleasure," Brandt replied. "What'll you have to drink?"

"Gin and tonic?"

"Coming up," Donnelly said, hustling to the drinks coolers to assemble the ingredients.

"How've you been, Greg?" Brandt asked, clasping Sampson's shoulder and giving it a friendly squeeze.

"A little better each day," Sampson replied.

Brandt led him to an open seat around the fire and introduced Sampson to the group, all of whom already knew him from the news.

"So, Gabriel tells us you're setting up a foundation," Chris said.

"I am," Sampson answered. "I think Peter would have wanted me to do something to help make sure that what happened to us doesn't happen to anyone else."

"That's a beautiful way to remember him," Chris said.

These Donnellys, Brandt thought. *They always know the right thing to say.* As he did every day, he smiled at how lucky he was to have Gabriel in his life.

"I'm glad to have these fine troopers as my partners in the effort," Sampson said, nodding to Brandt and Donnelly. "I was talking with the governor last week, and he was really supportive of a public/private partnership to work on this issue. He liked my idea of developing a seminar for law enforcement around the country on how to handle marriage and civil union issues, especially in emergencies. You two would be a critical resource in that effort. Until we get national marriage recognition, we have a lot of work to do. Even then, there are a lot of minds that have to be changed before marriage equality really makes people equal."

"We're honored to be a part of your work, Greg," Donnelly said, taking Brandt's hand. "Once we unleash Ethan Brandt on the country, everything will just fall into place."

"You don't need to flatter me, buddy," Brandt replied with a smile. "I'm already going to sleep with you."

"Crusader for justice by day, slut by night. Aren't I the lucky one?"

"Oh, the way you two flirt," Bryce exclaimed. "Please, continue."

It was nearing ten o'clock when the football game ended and the last guests drifted out of the yard. Donnelly puttered about, picking up bottles and putting furniture back. Brandt sat, staring into the fire.

"Oh, no, don't get up," Donnelly cracked. "It'll just take me a minute to finish up out here, and then I'll go wash all the dishes."

"Gabriel, come sit with me?" Brandt's voice was low and serious.

Donnelly set down the bottles he was carrying, and walked a little haltingly to the fire. "You okay?" he asked.

"I have something for you," Brandt said. "I was waiting for the right moment to give it to you."

Donnelly sat, a mystified look on his face. Brandt reached for something under his chair and handed it to Donnelly. It was a small wooden box, about the size of a deck of cards.

Donnelly looked up. "Is this some kind of occasion I forgot?"

"No. It's just something I want you to have."

Donnelly looked at the box, turning it over in his hands. "It's beautiful," he whispered.

"Open it."

He looked up at Brandt once more, as if to confirm that what he would find inside the box was something good. He opened the box slowly and found inside it a small stack of paper. He pulled it out and looked it over. It was a laminated sheet, folded like a map. He unfolded it, and read the title across the top.

"Durable Power of Attorney," he read. He looked at Brandt. "This is the document we signed at the lawyer's office last month."

"Yes, but it's even better. This is the prototype of something Greg came up with, working with the attorneys at Peter's firm. It's our power of attorney, but it's laminated and scored like a map so that it folds up and fits in your wallet. Plus, it has a picture of both of us, so if we end up in an emergency room, they can see right away that we're the ones named in the document. It even has the notary endorsement, so it will hold up in court. And look at this," he said, flipping the document over. "This is a scannable code that will download an electronic version of the document for the hospital or whoever to keep on file."

"This is amazing," he said. He folded it back up like an accordion and held it to his heart. "Thank you."

Brandt took Donnelly in his arms. "You will never be alone," Brandt murmured, kissing his stubbled cheek, dampened now with a tear of joy.

"Look at us, clutching by the fire, reduced to tears by a piece of paper," Donnelly said. "We have finally gone full Jane Austen, you know."

"Why, Mr. Donnelly," Brandt replied, his voice high and delicate. "I hope I can trust you to conduct yourself as a gentleman."

"If by 'conduct myself' you mean 'fuck you until you forget your own name,' then you have my word."

Brandt fixed him with a skeptical frown. "You are perhaps less of a gentleman than I had come to expect," he sniffed.

"I'll make you breakfast in the morning," Donnelly promised with a grin.

"Well then, Mr. Donnelly," Brandt said, holding out his arm, "shall we?"

Donnelly took Brandt's arm chivalrously. "We shall. Twice. Perhaps thrice."

"Fuck yeah," Brandt muttered, and, with a new appreciation for literature, he walked with his love into their snug bungalow.

Don't miss how the story started!

Frat House Troopers

A Brandt and Donnelly Caper

By Xavier Mayne

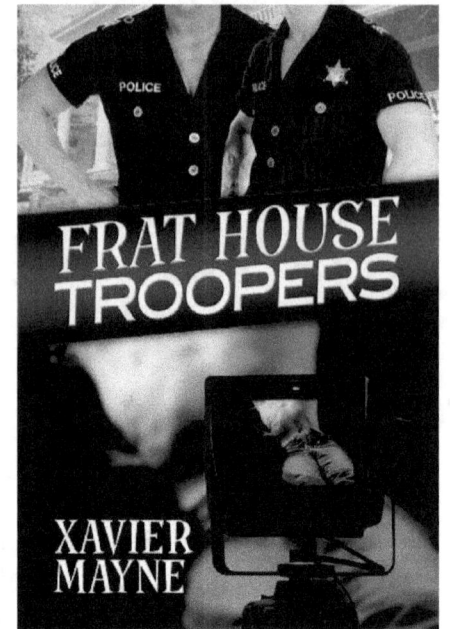

State trooper Brandt's new assignment to infiltrate a sex-cam operation puts him in a very uncomfortable position, especially since he'll have to perform naked on camera for his audition. Fortunately his partner and best friend, Donnelly, has his back—whether that means helping Brandt shop gay boutiques for sexy underwear or offering Jäger and encouragement while he researches porn.

Despite his mortification, Brandt gives the audition his best "shot"— and becomes an overnight sensation. But to meet the man behind the operation, he'll have to give a repeat performance, this time live on webcam opposite the highest bidder. Donnelly makes sure to win that auction for his partner's sake, but their plan has a flaw: faking it is not an option.

In the aftermath, Brandt is a humiliated mess trying desperately to come to terms with what he's had to do for the job and his own mixed feelings. But Donnelly has been on a journey of discovery of his own. Suddenly everything the two men thought they knew about themselves and each other gets turned inside out. Meanwhile, they still have a case to solve… but it may not be the case they thought it was.

Don't miss how the story started!

Wrestling Demons

A Brandt and Donnelly Caper

By Xavier Mayne

Jonah Fischer's high school wrestling career has been stellar, but now he's the unwilling star of a series of videos that have hit the web. The whole world may have seen the evidence that his best friend turns him on. Jonah's conservative family wants him cured, and his conventional town and school want him normal. The only person who still wants him just the way he is is Casey Melville, the same best friend who turned him on for all the world to see. Meanwhile, Casey begins to wonder if there's more to his feelings for Jonah than he thought.

Officers Brandt and Donnelly—lovers as well as partners on the job—have been assigned to find the culprit who posted the video. While investigating the case, they also help Jonah and Casey find their way through their feelings, and steer them toward refuge when Jonah's family turns against him. But the mystery remains: who wants to hurt Jonah badly enough to post those videos, and why? Thank goodness Jonah and Casey have found friends—they're going to need all the help and support they can get.

HUSBAND MATERIAL

XAVIER MAYNE

http://www.dreamspinnerpress.com

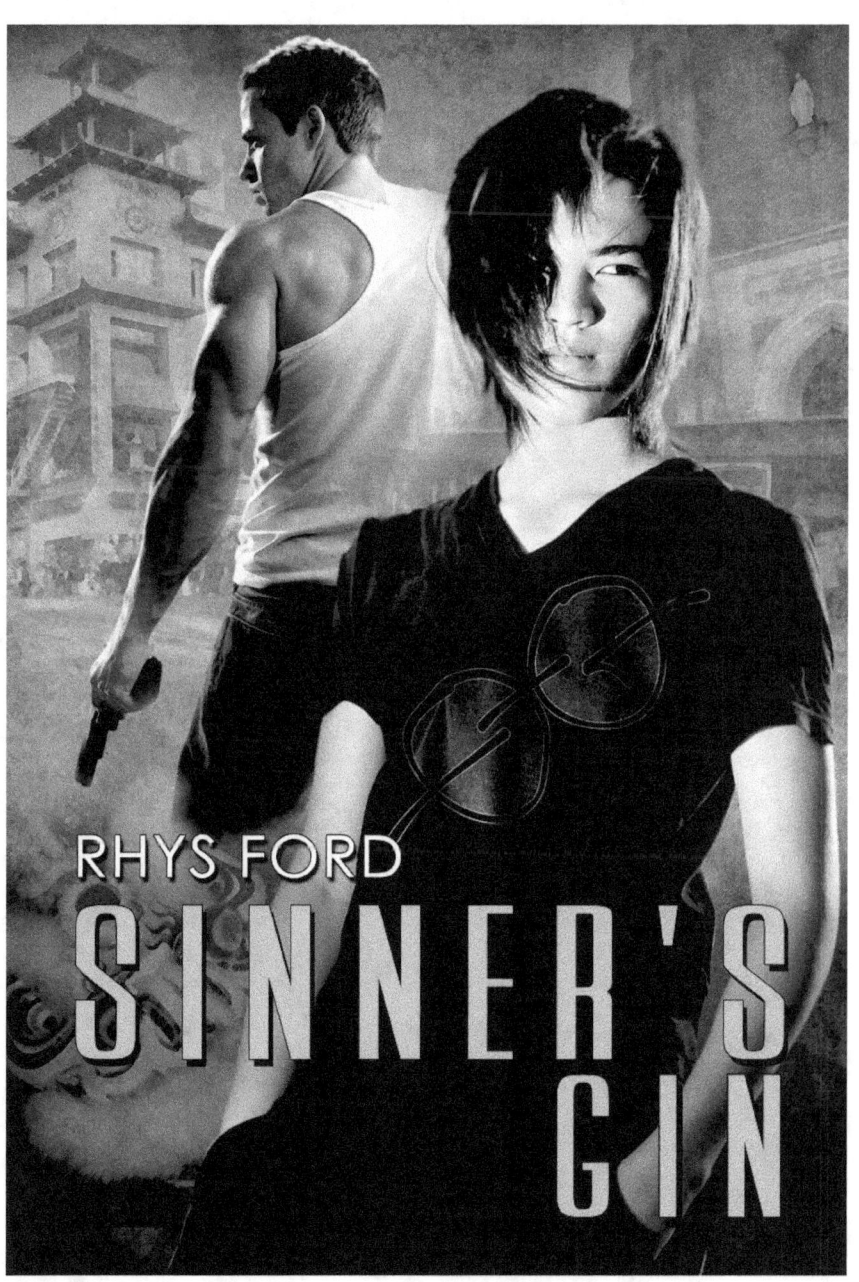

Hidden Gem
LISSA KASEY

http://www.dreamspinnerpress.com

PATCHWORK HEAVEN

Jaime Samms

http://www.dreamspinnerpress.com

MEMORY KICK

C.M. Torrens

http://www.dreamspinnerpress.com

I am the conductor,
leading the sweet symphony
of pain and agony.

SPLINTERED
SJD PETERSON

http://www.dreamspinnerpress.com